you lost me there

RIVERHEAD BOOKS

a member of Penguin Group (USA) Inc.

New York

2010

you lost me there

ROSECRANS
BALDWIN

RIVERHEAD BOOKS
Published by the Penguin Group
Penguin Group (USA) Inc., 375 Hudson Street, New York, New York 10014, USA •
Penguin Group (Canada), 90 Eglinton Avenue East, Suite 700, Toronto, Ontario M4P 2Y3, Canada
(a division of Pearson Penguin Canada Inc.) • Penguin Books Ltd, 80 Strand, London WC2R 0RL,
England • Penguin Ireland, 25 St Stephen's Green, Dublin 2, Ireland (a division of Penguin Books Ltd) •
Penguin Group (Australia), 250 Camberwell Road, Camberwell, Victoria 3124, Australia
(a division of Pearson Australia Group Pty Ltd) • Penguin Books India Pvt Ltd, 11 Community Centre,
Panchsheel Park, New Delhi–110 017, India • Penguin Group (NZ), 67 Apollo Drive, Rosedale,
North Shore 0632, New Zealand (a division of Pearson New Zealand Ltd) • Penguin Books
(South Africa) (Pty) Ltd, 24 Sturdee Avenue, Rosebank, Johannesburg 2196, South Africa

Penguin Books Ltd, Registered Offices: 80 Strand, London WC2R 0RL, England

Library of Congress Cataloging-in-Publication Data

Baldwin, Rosecrans.
You lost me there / Rosecrans Baldwin.
p.   cm.
ISBN 978-1-59448-763-7
1. Scientists—Fiction.   2. Widowers—Fiction.   3. Alzheimer's disease—Research—Fiction.
4. Memory—Fiction.   5. Marriage—Fiction.   6. Psychological fiction.   I. Title.
PS3602.A595415Y68   2010   2009048671
813'.6—dc22

Printed in the United States of America
1   3   5   7   9   10   8   6   4   2

Book design by Susan Walsh

While the author has made every effort to provide accurate telephone numbers and Internet addresses at
the time of publication, neither the publisher nor the author assumes any responsibility for errors, or
for changes that occur after publication. Further, the publisher does not have any control over and does
not assume any responsibility for author or third-party websites or their content.

to R.K.

prologue

The first night, obviously. Victor says it was love at first sight, but I was too tired that night to fall in love. It was after one of my little happenings. I remember I was exhausted, I wasn't out to impress anybody. Then he came up with a drink and I thought, Well, he's tall. The kind of guy who took himself seriously, straight out of Brooks Brothers, with pens in his breast pocket. Not at all my typical fan. But I could tell he wanted to kiss me. I made him want to kiss me. That was the whole idea.

New York, August 1971. I was renting a studio on West Eighth Street, back when it was dingy. Men found it avant-garde, the exposed pipes, the working bathtub in the kitchen. Victor and I caught a movie, then we drifted back to my place to listen to some Chicago blues records and drink whiskey sours (I only drank whiskey sours that year). I probably lit some incense and talked a big game. There was a point, I remember, when we discussed our favorite books. We had three in common—that seemed important. But he didn't come on to me. I started to worry I'd read him wrong. Then he asked me, after one of those prolonged quiet moments (I never liked quiet moments), "So, what's your secret?"

He had this earnest, really lovely look on his face. His seriousness didn't waver.

"Deep down, what's the one secret you don't share with people?"

"You first," I said.

After a second, he said, "I killed a friend of mine."

Not what I expected.

"Recently?"

"No, when I was a kid." He sort of laughed. He wasn't self-conscious, but it was a big deal. "When I was twelve. I'm not sure."

"Whether you killed him?"

"He killed himself. But I could have stopped him."

Well, I scrambled to think of something. "I hit my mother one time. I punched her in the mouth." After a beat, Victor said, "You might have something there," and then both of us started laughing, just crazy laughter, and that was that.

Normally I gave away my love in dribs and drabs, but not this time. As though I'd stumbled into a cause; perhaps not right for anybody else, but all mine.

Sara's handwriting covered both sides of the index card. She'd scribbled down to the last empty space. I put the card back where I'd found it on her desk, tucked into a book with dozens more.

She might have written it just after our counseling appointment, sitting in her car while I pulled out of the parking lot.

Weeks before California.

Some theories said the most accurate memory was one that's never recalled. The more the mind retells a story, the more that story hardens into a basic shape, where by remembering one detail we push ten others below the surface and construct the memory touch by touch. A sculpture between the neurons that looks like its model, just not completely.

But I hadn't brought this one up in thirty years. And Sara recalled that first evening perfectly: the movie, the music, the whiskey sours.

What we said. How it felt.

But I didn't remember that we'd gone to a movie.

I barely remembered that evening at all.

one

The ghosts of our research labs were old, clipped cartoons. Scientists treated them like Dead Sea Scrolls, as though nature's mysteries were best explained by *Far Side* captions. Comic strips were the relics of investigative progress. Scientists more esteemed than myself were probably above such things (if ranked, I would have made varsity within the Alzheimer's disease community, though not as a marquee player), but from Chicago to Cambridge, New York to Bar Harbor, I'd always carted along my favorites, particularly one that showed two scientists at a lab bench, one of them examining a fuming test tube, saying to the other, "What's the opposite of 'Eureka'?"

The best summary I'd seen of a researcher's daily life.

My lab consisted of a half-dozen rooms on Maine's Mount Desert Island at the Soborg Institute, a satellite campus for the state's university system. My office's eastern wall faced a faculty parking lot and featured three large windows, each of them blacked out by papers I was in the middle of editing (the better to see them with). The floor was a no-fly zone of archival boxes, FedEx envelopes, and stacks of journals. Sara used to say I worked in academia because OSHA would have banned my tidying habits from the private sector, but whatever I needed, I could find in twenty seconds.

Sherlock Holmes once said, "A man should keep his little brain-attic stocked with all the furniture that he is likely to use, and the rest he can put away in the lumber room of his library, where he can get it if he wants it." Perhaps my mind, like his, meandered. Other scientists were known for their impressive recall, but I preferred to rely on my judgment.

Science in school was horrible, though, a boot camp of memorization drills, except with one teacher, Mrs. Gill. Her hero was Charles Darwin, the garden explorer. She taught us about species evolution by lugging in her own butterfly crates. Our task, she said, was to assemble the world, to develop wondering points of view, even in the grass around a baseball diamond. I remembered a moment from that year when I was standing at the end of my parents' driveway while my friend Russell shot by on his bicycle, no hands, and I'd had an idea that seemed to make the trees shimmer: Was how I thought about things, the way things happened in my mind, the same as how Russell thought about things? If so, how could he ride no-hands when I was too scared? If not, then why not, and which one of us was the odd one out? What did it sound like inside his head? Was everyone's consciousness different? Were all of us equally full of thoughts, or some more than others?

I probably would have ended up reading Kierkegaard if there'd been a philosophy club, but instead there was Mrs. Gill's biology class, dissecting cow brains. And if my career since hadn't been Keplerian in magnitude, didn't rival Mendel's or Crick's, at least it reflected a life spent pursuing what had interested me for as long as I could remember.

Our lab's subject was Alzheimer's disease. Specifically, we were trying to develop neuroprotective strategies for sufferers, aiming to help their neurons fight back against or even prevent the disease. Unfortunately, our success was measurable among peers, not the public. Alzheimer's disease was still an excruciating illness for millions. It lacked a cure, and the popular spin on our genes as so many on and off switches didn't help. "Which one is the Alzheimer's gene? Which one causes cancer?" Even for experts, understanding gene expression was a shadows game, a spelunking mission where thousands of caverns were still dark. We simply didn't know much about genetics, and the ways both scientists and civilians behaved with uncertain information had led to straw men popping up. This misconception that humans were so many toggles was to my mind the new phrenology, and scientists themselves were responsible for bad marketing and spreading rumors, attempting to explain our mysteries with little data.

We certainly couldn't map memory function to a switchboard. Riddles abounded. I couldn't recall what I'd eaten for dinner the previous Sunday, but all the pretty girls from high school remained vividly in storage. Their figures, their hair color, their venomous voices.

Just that afternoon, a week before I discovered the index cards on Sara's desk, we'd wrapped up our Friday conference call and the team had cleared out, and I was checking my e-mail when my wife appeared: Sara the innocent, stepping out of the summer light to comfort a stranger. We were near San Juan, during a vacation in the seventies. We'd wandered a couple miles past the tourist beach and I was tired, but Sara wanted to keep walking. She left me in a concrete pavilion to catch my breath. I fanned my head for a few minutes. Far away, a young man was jogging toward her. I watched while he tripped in the sand, fell forward, and didn't get up. Imagine, I remembered thinking, if he died, just like that. Sara, in a skimpy white bikini, ran to him and stopped to help. I was shielding my eyes when he grabbed her and pulled her down to the sand, as if ripping a shirt in half. I ran out, shouting threats. He looked up and saw me just as Sara kicked him in the stomach; he fell backward, then ran over a dune toward some apartment buildings. When I got there, I turned to give chase, but she stopped me with a look: all her fury redirected at the notion that I would leave her. As if by being a man, I couldn't be trusted. That whatever genes were expressed in that boy had produced me, too, ready to stick my neck out.

Thoughts popped up while I shut down my computer: Why that particular memory? Why that event and those feelings, and why at that precise moment?

Questions like those were our lab's bread and butter. They stayed with me on my drive to Regina's house, at least halfway there, until other ideas took hold.

Regina Bellette was a few years out of the University of Michigan with a double major in chemistry and poetry, soon to return to Ann Arbor for her Ph.D. As far as I was concerned, her best assets were her cheeks, two moon pies round and white. Who knows why they did it for me. Probably some association with the girls I remembered from my adolescence, those peach-cheeked chorus singers in the movies.

Regina was a confident, contemporary woman who despaired of her time and place, a girl about town on an island of hikers. She had a crooked nose, curly hair, brown eyes, and pale skin. Very little of it was to her liking. She bemoaned her athlete's arms, the strong cord of her thighs. Regina had grown up on a dairy farm in Shelby, Michigan, the daughter of hippie scientists without a television in the living room. Their chores she escaped with books and magazines: Jane Austen, the

Brontë sisters, *Vogue*, *Sassy*. In Maine, Regina was a devotee of women's fashion on a graduate student's budget, particularly vintage pieces from the 1930s. I'd commented that she was showing signs of obsession, but secretly I admired all that thought put into beauty. Regina was simmering with ambition. She could be haughty, but not for long. She was quick to care and empathized reflexively, a headstrong girl of the midwestern mold and improving upon it: polite and grounded, but also willful, a tempest. Publicly modest but privately, in her bedroom's half-light, more imaginative.

"How do you afford them?" I asked one afternoon. I was lying on top of her comforter. A pair of shoes, poised in tissue, had caught my eye: two gold high heels studded with costume jewelry.

"*Chéri,*" Regina said, and grabbed the box, plopped down next to me, and spun one shoe like a mobile above my chest, "it's not about the having. It's about the hunt."

Regina Bellette, my obsession, and one whom I regularly failed to please. Her rented house was on the outskirts of Otter Creek, one of Mount Desert Island's smaller villages, with a year-round population approaching six. Not where you'd expect to find the great La Loulou, but then rarely in her bedroom did Regina seem her age. Instead, she was more like a Toulouse-Lautrec dancer transplanted to the sticks: innocence and worldliness slouching in a complex bustier. I never knew where Regina's interest in burlesque had begun, but as a fellow researcher I admired her dedication to the data, to the vintage Hollywood fan magazines she printed off the Internet and studied closely.

She was Barbara Stanwyck one week, Betty Grable the next.

"Listen to this," Regina said one night over the phone. "Straight from *The Wall Street Journal*, guess on average how much Parisian women spend on lingerie, what percentage of their clothing budgets?"

"Five percent."

"Twenty-five percent. *Chéri*, why wasn't I born in France?"

But La Loulou was a role reserved for our secret Friday afternoons. The Regina I saw more often was at work. In 1936, a rich Danish immigrant, Søren Soborg, donated enough money to the State of Maine to seed a campus on Mount Desert Island, hoping to find a cure for his daughter, who had been blinded and deafened by a mysterious illness, later identified as osteopetrosis, marble bone disease. Over the years, The Soborg Institute broke ground in genetic science, particularly in gerontology, with an emphasis on Alzheimer's disease. By the time I was being recruited from NYU, Soborg was setting pace with the field's biggest leaps. Like the rest of academia, though, it hewed to certain standards of professor-student relations. On campus we pretended not to know each other. Regina didn't work directly for me, but research fellows were occasionally shared between labs and they fell under our collective oversight. Incidents had occurred. Precedents had been diligently constructed by lawyers and administrators. I'd looked it up in the employees' manual back in April: *Any sexual relationship between instructors and students jeopardizes the integrity of the educational process by creating a conflict of interest and may lead to an inhospitable learning environment for other employees.*

But sex between us, I would have told my jury, was never as vital as La Loulou's performance. Especially now that I'd lost my erection three times in as many weeks.

It was dusk on a beautiful June Friday, warm and bright. I found Regina propped up on an elbow with her legs fanned out over the yellow duvet. Pouty and dressed in royal blue lace. The curtain was drawn, the lamp shaded with a scarf. After half an hour, we both ignored what hadn't occurred. Regina poured herself a glass of wine and slid away. Twilight snuck in through the window and brought the forest, the smell of thawing ground. I still had another appointment that evening, but I lay there in my underwear, staring at Regina's ceiling.

How many other men had occupied my place? Was there a Thursday date? One who could make love properly?

On the wall was a poster of a young female singer dressed like a Japanese robot, her hair tied up in two buns. I reached out for Regina, but she snorted through her nose and scooted away, slurping her wine.

"So how's work?" she asked, crawling back.

"Fine. You?"

Truthfully I was thinking about that beach moment in Puerto Rico. I remembered feeling slow to the rescue.

"Oh, please, come on," Regina said, changing into an old T-shirt with "Kiss Me" scrawled on the front, promising "The Cure."

"What?"

"At least complain about someone. You never talk."

"Maybe I'm not the gossip type."

"Aren't you high on the hog."

Regina wiped her lips with the back of her hand and smiled. "Well, don't you wonder what people say? Aren't you curious?"

"Believe me," I said, "by now I am too old to care."

Regina stared at me as if she wanted to share something, then turned away. Not many women, I thought, can appear wise and naive simultaneously.

"All right, what?"

"Forget it."

She unclasped two barrettes and threw them at the wall, one at a time.

"Well, what do you want to talk about?"

"Oh, Christ. You know you sound—" She watched me for a minute while I dressed. *"Chéri,* the least you could have done was clean your wife beater."

"My what?"

"Your wife beater."

"What's a wife beater?"

"Oh, don't tell me."

Regina laughed deep in her throat and pulled her T-shirt down against the breeze. Such chubby baby cheeks, I thought, staring from my position by the door, and grabbed my keys off the dresser.

I was leaving when she said, "You really don't give a fuck about me, do you?"

Out of the blue, just like that.

So flat it could have been her alarm clock going off.

Friday evenings, I had a time-honored date with Aunt Betsy in Northeast Harbor, preceding Regina by several years. Aunt Betsy was virtually my only companion. She was an eighty-six-year-old gossip who shredded other people's lives between her fingers over breakfast. Her family had long inhabited Mount Desert Island and she knew everyone, year-rounders like me as well as the summer people, and collected our personal affairs not for wampum, but like a pack rat, for the joy of hoarding. No one was beyond her reach. Her dispatch board was a dining table cluttered with newspapers, coffee cups turned into ashtrays, and a large black office phone. In town, she'd pick up tidbits at the post office, the hardware store, and from the owner's twin daughters at Pine Tree Market, who'd inform her which customers were doing what and to whom. As an amateur anthropologist, Betsy studied misbehavior. She tracked her stories doggedly and did not hesitate to use them. She loved playing vigilante. A few years earlier, when one of her neighbors, Tim Winston, hit the lotto, he'd secretly financed a breast augmentation for his girlfriend, while his wife, Maureen, still worked two jobs. During the winter, Maureen had shoveled out Betsy's car a few times and helped carry in her groceries. When Betsy got wind of things, Maureen soon was filing for her share, represented by one of the area's most expensive divorce attorneys.

But Aunt Betsy didn't know everything about us. If she suspected where I'd been before dinner, I would have seen it in her face. Aunt Betsy rarely blinked. Her eyes behind her glasses were always wet.

"You look terrible," Betsy wheezed. She patted my arm. "Did you watch the tennis?"

"I have a job," I said. It came out short. After Regina's, though, I wasn't in the mood.

"Not much else besides, I'd say."

That made me laugh.

"Anyway," she said, "you're too skinny, dear."

We were standing together on the front porch at Cape Near. From Betsy, "dear" was pronounced "dee-ah." "Work" came out "wairk," "hard" was "hahrd." Her accent was a classic mid-Atlantic, a coastal Mainer's, except with a highbrow, Anglican lilt. "Now, Agassi, the poor boy," Betsy said, "you should have seen him, up against some Croatian, oh just *awful*, Victor. And this one wears his hair long to rub it in. You know how Andre shaves his head now, just like you, dear, well, poor Andre!" She fluttered her hands around her hat. "He barely squeaked it out. You can tell it's his final season. Krackalovic, Milokavic, some nonsense. Victor, weren't your people Croatian?"

They were, but I wasn't listening. The gin on Betsy's breath said we wouldn't be drinking the wine I'd brought. Mixing her liquors, Betsy always said, made her blue.

Typical of the neighborhood and of Maine's coastal resorts, Cape Near was an oversize shingled cottage, a musty and disjointed Victorian with cedar siding. The name, coined by Betsy's father, referred to a cove past the front yard. In August, the smells turned rank indoors. A cigarette was always burning somewhere. The area's heyday dated back to Aunt Betsy's teen years, when Mount Desert was able to peer down its nose at Newport or Tuxedo Park as an enclave for the wealthy. Now the house just felt deserted.

I fixed drinks and went outside to the terrace, where the lawn was overgrown, rolling down a hill wild with beach plums. Sounds of summer rang through the dusk: children playing a few yards over, somewhere behind the hedgerow. And then I sat down, covered my eyes, and slipped back to that bedroom in Otter Creek, halfway across the island, to the late-afternoon revue starring Ms. Bellette, twenty-five, and her headlining question: Did I or did I not "give a fuck" about her?

It was all a bit too much.

"So how have you been feeling?" I called out.

"Stuff it, Victor," Betsy shouted. "You're a medicine man now? Why, poor Agassi, think how he's doing."

"Isn't he married to Steffi Graf?"

"Who's no Brooke Shields."

Betsy turned up huffing through the screen door. "Who would you pick?"

"Brooke Shields."

"Now to be fair, Graf was a *marvelous* player." Betsy paused to reflect. "In the modern game, Graf was best, bar none. Review any numbers you like, I don't care if she lacked rivals. Now this was before the Williams sisters powered through, *n'est-ce pas*, but Graf really played like the men did, you know, and very much to her credit. But that nose of hers, imagine waking up to that in the morning."

Regina's nose was crooked in the middle from a childhood break. I unconsciously rubbed the stubble on my head, where it prickled around the crown. It had been Regina's suggestion that I start buzzing my hair, a younger look for an older man. "Time to ditch the power doughnut," she'd said.

Betsy settled herself in an upholstered patio chair.

"So how are you, really?"

"You know," I said, "busy."

She puckered her lips. "One day it will be important to surprise me."

"I have a grant due soon, on top of one we just submitted."

"You've had a grant due since you were twenty."

"Well, you asked."

She picked her teeth with the side of a fingernail. "And how's the swimming?"

"I'm fine," I said. "Are you worried about something?"

"Be honest, dear, am I all you've got?"

"For what it's worth."

"Oh, I'm nosy, I know," she said a moment later, gazing down the lawn, like we'd been lying out tanning all afternoon. "Now, Victor, did I *tell* you about Margaret's David? So, apparently David ran his Mercedes into the picnic table again."

Behind the trees, the sunset was really something, going from hibiscus to rose. Someone should take a picture, I thought. Sell a postcard to the tourists. As a destination island, we attracted four million visitors a year to smell the lupine. It was Aunt Betsy who'd told me how, around the end of the nineteenth century, a planning committee had renamed the town Bar Harbor, to attract rusticator money and sound more resortlike.

Previously, the town was called Eden.

Betsy reached out and pinched me.

"I've been meaning to tell you, I found a poem of Bill's you'll like. Remind me, I'll give it to you when you leave."

"That hurt, you know," I said, and massaged my hand.

"You're a fart. Now go inside and set the table."

Funny thing was, Betsy Gardner was Sara's aunt, not mine. Yet I was the chauffeur to Betsy's doctor appointments, her lunch date on Mother's Day, her every-week Friday-night special.

The Gardners had been some of Mount Desert Island's earliest settlers. They'd gotten a head start on tourism by planting hotels on bedrock, and then turning enough profit so they could bet on steel. Come another generation, the family focused on their daughters: socializing in higher circles, breeding with Hookes and Pughs. There'd been an admiral, Betsy's father, whose portrait hung above the guest toilet. He was also the author of a family genealogy he'd self-published in four volumes, a Social Register for the extended Gardner clan of which Betsy had recently bequeathed me a copy. My own story wasn't much to note, just a chain of Long Island pharmacists and roofers trailing back to the Balkans. I was named Victor after my mother's father, a wife beater no one liked to sit near during holidays. My last name, Aaron, was incidental: it had been assigned to an ancestor by an immigration clerk, since Cikojević didn't sound much like baseball.

None of my relatives ever had a head shot of FDR above the fireplace, signed, *"Dear Betsy, who ever swam with more grace? Adoring, Franklin."*

From her end of the dining table, Betsy related the scoop of the week: A famous fashion designer was whispering about dredging Bass Harbor so that he could park a yacht off his backyard. Fishermen were outraged and neighbors were bearing arms. It would be the scandal of the summer once it broke in the newspapers, Betsy said, with town, gown, and sea rights in a single basket.

And all I heard was, "You really don't give a fuck about me, do you?" as if Regina were throwing out a clue for a crossword puzzle.

More than cartoons, more than an addiction to diet soda, most researchers I knew shared a knack for submerging into musing—or worrying, to be honest—at the cost of social graces. We were well-trained minds, but poor dinner guests.

Betsy shouted, "You must know Martin Filsberger, Victor, for Christ's sake!"

"What?"

"The *Washington Post* reporter? No, you're too busy with a microscope up your fanny." Betsy threw her napkin down and lit a cigarette. "See here," she said, "now, Martin was married to Jane Paul. Sort of a canine girl, Jane, with a snout. Martin and Jane used to summer in Pretty Marsh until Martin started running the Jerusalem office. But listen"—she blew smoke across the phone—"one afternoon I ran into Martin at the post office. Now, remember, this was the year of Monica Lewinsky, so I said, 'Martin, what is the *story* here? Clinton was a Rhodes scholar. The man was an *Eagle Scout*. What in God's name's happening?' And Martin took my elbow, we walked outside, and he said, 'Betsy, I am forced to swear you to secrecy or my editor will have my neck,' and I said, 'Martin, if anyone can keep a secret, it's not me.' And he liked that, he gave me a nice smile, he leaned down, and whispered in my ear, 'It wasn't just a blow job. It was *one hell* of a blow job.' And oh, I was dying, Victor, what a card, what a *card*!"

Betsy made off for the liquor cabinet. A boat horn tootled from the harbor down the road. Outside, through the window, the night was full of fireflies and searchlights, children running around the street playing flashlight tag. I did the dishes while Aunt Betsy paced the kitchen, stamping the tiles with her cane.

"So why don't you come out to Cranberry this summer?"

"What? You know I can't do that."

Little Cranberry was a smaller island south of Mount Desert, where Betsy kept a cottage.

"The camp is just to pieces," Betsy said. "Or perhaps I shouldn't go out this summer, is that what you think?" She stopped by my elbow. "But you must come, Victor, visit for a week. You could commute by ferry."

"I'm working all hours as it is. Plus, I have a conference in New York."

"New York isn't going anywhere. Oh, listen to me for once. You promised."

I stared down at my hands.

"When? Exactly when did I promise?"

She ashed her cigarette into the sink. "Anyway, you work too much as it is. You'll be reminded that Uncle Bill worked too much, too. Aside from work, Victor, what have you got? Just look at your forehead."

"What's wrong with my forehead?"

"Dear, you are inhumane." Betsy sat down and folded her arms in her lap like two mannequin limbs. She'd won, but the fight had drained her spirit. I wondered if one of her spies had told her something about Regina. Was this how she'd exhibit jealousy, by nagging?

I finished the dishes, poured a scotch, and escorted Betsy out to the screened porch. We watched TV on a wheelie cart, an hour with the great Belgian detective Hercule Poirot while he investigated murders on public television. At a scary point, Betsy grabbed my hand.

"Tell you what," she said when the program finished, "I found an old draft of Sara's movie that she gave me. You should have it. That one I saw at the Criterion."

This was a new habit of Aunt Betsy's, giving away things she'd unearthed around the house.

"The Hook-Up," I said.

"Shame she never wrote another."

"She wrote several, you know that. They just weren't produced."

"Well, I never saw them," said Betsy. "I'll give it to you with Bill's poem. Remind me."

She squeezed my fingers and held on. It was understood but never spoken aloud that our Friday-night dates, figuring out how Poirot could know so much from so little, were our weekly shift at the widows' walk. Seven years earlier, Betsy's husband, Uncle Bill, had died from a stroke at the Harbor Club. Four and a half years after that, on January 5, 2004, Sara, my wife and Betsy's niece, was killed in a car accident on the island, above Seal Harbor. We'd been married thirty-three years. Pipes had burst in a summer cottage and flooded the street, and Sara spun out, crashing her BMW through a metal barrier.

She'd grown up on the island and had known the roads as well as anyone, but this was black ice, impossible to spot.

At the time, Sara had just returned from six weeks in California. Our marriage was going through a rocky patch, and what could never happen became indelible over the telephone. Instant history. Called to the hospital, I cried over her face. I lost my balance in a corridor. Betsy was driving me home that evening when I insisted on visiting the accident site. It was a curve of road with a southern view, where in daylight you might see cruise ships. The full moon made the ocean look frozen.

Back at the house were groceries to be unpacked and Sara's Ray-Bans by the telephone. Near the answering machine was an envelope from American Airlines. We'd been scheduled to go to Italy in February for a two-month sabbatical. A second honeymoon. She'd thought of it on the return flight from Los Angeles.

According to the police report, Sara's not wearing a seat belt was a determining factor in her death. It was the kind of detail she might have used in one of her movies. Sara never wore a seat belt. She refused to, all her life, and I let it slide, the way some spouses will tolerate a smoker. But it drove me crazy. A year before the accident, on a trip to Boston, she'd proudly labeled not wearing a seat belt "my thing."

It remained the clearest thing I could hear her saying.

Regina's voice played louder than the radio on my drive home from Betsy's. For our Friday afternoons, I'd been ready to sign over my house and my car, chop off my hands and leave them as offerings, remove my head, extract the calcium from my hips, whatever Regina found of value. Now, driving through the dark, I was prepared to toss it all out the window.

For two and a half months, Regina and I had had our own island. But I'd had that before, for thirty years. She's twenty-five, I thought, she wears corsets for fun, no wonder she's moody. She needs a companion who can share her vocabulary. If you call that a vocabulary.

After showering, I gave "wife beater" over to the Internet. A moment later I was running back upstairs, grabbing my undershirt from the laundry basket. On the stomach was a good-sized stain I hadn't noticed before.

I thought of my grandfather, the wife beater.

Later, I was falling asleep when the telephone rang.

you now know something that no one has known before—that's when the blood's pumping, and all the hours, all the sacrifices, assume a much larger value. Those moments were fewer in recent years.

Instead, there were banquets to attend, too many banquets. Departmental politics, silent auctions, air travel to foreign conferences. And the environment was colder, less collegial. Colleagues were more frequently in other countries than down the hall. There were a few researchers remaining in our world who had their own lab and two technicians and they wrote their own grants and spent their days ruminating, but for the rest of us, we competed for bread rolls and rollover funds, we worried about inflation, we got into bed with the wrong partners and had to get out again. It was mechanical and political, and it made accounting sound fun.

Partially I blamed it on technology. I hadn't signed up to become a computer programmer. Strong friendships had dwindled in the age of e-mail. Some colleagues had adjusted, but I knew many who refused to read their e-mail at all. Others asked assistants to print out their messages, passing along only ones deemed significant. Some got trapped in loops of responding to people who couldn't compose logical sentences, and felt compelled to reply, "By saying that, did you mean this, or this, or that?" But we were dying out, those of us who felt encumbered by all the data. E-mail was necessary now that research was distributed globally and then published on the Internet, and my staff was comfortable in the new channels, thrived in them, and claimed that they improved their work. I didn't say so, but I found it all isolating. Brain science as I practiced it meant studying mental processes in the context of a human's experience of the natural world, not a virtual one. I longed to return to my graduate days in Chicago, working beside short Austrian men in three-piece suits. Back when our mysteries demanded magnification and the axons of giant squid, not Microsoft Outlook.

As a full professor at fifty-eight, a tenured graybeard at Soborg's Aging Research Center, I was to be a master of memory, an expert at our mechanisms for retaining information. And half the time I couldn't remember the log-in password for my own computer.

After lunch, I spent an hour reading e-mails, then settled down for an afternoon of grant review. But I couldn't focus. In the glare of my desk lamp, a vision of youth and lingerie intruded. I could easily dial Regina's extension. The risks of our affair were gigantic, they might cost me the legacy of my career. But excitement lingered.

I put my hand over the keypad and noticed the voice-mail light blinking.

"Victor, it's Russell. Look, I'll be in Boston Friday, thought maybe you could put me up for the weekend. Let me know. Oh, and I had a question: What was that restaurant we went to last time, you knew the guy? I think I saw something about him in the paper, figured maybe I could fit in some business. Anyway, call me, dearie, hugs and kisses. And Connie would say she misses you, except she only instant-messages. She has dreadlocks. My daughter the Jamaican, believe you me. Ciao."

Russell Caratti, wine dealer, womanizer, I'd known since we were kids. He was my closest friend, by that point probably my last remaining one outside the lab. My schedule didn't allow for much of a social life. Connie was Russell's daughter from an earlier marriage, also my goddaughter. Her real name was Cornelia, but Russell insisted on calling her Connie, to spite his ex-wife, who'd named her at the hospital.

It reminded me, I still needed to thank Russell for his birthday present, an unopened case of wine in my garage.

My associate director, Lucy, walked in without knocking.

"If you are not busy at the moment."

"I'm yours."

"Well, this is potentially groundbreaking," Lucy said, swinging in, her voice sounding hoarse. "In the big scheme of things?"

"What am I looking at?"

"What's your expertise on dating?"

I laughed. I'd been expecting a conversation about genetic mechanisms. "What are we talking about?"

"Say we swim upstream. So, what was your line before you met Sara? For picking up girls. Courting, they would have called it."

"You know, I don't think I had one."

Lucy unlatched her watch, some heavy global-positioning machinery, and set it on the coffee table. She'd recently taken up mountaineering.

"I picture you sweating."

"Interesting."

"How many, would you estimate?"

"What?"

"Women. Dates." Lucy paused, scanned the room, and pushed her hair back with two hands. "So I would like you to surgically remove my head. Whatever skills you've picked up. Actually, know what, forget it, I'll work this one out on my own."

"What are you talking about?"

Lucy collapsed lightly on my couch.

Lucy Sejung Park was in her early forties, a Ph.D. and senior scientist, my longest-serving employee. She was also my co–principal investigator, a heavy-lidded workhorse who rarely left campus. Lucy was demanding, reliable, quick-witted, and born caffeinated. Generous and considerate to her coworkers, a gifted researcher, but also caustic and sarcastic, the office gossip, and easily wounded when her defenses were down. Neither scientist-as-wonk nor a madcap genius cliché, Lucy was a second-generation Korean-American from Newark who liked horror movies. She was five-seven, with a marathoner's figure; a health nut; a body-as-a-temple type. Lucy was permanently agitating toward becoming someone new, one of those people who never completely graduated from adolescence. When she did leave the lab, it was usually to train for whatever new sport she'd picked up that season, pursuing it to an expert's level before abandoning it for something else. Over the winter she'd started rock climbing and gotten a double-helix tattoo on her left biceps, which she liked to show off when we were interviewing job candidates. As far as I'd seen, she kept few friends. Her love life was shaky. She had all the aptitudes necessary for complex analysis, for competing in triathlons or playing violin, just not for human relationships.

As coworkers, though, we had an unusually close bond, and one I treasured. Lucy was my vault, my institutional memory. No one else had worked for me so long or knew me better. New hires were always surprised by how we teased each other, which some around Soborg found off-putting, even flirtatious. But Lucy was a daughter to me. Technically she was under my direction, though she had earned a high level of autonomy and ran her own projects. Her name someday would be better known than mine, especially if her most recent experiments played out.

Our work at that point concentrated on isolating the protein fragments that nurtured brain cells. The hope was that we could prevent the loss of brain function caused by Alzheimer's with a medication based on those isolated pieces. But we were a long distance from our goal, and we'd run into a problem: the fragment we'd isolated was obese. On a molecular level, the resulting drug would be too large to pass through the fine mesh of a human's blood-brain barrier.

Basically, our pill could work, but it was too big at the moment for the brain to swallow.

Lucy, on the other hand, had struck a eureka moment the previous autumn in her own research. The current thinking in the Alzheimer's community held the disease to be caused by a knotty protein called Abeta. Because Abeta was sufficiently complicated, we assumed there to be multiple and complex Abeta mechanisms involved in causing Alzheimer's. But Lucy had isolated a single mechanism, a sole receptor in mice that prevented them from developing the disease. Treating Alzheimer's therefore could become relatively simple: Design a drug that would block the identified mechanism, and all would be well. Since then, Lucy and her technicians were pulling all hours, figuring out exactly how such a drug would work. For that type of achievement, though, whether or not it panned out, Lucy deserved her own lab, her own glory. But she'd yet to show any interest in establishing herself. When I'd moved north from New York, NYU had said they'd find her space if she locked down a grant. Instead, Lucy packed up and drove to Maine.

Also, Lucy had known Sara. They hadn't been close, but friendly enough. And no one had been more supportive after the accident, no one more hands-off.

"Fine, try me," I said, leaning forward in my chair, attempting to block out an image of Regina dancing. "But tell me it's not Deke."

"Deke?"

Deke was Lucy's on-again, off-again boyfriend, a radiologist at Maine Coast Memorial Hospital. He'd proposed to her back in January, without success.

She laughed lightly with a scratchy voice, humorlessly. "No, it is not Deke. Enter Terry, stage left."

"Tell me about Terry."

"Terry is a senior-grade ranger with the Acadia park service. He has a name tag that will explain this to you. He is thirty-seven. I met him online three weeks ago. Turns out, Terry is a musician of considerably mediocre talent. Also, he has a lip ring."

I laughed. "Very interesting."

"No, because Terry is neutered, except he's able to compose twenty songs about his ex-girlfriend." Lucy picked through a bowl of cashews. "'Amy slim as grass, sweet as cream,' that's one of his lyrics, about Amy the perfect girlfriend until she left him for some ski bum in Idaho. Now Terry plays the orphaned lover anytime there's an open-mic night. How do I know? Because that was our first date: an evening featuring Terry and his guitar, and all the chai tea I felt like buying for myself."

"There won't be a second date."

"He has a song called 'O Death.' Victor, tell that to your mother, next time she calls wondering when you'll be married." Lucy stood up and stretched her hamstrings. "So, what about you, how are you, I haven't seen you all day. You talk to that guy from Chemistry yet?"

"Me, with a dozen evaluations to complete?"

You try not getting an erection, I wanted to say.

"Fine, run your scorecards," Lucy said. "You know, for a genetic sample, the middle-class single male? This could be a fire sale for research. I mean, as a consortium, progressing from Neanderthal to, what, passive-aggressive North American. You should see Terry's MySpace page, it's like an Elliott Smith memorial."

Lucy picked up her watch.

"Tell you what, I will leave you to your assessments. Some of us have real work to muddle through."

A minute later, I heard her on the phone in the hallway, bawling out Soborg's IT department about another PC on the fritz.

Gradually the rest of the team left, and Lucy and I ordered pizza and revisited our recent grant. The application had already been submitted, but considering the new budget cuts, we wanted to amend a few pages. Around eleven I called Russell and left him a message saying he was welcome to visit for the weekend. At one in the morning, we smelled chimneys from the parking lot. Bar Harbor was quiet. The mountains behind us were transformed by clouds into pillars of black salt. And suddenly there was Regina. Under the phosphorus lights, wearing a puffy down vest, walking to her car beside an older woman on crutches, her lab director, the two of them laughing in conversation. Regina as the opposite of La Loulou: a modest acolyte in glasses, striding by her director's side, jogging to reach the car first, to unlock and open the door and sweep her arm out, fully stretched, like a valet's, my Regina, the amicable junior scientist, leaving work after a long day's slog.

But actually not mine at all.

"The young ones always *are* eager," said Lucy in my ear.

Regina was startled to see me, but she masked it. Her large eyes didn't change, except to intensify behind her glasses. *Not here*, they messaged to me silently across the parking lot. She rapped her knuckles on her boss's window and I kept walking.

Why not just call it what it is? I watched through my windshield, listening to Ravel, as Regina waved good-bye to her boss.

I turned the key, but left the headlights dark. The other cars pulled out and drove away. I put in a Schumann CD, his Piano Concerto in A Minor. It had been a favorite of my mother's: my mother, for whom music supplied the passion lacking in her marriage.

Regina: now somewhere driving, heading home, listening to Japanese robot rap. What did we have besides a standing sex date? One no longer involving sex, that wasn't quite so eager? A few telephone calls where I rarely spoke?

No wonder she wasn't sure if I cared.

I shifted into reverse, then a secret cave opened inside my chest, and I was about to cry. I re-parked the car. My body went liquid. I punched the steering wheel. There was nothing I could do. By that point I knew what to expect: the comic waves of sobs, a pit in my stomach, and the craven hope that no one had seen me.

The first episode had struck in February, two months before I met Regina, the morning of my birthday: fifty-eight, lying in bed in tears.

Pathetic.

Night frogs were still singing at three in the morning. I pulled on sweatpants, uncorked one of Russell's bottles, and returned to the music room, where I slept most nights. From floor to ceiling, I had a wall of records, LPs I'd collected since high school and stored in pristine condition, plus a few thousand CDs and a couple of old cassettes. As a boy I'd hoarded bugs, toy metal soldiers, postcards from foreign capitals. Perhaps scientists were necessarily collectors first: Darwin with his favorite beetle, Fleming with his bacteria. I considered Schumann again, but picked *Graceland*. Better Paul Simon to treat my insomnia than a composer who'd been kept awake by visions of his own concertos.

When Sara and I met, she'd never seen a stereo receiver that cost more than a car. Nor had I, except in audiophile magazines that promised pleasures like I'd never experienced, which became a party joke of Sara's, whether I preferred aural to oral.

Certain memories persist.

In 1971, I was pursuing my graduate work in New York and not much else. I swam at the university pool in the morning, worked through the night, returned late to my apartment, and played records until I fell asleep. Pretty much the same schedule I'd keep for thirty years. Sara at the time was much more active. She had a circle of friends and lovers downtown whom she saw in the evenings, the most out-there individuals from New York's avant-garde. For a day job, Sara was a copy editor at Macy's, fleshing out the circulars. The first time I saw her, it was in the men's department. She floored me. I was trying on a marked-down blue plaid jacket when Sara walked by with a girl-friend and said in my direction, "'It's tough to match plaid." But she stopped. Perhaps she felt bad about the comment. She was wearing cowboy boots and a buckskin jacket, her hair fell straight down, the blackest black. She was beautiful, like Joan Baez, with olive-colored skin and dark eyes tuned to an intense focus. She hesitated, about to say something, then thought better of it, and reached out and slid a flyer into my jacket's right hip pocket.

"It'll mess with your head," she said, laughing, and walked off with her friend. Dumbstruck, I wondered if she was talking about the jacket. The card advertised a "happening" on Waverly Place that Friday evening, *Goodnight, Icarus*, written and performed by Sara Gardner.

Later on I learned Sara did this to fill seats—she'd hand out a dozen cards by breakfast—but at the time it seemed like a memo straight from Fate. I couldn't get her out of my head: the cowgirl at Macy's with the long black hair. After the performance, a nonsensical monologue performed for an audience of twenty, which I didn't understand at all, Sara was surrounded by admirers. I followed them to a bar nearby and drank two whiskeys sitting on a barrel, watching her when I felt unobserved. Finally, I got up the courage to buy her a drink.

"So did you buy the jacket? I mean, I hope not," she said. "Please say no."

Later, I wanted to tell her everything I'd ever known. Everything I'd seen, all the facts I'd memorized in school, all my stories.

The next morning, I walked more than a hundred blocks back to my apartment. I called her that afternoon. We began spending our nights together, proof that opposites attract. Sara's world, I would discover, was fantasy like I'd never seen, the city's floating French Quarter, an inverse New York limited to a dozen fluctuating locations, a map of small box theaters and crowded parties, where the action was in the kitchen, and it was drugs, boxing, and the latest wave of Floradora girls influenced by Italian neorealism; a world of hangers-on and drunks, of sculptors and painters who were union guys by day, revolutionaries at night; of next-morning phone calls for gossip roundabouts followed by three-hour brunches, always in the same SoHo diner, in the same booths; and several times each week—the likes of *Twelfth Night*, every night—these high-octane, intellectualized, often hair-raising performances with academic mission statements done in old sewing factories in the West Thirties or down near Chinatown in second-floor shops, put on by singers or actors or roughnecks from Oklahoma whom nobody knew, who had just arrived in New York that afternoon, each one falling over himself to impress the next, to one-up whoever had been crowned emperor for the week; and Sara, my Sara, standing slightly apart, sticking with me in the corner, near the fire escape; Sara, their secret Euripides, who dreamed of writing Broadway plays, instead of installing performances off Wall Street, taking notes on a tiny pad she kept in her purse, wearing high heels she'd decorated with glue and costume jewelry.

Sara was my passkey. She'd found a way to wrench open my cerebral cortex and prop the doors. It was the disturbance of the new.

I was shocked by how fragile these artists were behind closed doors and yet so intimidating in public, Sara most of all, Sara whose ego in those days had only sarcasm for scaffolding. We'd stay up late practicing dialogue, and if a section of her latest piece didn't work, she'd throw the pages in the bathtub and run the water. But after her first real play was produced, in a theater for an audience of twenty-five, with me in the wings in my only suit, bearing lilies, her ego got an enormous boost. The typewriter needed new ribbons, and Sara began to write more often than she talked about writing, and her writing improved. I loved her there: typing at the pygmy desk in the kitchen, her hair tied in knots, jeans rolled up to her knees. She started passing me her drafts for notes, and I'd pore over them devotedly, determined to prove my worth. I couldn't believe my luck, that she'd picked me.

Frankly, I didn't understand why any better than I could predict her mood swings. Sara's confidence could vanish in an hour. Some mornings she'd wake up feeling too low to get out of bed, moored under the covers, crying over something she'd read in the paper, and she would call me at the lab, begging me to come downtown.

I waited a year before asking her to marry me. What Sara saw in me I didn't know, but I was desperate to live up to it. I picked a folk club turned into an Italian restaurant with sawdust on the floor. I managed to wait until after the bread arrived before I went down on one knee, feeling for the puny diamond in my pocket. When Sara refused me, the shock made my leg jump. She was infuriated. Said she belonged to no man, particularly not one so square. After only a year, I wanted to claim her? She marched out. Sawdust stuck to my pant leg when I stood up. Then, a few weeks later, it was Sara who proposed on a crowded subway train. Victor Aaron is the most solid element in my life, she announced.

You disarm my mistrust, she said, kneeling on the subway floor.

She had diamonds on her shoes, from the toes to the heels.

Decades later, the music room was my only wish when we finally left New York to build our dream house in Maine (our dream everything: my lab at Soborg, Sara's office with a garden outside the door), and Sony Pictures gave it to me. A fantasy I'd harbored since I was Regina's age, a room just for listening, equipped with top-of-the-line equipment, a comfortable chair, and my record collection. A room designed for one purpose with nothing rational about it, but everything planned to the centimeter. When construction began, I monopolized the contractor for weeks. I sent away to Thailand for wood samples with different resonances, and I spent thousands of dollars on a stereo and nearly as much on a recliner I'd seen in designer furniture catalogs. Sara probably thought it was frivolous, but she held her tongue when she was well within her rights to complain.

It was her money, after all.

Decades after Sara had withdrawn her membership from the avant-garde, a screenplay of hers, *The Hook-Up*, turned into one of the nineties' biggest-grossing films. A mega-movie filmed on a minuscule budget, and written by a relative nobody. Now I received residuals for every Saturday-night replay, every DVD sale in Japan.

And if I'd been asked, when Sara and I first met, based on *Goodnight, Icarus*, if I could envision her becoming one of Hollywood's most talked-about names?

At one point an entertainment magazine wondered whether Sara might be the next Nora Ephron, back when the "little movie that could" was still astonishing the snobs. Sara's answer, confessed to me in bed one night in New York, was that she wanted to continue writing on an island, just not Manhattan. She was finally ready to return to Mount Desert, to the low-lying coastal Maine mountains she'd fled when she was eighteen. I started looking into ways to move my research, to establish a new beachhead, and fortunately the timing was good: my track record spoke for itself, and soon a generous offer appeared from Soborg. Everything seemed to be falling into place. We moved when construction was three-quarters finished: down 102, over the bridge, and right by the drained swamp to our isolated six acres.

The town we chose, Somesville, was Mount Desert Island's first settled community. Fitting, since we were finally settling down. We built our retirement home exactly to Sara's tastes, except for one room overlooking the woods, perfectly balanced acoustically, where I'd recently taken to sleeping. Or trying to sleep, depending on the night.

Betsy called at five-thirty in the morning. The French Open was on, and dear Agassi had advanced to round three. "Those boys are teenagers now, Victor, and he's just ancient. He's Theseus and he's killing them. He's the tour's Superman!"

"Aren't you happy to hear from me, dear?" Betsy added before hanging up.

I stumbled, trying to stand. My right leg was pins and needles. Paul Simon was singing and Betsy's voice rebounded inside my head while I focused on my breathing. Old age whistled near my heart.

I remembered how Sara had once tried to convince a producer friend to cast Bruce Willis for the next Superman sequel. "You'll have to wait until Christopher Reeve dies," she said, "but in terms of charisma? Superpowered, but with human weaknesses, who else could pull it off?"

Regina had brought up Bruce Willis the night we met. It was her way of convincing me to clip my hair down to stubble, in lieu of the wispy laurel I sported at the time.

"Buzz it down the way Bruce Willis does. It'll look imposing."

When she'd wanted to say "less elderly," or "not lame."

But that's what age brought, the power to name things properly. I pushed myself up. Lucky me, to live in an era when the superheroes were balding and over thirty, still able to excite multiple generations of women.

Three days since I'd seen Regina in the parking lot. Seventy-two hours of insecurity, with Regina as an Edmund Leighton portrait hung between my eyes. I tried to maintain my routines. Swimming, work, bad sleep. The clock radio announced a program of "down-east bluegrass," "down east" being a Maine regionalism referring to our neck of coastline, our wild-rose towns beside the Atlantic fishing routes. I'd always found the phrase a touch too quaint, especially the way "down" was invoked.

Did our credibility really need defending against the cosmopolitan Bangor hordes?

Red spruce trees in the yard swung to a northwest wind. The same kinglets and song sparrows I heard every morning chirped from the same boughs. After half an hour, I peered beyond my laptop through my reading glasses.

How old would Agassi be when he retired?

What about Bruce Willis?

I had no desire to review spreadsheets I knew by heart, none to imagine the remaining years of my career. Retirement felt impossible, but what kind of work was I doing anymore, really? One odd thing about AD, we couldn't yet diagnose a patient conclusively, not until after death. Most of us believed we knew what caused Alzheimer's— plaques in the brain that caused diminished function—but it took an autopsy to find them. Plaques, cloaks, caulking. There were evaluations available to people who went in for a workup. One was a test in which a person would receive four words, each belonging to a different set. For "sweater," the category could be clothing; for "dog," animal. A few minutes later, the examiner would repeat the category name, and the patient would need to remember the related word; people with dementia or Alzheimer's often got stuck trying to relate one to the other.

So what did it say of me that when I thought of science, of my passion for research, I no longer saw a connection to what remained of my career?

Between seventh and eighth grade I grew seven inches. That rapid development led to painful knee problems, which caused my doctor to ban me from gym class. So I sought competition in academics, validation in my teachers' esteem, though in college I discovered swimming, and took to it as a meditation, a way to wring out stress. These days I did my laps mainly with a kickboard, but when it was warm enough I skipped the Soborg gym for the island's ponds and lakes, sometimes even the ocean.

I grabbed a dry pair of swim trunks and started the car.

How comforting it could be, being alone. It prevented the scenery from blending in. The drive to Little Long Pond was a winding road by the sea. The ocean charging in over the rocks was blue paisley. The pond was deserted. I did laps back and forth, setting a goal for twenty, and focused on listening to my lungs, trying to feel my muscles warm up and relax.

But there was Regina, throwing her barrettes at the wall.

At least complain about someone. You never talk.

You really don't give a fuck about me, do you?

So did Regina want us to become some conventional twosome? Dinner and a movie, and afterward, banana splits? But it was true, recently I'd noticed her withdrawing more into herself: moodier in bed, more sarcastic on the telephone. Fewer Fridays where she'd prepared a routine.

But maybe something else was upsetting her, I wondered. Maybe there was someone else.

After half an hour, I toweled off and drove up the road to the beach in Seal Harbor. The view there included a small bay, some bobbing sailboats, and a swimming dock. Fog clung to the water. An older couple was walking the beach, collecting litter in a child's sand pail. Once, when we took coffee and newspapers to the beach, Sara found a used condom wedged under a pile of rocks. Some gay teenagers had buried it as a cairn for their love, she said. Another morning, Sara called me out to the backyard. A condor was trapped in a tree, its wingspan snared by the branches. Sara was crying, and I remembered trying to hug her, when she snapped, "Oh, get away, it's just a bird, this is the fucking menopause talking."

But when I reminded her of that morning a few months later, her line about the menopause, which I'd found quite funny, Sara insisted she never said it. That I had it wrong. She'd been worried about the condor was all, that's what had made her cry, and wasn't it typical both of me and men that I should misattribute emotion to menopause.

I swore, though, I remembered it correctly. In any case, we called the fire rescue squad, they extracted the vulture, and it clapped away. So maybe Sara had it wrong, I thought. About the condor *and* the condom. Maybe some kid spent a quarter in a gas station bathroom, then hid the rubber out of shame. It was just one clue. A buried condom, a stained wife-beater: What would the great detective Hercule Poirot do with such clues except laugh?

How about: Poirot and the Case of the Vanishing Erections.

A green Oldsmobile Cutlass Ciera drove into the parking lot and rammed my bumper at five miles an hour. The doors sported fluorescent orange racing stripes. Betsy had painted them on herself, to make the car easier to identify in parking lots.

"You idiot," she shouted hoarsely, "no one swims until August. You'll catch pneumonia!"

Betsy grasped my wrist through the window and snapped her cigarette into the rushes.

I said, "You're going to set this island on fire. Again."

In the 1940s, most of Bar Harbor had burned down, cause unknown.

"Oh, go to hell."

I was actually very pleased to see her. "How did you find me?"

"How do you think? I call the office, your lab manager tells me you're working at home. I call the house, no one's there. It's too late for you to be swimming at the gym. Where else would you be?"

I conceded the point. "But why?"

Betsy stuck out her lips, pulled a lipstick down from the visor, and applied it slowly in practiced loops. Her white hair was pasted flat on her head, with a slight flip at the ends, as though she'd been wearing a swim cap. Her trusty beach hat lay on the passenger seat.

"My boyfriend wants to know why I want to see him. Well, I need assistance."

"With what?"

"Oh *forget* it, Victor."

"Now what?"

"Will you buy a lady a drink?"

"How about coffee?"

"I don't want coffee."

"Well, all right, then."

Betsy snapped the top back on her lipstick.

"You've stopped drinking beer, prig? But after we finish working, let's go."

I was about to ask, and then I noticed the picket signs.

Downtown in Northeast Harbor, along the boardwalk, I insisted on staying in the car. I'd told Betsy before, hers was a solo mission, but I did help set up her station: a card table, a folding chair, and her hand-lettered signs: GEORGE BUSH, AL QAEDA RECRUITER OF THE YEAR and YEE-HA IS NOT FOREIGN POLICY and GUESS I DESERVE WHAT YOU MORONS WANTED. Not that I disagreed with her politics, I just wasn't the protest type.

Aunt Betsy and Sara used to stay up late discussing the news, Betsy taking the socialist fight to Sara's gradual, resentful right-leaning (Clinton had ruined her liberal side). When there wasn't enough gossip to fill the day, Betsy clipped stories from the newspapers and added them to a Bush-Cheney conspiracy map she was building on her dining room wall from Post-it notes. Recently, she'd begun speaking truth to the sidewalk. Her argument, that Northeast Harbor saw more policy makers than K Street on an average summer weekday, wasn't illogical. Both the Cap Weinberger estate and Senator George Mitchell's house were down the road, though in opposite directions.

She returned twenty minutes later. "Roll down the window!"

"Do you want a hand?"

"Too late. Nobody's listening. They think I'm a skinny old joke." Two hikers walked away, smiling to themselves. "Besides, Bayne says I'm driving away customers, isn't he smug."

Bayne Gifford was staring at us from inside his ice cream store, hands in his apron pockets. Betsy stared right back at him. Both were the geologic embodiment of traditional Maine obstinacy, like Sara refusing to wear a seat belt.

"He doesn't understand we're at war," Betsy said. "Sacrifice is expected."

I suggested we sacrifice my Visa over lunch. Northeast Harbor was a small village with a single main street, where wealthy people went to feel quainter about themselves. Some old folks stopped Betsy on the sidewalk to say hello, twenty-five minutes of hello. We passed a jewelry store, and Betsy admired a necklace in the window made from lacquered coral. An hour later, after lunch at a seafood restaurant, I presented it to her across the table, feeling quite pleased with myself.

From my view of the harbor, it looked like there were only five docks. At that moment, losing my sexual capacity seemed a bailout. Now I could enjoy the simple pleasures in life: work, music, nature, my elderly girlfriend easily and not too expensively satisfied.

"You're a damn nuisance," Betsy said, and dropped the necklace on the table. "Oh, Victor. You know, I was thinking about Sara this morning," she said a moment later. "I had a dream. It was that night she showed up on our doorstep, when she was sixteen."

"The big fight."

"Now, it wasn't the shock you'd figure. Ginnie *always* was drinking, you never knew what would happen next." Ginnie was Betsy's sister-in-law, Sara's mother, who had long since passed away from cancer. "But it was terrible, this plan of Sara's. Three in the morning, a bus ticket for San Francisco. Sara ringing the doorbell like she's the one who's been drinking. She was there to say good-bye, you know. Personally, I felt like I was losing Joel all over again. Good-bye forever, she said. Because she hit poor Ginnie."

Joel was Betsy's only child. As a teenager, he'd run away from boarding school and vanished, drifting with druggie friends through

California beach towns. Subsequently, though, he'd surprised everyone by becoming an accomplished chef. He now ran a restaurant on
the island where I ate frequently, at least when I could afford to.

But something sounded wrong about Betsy's story. I said, "She
was hit, you mean. Ginnie hit Sara. That's what made Sara want to
leave home."

Betsy put down her coffee. "What are you talking about?"

"Her mother was the one—"

"Ginnie was punched straight in the craw, is what happened.
Her mouth, Sara's fist, and she deserved it. If anyone in our family had
had an ounce of nerve, she would've been locked up in a drunk tank
years earlier. Think of the embarrassment, Victor, being *sick* on the
floor at the poor girl's school play? I don't blame Sara a smidge."

"See, I would swear it was the other way around," I said.

"Well, you swear wrong. Check, please."

"You don't want dessert?"

Betsy leveraged herself to a standing position and unwrapped a
toothpick, pinpointing me with her stare.

"You need to get yourself a girl, Victor."

Two months after Sara's funeral, I was taking the garbage out in the
rain when I discovered that someone had left a pile of leaking trash
bags in the shed. The place stank. Someone must have unlocked the
door and dumped his trash, even made a routine of it, but who would
do that?

I was gathering up coffee grounds with a dustpan, angry and wet and
late for work, when I realized the culprit was me. I'd canceled the pick-up
service. The week after Sara died, I'd been in the kitchen and remembered her saying how we could save money by driving the trash to the

two

*Change of direction two, and I don't know where to start.
Well, that's not true. I knew as soon as you proposed this idea what my first
three turns would be. But right now I'm parked outside a CVS, I'm sitting in my
car, I just bought a package of index cards like they're Kleenex. Like I'm about to
break down.*

Perhaps I am about to break down.

*Victor's voice is still ringing in my ears from the parking lot outside your
office. That was just twenty minutes ago.*

*Between this card and the first one, when Victor and I met, there's a gap
of twenty years. Two decades reduced to a thirty-second montage, a flip book of
cities, apartments, friends, vacations, birthday parties. Marriage as a product
of mass and velocity, traveling in a single direction forward. Of course, though,
with peaks and valleys. My mother passed away from cancer. Victor's father died
from a stroke. I miscarried. September 9, 1978. We named her Elizabeth, after
my grandmother. Victor and I went to Puerto Rico for a week and decided not
to try again. We talked vaguely about adoption, it was something we might do
someday, like a safari we'd take when we had the money.*

Twenty years of motion. Each time Victor wrangled a new appointment, we moved. And we were young, we had fun. There were wonderful weekend trips, outdoor concerts, and long city walks. It felt as though society were shifting, but as a team we were grounded. It was the two of us moving across a moving world, both of us striving so hard. I even got Victor to grow out his hair. We went to Paris and to Crete, a romantic week in each, and then came Boston. Victor got the call from Harvard, his big break, and so began the Cambridge period: Victor, in his early thirties, the relentless seeker, hard-charging in the lab, and me taking afternoon strolls with graduate students, who quizzed me for their theses on performance art. Furloughs when Victor had a conference, but he rarely had a conference. There was too much work for that. I never saw him. He was so focused on research and making a name for himself that we were landlocked by his lab schedule, him at sea and me in the window. I tried playing housewife for a year to an empty house. Then I got a grant to start a tiny theater in Somerville, sandwiched between a hardware store and a salon. We ran eight productions in twenty-four months, none of them mine and every one a stinker. By that point, though, I was visibly weakening. I was tired of life, what we called a life. I was exhausted from avoiding putting demands on my husband, the workaholic. I bought a biography of Emma Darwin at one point to please Victor, thinking it could be adapted for the stage, and threw it away after reading ten pages. Honestly, deep down, I was simmering with rage, prepared to light Cambridge on fire, and meanwhile my husband was beaming with success. He was part of the team that helped figure out Alzheimer's core mechanism. For me, though, every month there was another knuckle in the fist pinning me to the floor.

Then Victor got an offer. Our fortunes lifted, as if from Fate: associate professorship, support for a lab and in New York no less. I may as well have drunk champagne the whole way down I-95, this glorious spring day. Victor clipped the car over to the Merritt Parkway, and both of us were happy and in love again, laughing, passing glances back and forth, fully knowing we were on our way.

And knowing I would, I regained my groove. Soon I was writing again, hav-

laughed louder at his jokes. I was forty years old, and damn if I didn't want to feel sexy, if I didn't like looking young in his eyes.

Then at some point Victor asked me pointedly, "So how was rehearsal?" And I remember sobering when he said it. Because all it took was the change in his voice. Between the appetizers and entrees, this quiet moment when his tone stood out for its openness, and so did his face, and I dived in, when with just that one little question he'd made us "us" again, the us I loved. Well, I took him up on it, made some dumb joke before getting to anything real, but just when I stopped joking, when Victor inquired again and pressed me and put his hand on the table near mine, this time asking something more specific, about a certain actress's tendency to drop lines, Russell interrupted, wanting to know if Victor understood what a hot piece of ass he'd married.

Russell laughed at his own comment and started telling some story. A minute later, Victor excused himself to the restroom, and Russell took the opportunity to tell me what knockout proportions I had, like I was an apartment he wanted to rent.

"Honestly, Sara, you know if Victor wasn't my best friend—"

Victor came back. The two of them spent the rest of dinner discussing stereo equipment.

How many cards has this taken?

Twelve cards.

I'm staring at the plastic wrapper from the cards balled up in the ashtray, threatening to uncrinkle and pop out.

I wonder if that night meant anything to Victor. If he ever thought of it again. If it was more than just another dinner out, another New York night, while for me it was an era collapsing by the time we got the check. An evening bigger than a decade.

Victor will never see these cards. I can already hear the Socratic inquiry, his careful investigations, to pry and soothe simultaneously. He'll say I've got it wrong. He'll say my remembering is incorrect, that I'm over-emphasizing, under-

analyzing, the typical dramatist's approach: emoting. Besides, he's not coming to counseling again anyway. An hour ago, we had a fight in the parking lot about psychology, "pseudoscience." He blew up, and one thing he didn't see was that I loved it. Just to get him shouting, part of me was happy. A lot of me. That was psychological progress I'd pay triple for any day.

Victor listens to neurons, not people. Something he'll find frustrating or unnerving about someone at a dinner party, he'll label "interesting" and leave it at that. Right at the moment when anyone else would vent normal human frustration, Victor shuts down, or clasps his hands behind his back and observes and labels. As though to say, never get involved. People don't change. You can't bring about evolution, the point is to watch and ponder. And yes, in my exasperation there's still part of me that likes that side in him, since it's the opposite of my tendency to pounce or explode.

It was something I once wanted for myself: to step out of myself into the cool-blooded post.

But for all of Victor's powers of analysis, he never turns them inward. I remember I once urged him to keep a diary. He said, "What would I write about? I don't spend much time reflecting why I do anything."

Woman Hits Forty was a big success, up in lights nine months, a great run. The producers got paid, the actress got an Outer Critics Circle Award, and I found my voice and some big paychecks. Late bloomer, but I bloomed. I gave myself four hours at Saks. I called Mark, my new agent, out in Los Angeles.

First thing Mark asked me, "How come you're not writing screenplays?"

Know what Victor said? "What do you know about writing screenplays?"

Regina's town, Otter Creek, where Indian campfires once attracted the sights of Mount Desert Island's first European visitor, the French explorer Samuel de Champlain. Sara bought me an edition of his journals when we moved to Maine, so that I'd have an idea of the island's history.

"This island is very high, and cleft into seven or eight mountains, all in a line," Champlain wrote around 1600. "The summits of most of them are bare trees, nothing but rock. I name it l'Isle des Monts-déserts."

In April, when I first met Regina, there was still a foot of snow on the ground. By five on a Friday, in the basin of a mountain range, her bedroom would be a glowing box, a lighthouse in the woods. I'd hang a right by the motel, go two miles on a dirt road, and turn up a gravel drive, and there at the top would be Regina's cottage, with the sagging roof, shingles in the yard like litter. Shutters off their hooks. Her bedroom light would be on, first floor, southeast corner, and so would the porch light, and I'd walk inside without knocking, knowing the room-mate was away, the curtain about to rise.

But that Friday, there'd been no invitation. No e-mail from Regina commanding me to attend. If La Loulou's show was going up, some-one else held the ticket. Russell's plane would arrive in an hour, and I was still at the lab with my staff gathered for our weekly Friday status meeting, trying to stay focused.

"The point is," Lucy said, pacing beside my whiteboard while she dug her fingertips into her arms, "what are we looking at? Too many holes. Gaps and flaws. If you make a mistake, just let some-body know. Copy me on the e-mail. Put up a red flag. We're gathering an enormous data dump here, of course slips occur. But if Dr. Aaron and I aren't warned to catch them, we'll have big trouble down-stream."

Recently we'd experienced quality-control problems. Crammed around my office, sitting on folding chairs or perched on the radia-tor, our team of fourteen was more than half composed of recent ad-ditions, many to leave in the next year or two for other labs, med school, further training. Listening to Lucy, I tried to concentrate on the milestones rather than the headaches. I knew too many researchers who'd been undone by the pressure to publish, raise more money, swim faster. And what was lost was the satisfaction of knowing truth: the thrill of discovering an answer to the question each experiment posed.

Each airtight, flawless, beautiful experiment.

Half an hour later, I thanked everyone, proposed a revised sched-ule for incorporating new data, and called it a day. Five minutes later, Lucy was back in my doorway. She said calmly, "Tell me, why do we have to go through this every time?"

"Just the way it goes."

"We hire too many gunners, is what it is, not enough plain-Jane control freaks. But why?"

"Why what?"

"Do this," said Lucy. Her features and shoulders sagged. "All of this."

"Listen, I'm late picking up a friend."

Lucy stretched her forearms on the doorframe. "You should see yourself. You look like three bucks."

"I'll take it that's not a compliment."

"What I would give, Victor," she said, turning away, "for the NIH people simply to magically appear and say, Yes yes, take the money, have fun."

Ten minutes later, I was stuck in a line of cars. I nearly slammed on the horn several times out of frustration. A few years earlier, they'd built a Walmart in Ellsworth, and now it caused traffic jams for miles along the one-road concourse off the island. I stared at the wipers, wondering if Regina was burlesquing somewhere miles behind me.

Years in the past, someone thought my wife was a knockout, one night long ago in a restaurant. A night I didn't remember.

Since Wednesday I'd kept some of Sara's index cards in my shirt pocket, her notes about how we met, how I'd neglected her apparently just when Broadway called. I'd stayed up nights rereading them. One night I tossed them in the kitchen trash with the tangerine peels and coffee grounds, only to run down to retrieve them the next morning. Having them on me meant I could avoid going back to Sara's office to read the rest.

And she was right: in some cases, I didn't agree with how Sara remembered things. I remembered celebrating her success in our little living room by the fireplace with champagne. I remembered lovemaking, late-night conversations, snuggling in bed. Our unspoken signals: the hand-squeezes to silently say I love you. Me playing the bleary-eyed bulwark when Sara was overcome with anxiety and couldn't sleep. I remembered her nerves, and how I took care of her. How I went to the drugstore at two a.m. because she'd broken out in hives, worrying about that play. And if I had been neglectful, balanced against Sara's enormous need for attention, for regular, escalating affirmations, then surely there was a good reason we both were forgetting: a grant, a paper, something at the lab.

But about that dinner she described, I drew a blank. Which didn't necessarily mean much. We probably had dinner with Russell a hundred times in New York. But for this one night to have mattered so much to Sara that she chose it as a point when our marriage turned a corner, and yet to figure so lightly in my own recollections?

There was a moment in New York that she hadn't mentioned, a night we had a terrible row. I was home late from work and Sara confronted me in the front hallway with a simple question: "Why do you ignore me?" She'd been crying. It was midnight, she was wearing an old Chicago sweatshirt of mine with rips in the underarms. It had been a terrible, arresting shock. She walked away and I stood in the hall fiddling with some mail in the key basket, wondering a storm of thoughts. It took me a few weeks to recover and then grasp how I needed to change, which seemed pathetic now in retrospect, but I'd dedicated myself afterward to a plan of evolution: engaging, listening, spending more time at home; being better about leaving work behind when I locked up at school; worrying fewer nights away in the lab or on the phone from home, and stopping weekend work altogether; being a better husband.

But it must have been around the time that Sara started writing *Woman Hits Forty*. Because just when I changed to be more of a homebody, it seemed as though she didn't want a husband at all. I thought I'd simply read her wrong. How else to explain the short temper, her lack of interest in sex or conversation? And then the play took off, Sara rocketed up to Broadway, and soon it was she who wasn't coming home after work, leaving messages saying I should order take-out.

A change of direction for me, not for her.

The airline representative said Russell's plane was late, due to rain. A thin fog was drifting through the meadows surrounding the tarmac. I went back to my car and put in a John Dowland CD and turned up the volume. Sixteenth-century lute songs to wake the drifting dead.

The night I met Regina was foggy, too, at a party of Soborg people where I'd snuck out to escape the band. When Regina appeared, I was leaning on a railing, remembering how it had always been Sara's job to lead at parties, particularly after *The Hook-Up* was in the works: Sara tugging me behind her, like a teddy bear, her husband the "famous" scientist, hadn't they seen the latest issue of *Nature*? But whoever it was, whether some agent or producer, he'd often seem more pleased than I expected, as if here was a chance to be normal, show off he'd once taken a science class. "The genome project, now, that's real magic," one would say, and then we'd leave for the next group of strangers, our chain of hands yanked by Sara's agent, Mark, who was constantly whispering, "But you must meet Arlo, you must know Thaddeus, you must know Jude."

Except Victor, who needed to know Victor?

"You should shave it," Regina had said from somewhere behind my left shoulder. Her voice was bored, affected to sound worldly. "Like the way Bruce Willis does," she said. "It would be more imposing."

The party was held in honor of Soborg's president, the man who'd recruited me in the first place. Almost the entire institute had gathered to celebrate his ninetieth birthday, Dr. Solomon Low's, a former Dartmouth dean and renowned biologist, well known for his crotchety temper and his humpback, hence his nickname, Toad.

I was not Toad's favorite. Academics demonstrated status by hoarding information, displaying that behind their peacock feathers they owned something no one else possessed (and thus our fields of study had over time become more specialized, more competitive, and less able to communicate with one another), and in the same fashion, academic institutions prized notable names, the better to flaunt their standing. Basically, Toad would have liked me more if I were cited more frequently in *The Boston Globe*. He was an old-guard New England aristocrat who took his favorite employees sailing. The time I went, I was seasick in the hold, and when we docked he was still laughing about it.

"I met him, actually, Bruce Willis," I said to Regina. "At a party in New York."

"Nice guy?"

"Nice enough."

"Wouldn't you want to look like Bruce Willis?"

How did she know?

"People here get hung up on not caring about their looks," Regina said. She leaned on the railing. "It's like everyone's deciduous. No one knows how the island repopulates itself."

Past the lawn, the ocean stewed under the moon, crashing with foam like magnesium bursts. "Maybe," I said, "it's because there's no sex ed in the schools."

"Maybe it's because there's no one to have sex with."

"Maybe it's just too cold."

Now she laughed, a surprisingly sincere laugh, and I felt as if I'd won a prize. I'd never seen anyone like Regina. She wore a black crepe dress and gold shoes, and spoke on the cusp of sneering with a hushed, deep voice. Big legs, broad shoulders, painted lips. Aware of her effects, but not quite in control. Probably too much for boys her age.

Next to the kitchen was an empty sitting room full of plants. We sat on a love seat. Regina told me about her undergraduate years in Ann Arbor writing poetry and organic chemistry papers. Her parents had been free spirits, both trained as biologists but practicing as hippie farmers. They took family trips from Michigan to study marine life in Florida, one summer joining an archaeological dig in Montana. After graduating from college, Regina spent two years working for a pharmaceutical company outside Boston, and then moved to Maine to work at Soborg.

"Now everyone I meet wants to play country bumpkin, to try their hand at the plow. And I want to join the Velvet Underground."

"Then why here, of all places?" I asked. I had a hard time picturing her in Bar Harbor during the busy months, never mind the winter, when the island emptied out, when the passes filled with chest-high snow, and the forests were more congested than the towns.

"Well, the work." As though this were a stupid question. "Soborg's not exactly bush league. Do you know how many people applied for my position?"

"But you'll do your Ph.D. somewhere else."

"Sure, I'm hoping for Michigan. I mean, I love the work, I just don't know if it's my life's ruling passion. Maybe I'll make out for Broadway. You know I played Ophelia once; I still remember the lines."

She laughed at herself, and then her eyes lit up; she turned toward me, pulled her feet underneath her, and asked about my favorite movies. I mentioned *The Blue Dahlia*. She slapped me lightly on the leg.

"Come on, you're lying."

"Why would I lie?"

"Whatever, it's one of my favorites, too. George Marshall? Veronica Lake?"

"No, you're teasing," I said. "You're too young to appreciate it."

"I'm not so young."

Twenty minutes later, Regina stood up, smoothed her dress with both hands, and excused herself. "E-mail me sometime. Or don't." She smiled. She pronounced, "Rich gifts wax poor when givers prove unkind."

Decisions have multiple origins, neurologically. If we used only our brain's rational side, we'd analyze without stopping, dissect our options into ever smaller pieces, and follow out their logical options, step by step, until we were so distant from the original impulse that we'd forget why we began. Without our emotional voices, without the gut, without sentimental gales and whatever mute instinct governed (or not so mute, considering the loudness of hunger, a sex drive's roaring static), there'd be only dithering.

I spent the weekend composing a letter in my head. I found Regina's e-mail address in the Soborg directory. I e-mailed her Friday morning, a week later, surely too late. *Dear Miss Bellette*. I wrote that I had enjoyed our meeting. Perhaps we could have coffee sometime in the Soborg cafeteria. Or not. Yours sincerely, Victor Aaron.

She responded after lunch.

Try again. Write this. Dear La Loulou, I'll be by at five, see you then.

I laughed from shock. I read it and couldn't believe what I was reading. I sat back, then lurched forward and did as she commanded. I clicked REPLY and typed through a daze, *Dear La Loulou, I'll be by at five, see you then.*

The same reply I'd send the next nine Fridays in a row.

Try again. Write this.

I stared out through my windshield at a low band of trees. A plane was just landing in the mist, bouncing down the wet black strip.

Russell and I got back to the house around ten. The answering machine in the kitchen said I had a new message. I pressed the wrong button and a voice shouted, *You have selected Daylight Saving Time.*

Betsy wanted to know how I'd forgotten about our dinner date. At least, why didn't I call? "Never call me again, Victor," she said. There was a long pause. "Good night." Another pause. "This was Betsy."

One of my regular Friday dates I hadn't been invited to, the other one I'd failed to please.

"Was that the aunt?" Russell asked. He had big arms but small hands, the frame of a lineman squeezed into a gymnast. He looked like he might tumble off the counter stool. "Wait," he added, "I remember. The nut-job."

"Be nice," I said. "She's eccentric."

"Eccentric, right." He got his thumb under the peel of a tangerine. "Like putting a beanie on a serial killer. I mean, when it's my time, call me crazy, please. People respect crazy."

Russell bounced off the stool and took his suitcase upstairs to the guest bedroom. I put a Post-it note on the refrigerator reminding myself to call Betsy in the morning. I heard the shower running and then a squeaky tenor, out of tune, screeching through "Satisfaction." I went outside and collected kindling.

Russell had begged for a fire. One of Sara's best ideas when designing the house had been to install an outdoor fireplace, this pit contraption from a gardening catalog that stood next to the deck. Now that the rain had blown away, the night was cloudless. I was shuffling out to the log pile when Russell called from his window, "Check that shit out!"

Stars covered the black distance: Ursa Major, Virgo, Hercules, the names came swiftly back to me. I'd been bonkers for my telescope when I was ten. I loved knowing where to draw the edges and shapes. In school that year we'd been forced to memorize the state capitals, and I'd approached the task by reassigning them as dots in the sky, simply more stars I should remember. Lessons I learned on my own about differentiation, about the comparative scale of my desires. The idea being that if I was so extremely small, then I could do almost anything, because what impact would I have, really? What damage could be done, being so puny in the big scheme?

Yet the dinner Sara mentioned in her cards, I couldn't retrieve. It wouldn't light up. As though as soon as the three of us crossed Third Avenue at a walk signal, it disappeared and no outline was left behind. A fragment of experience my brain found no reason to bind to any others.

"Seriously, is it always like this at night?" Russell yelled, and then ducked back inside.

He appeared downstairs ten minutes later, his sleeves scrunched up, carrying a bottle of wine. Russell's great-grandfather came from Naples, his grandfather from Uniondale. They were Italians on the lean side, slimmed by the depression and emigration, but Russell had been their pride's rebirth, built like a hog. One of the high school toughs, he'd also been my best friend and my protector in those years, a fellow outcast before he filled out, and then simply an A student who happened to wrestle. Now in his fifties, he had a lined face, permanent stubble, soft lips, and close-cropped gray hair. A jolly miniature giant devoted to triathlons, he cycled miles around Central Park in the mornings, a rhino on a tricycle. His gut was his only handicap: it was shaped like a cube, as if he'd swallowed a small moving box.

He waved the wine bottle at me. "Let's get to it already."

"What are we drinking?" I said, banking the fire.

"Cherry pie. A rare California Cab. Trust me, it's a lot better than you deserve."

"Thank you."

"I'm serious, you won't appreciate it," Russell said. "Your tongue is tone deaf. You'll get strawberry jam if you're lucky." He'd swapped his blazer for a thick black turtleneck sweater, his distressed designer blue jeans for a pair of Levi's. I put on Brad Mehldau, something pleasant.

Russell stuck his nose deep in the glass after pouring. "A friend of mine in Sonoma makes this in his garage. Huge in the game. Look for tobacco notes. What do you think?"

"Cherry pie," I said, swallowing, and sat down. Wine was Russell's music, not mine.

"Here, let's toast," he said, thrusting his glass at me. After a pause, he dropped his head two inches: "To Maine skies."

"To Maine."

"So, okay, give me something."

"What?"

"I'm up here from New York. I've earned it."

He squinched his eyes.

"Get out of here," I said.

Russell took my hand. "Vic, I want to know how you are. How you're doing. Who you're sleeping with."

I laughed. "I've got nothing. Work is about it."

"The monk. Well, you look awful." He spread his hands over his knees. His fingers were baby pink and stubby. "Honestly, you've got bags under your eyes. Don't forget, I've nursed you, I've seen you at your worst. You're worse now, swear to God."

Part of this was true. After Sara's accident, Russell moved in for a month, despite my refusal to have him: he did the cooking, cleaning, making arrangements I couldn't possibly. Calling me every morning for a month afterward to check in. Calling me each year on the anniversary.

It came blurting out: "Well, I've been seeing someone."

Jesus Christ.

"Bullshit."

"She's younger."

"What's young?"

"Twenty-five."

Russell cracked his knuckles.

"What?"

"Go on."

"She works at Soborg. I'm crazy. It's crazy."

"What's the sex like?" Russell asked.

"No, it's more than sex."

"So describe the sex."

"It's not about sex. She dances."

"All right, you're a magician. She dances?"

The words just came out: "Burlesque. You know, those old strip-teases. It's cool now."

"Cool now."

"Honestly, we don't even have sex anymore."

After a moment he leaned over to whisper, "Because you can't get it up."

"I'm crazy about her," I said.

"Yeah, of course." He refilled our glasses. "Of course you are. 'Crazy' is the billion-dollar word up here."

Russell kicked a log back into the fire.

"So what are your erections like? I'm being serious. Medium-soft? Full-bodied when you're by yourself?"

"Fuck you."

"Are you on the pill?"

"Viagra? No."

He sat there, staring off.

"Has she taken you shopping yet?"

"I don't get it."

"Hey, neither do I. Though where a girl goes shopping around here, who knows. I'll take that as a no."

"No."

"This has been going on how long?"

"Beginning of April."

"These days that's a decade. How often do you take her out?"

"We don't," I said, "it's just Fridays," and already I was regretting every word, confessing to the man who once compared my wife to real estate, assuming Sara had it right.

"*It's just Fridays.* You sound like one of those in-flight magazines." Russell rolled his shoulders. "You don't see it, do you? You are just about toast. I give it three weeks."

"I think she's seeing someone else."

"Oh, do you? Of all the out-of-touch scientists in the world." He clawed for my arm and I let myself be pulled down. "Listen to me. What juju have you got? What is your pull, exactly?"

We were inches from each other. I went back to my chair.

"You're not bankrolling her, you're not dating, you're not fucking her."

"You don't get it."

"I don't get it? Victor, you haven't dated since Haight-Ashbury.

These are women of the next century. Two months ago, I live and breathe, listen to me, I had a twenty-six-year-old, I thought I was going to marry this one. Me. Let's imagine here that I'm not kidding, imagine me seriously considering being married again. Now picture the girl it would take: beautiful, intelligent, vivacious. Already at her age she's running her own PR company. Beautiful clothes, jewelry, I mean, great taste, she didn't need shit from me, and not for love or money would I let her go. We met at a charity auction, and three weeks later I'm on the Tiffany's website. Fuck it, listen, I was serious, then this past week she *informs* me we're through. Monday morning. That's it, up and done. And never mind that she's dumping me, it's the ratio-nale that gives us clarity, because she used me. She drained me dry and was ready to move on. That's how they operate now, Victor, I'm telling you, *vampirically*. You are to be tried and returned, like she bought you off the Internet. Because I'm too old to marry, is her excuse, I'm a charity event. I'm not the type she would marry anyway, she says, for clauses A through K, plus she has her own money, her career, plenty of other men she can call for sex, and the sex was losing steam, she points out, fine, but listen, this was over e-mail. With bullet points. How the fuck do you format bullet points? Buddy, her generation had e-mail *in elementary school.* Monday morning, seven a.m., I'm standing in line at Starbucks reading my BlackBerry, I haven't even gotten my fucking coffee yet." He paused. "You think I'm up here to see you? Shit, I had to escape. Manhattan's for the Amazons now."

He said, "You know what a BlackBerry is, right?"

The fire would need more fuel to keep going. We finished our wine. Russell shivered and rolled down his sleeves, staring out into the forest. "See, I worry about you. These are not your woods. Hell, I'm surprised your jackets don't turn camo."

"So you're saying what?" I jammed my hands in my pockets. I was up, pacing again, kicking the logs around the firebox. "Because I could stand here for some clarity."

"What are you, freaking out?"

"You're the ladies' man, you're the goddamn expert."

Russell watched me with his fingers laced behind his head. "Brother, this is your rebound play. Find a nice innkeeper. Find some fifty-year-old divorcee who will listen. You're out of your league with Gypsy Rose, you're fucking it up. Just act your age. Be steadfast for once.

"Shit, your dick must be killing you," he added, "all blue-balled up."

There wasn't anything to do but finish the wine. Russell laughed quietly and lit a cigar. Afterward, he went inside to make coffee, real coffee, assuming I'd join him, and I said sure, but I didn't want any.

Two in the morning, I was tired of staring at the ceiling. I padded over to my office and booted up the computer and sat down heavily in the chair. One e-mail I read twice: *Sorry, schedule fuckup. You can come over if you want. Reply to this first tho.*

I typed: *Too late?*

Five minutes later: *Not too late, no.*

Russell's snoring was loud enough that I could hear it in the driveway. I quietly rolled down the gravel, past my neighbors, then on Route 3 I floored it, hitting five thousand RPMs in third gear. With most houses set back from the road, the route to Regina's was a canyon ride, a night race through the desert. For the last mile, I turned off the lights and drove by the moon.

Then, just before Regina's cottage, deep in the woods, a car came flying at me, its lights out like mine. Time seemed to slow. I threw my headlights on and swerved out of the way, barely avoiding an accident, and a Ford Taurus sedan glided by in black and green streaks, as though in a dream. Maybe it was a dream. In the headlights' punch I saw Regina's roommate, Lindsay, glaring back at me.

I'd seen her only once before, over Regina's shoulder, a tall girl with dyed green hair, back in May. Regina had been standing in the door explaining how Lindsay had come home from work with a stomach virus. "Didn't you look at the porch light?" Regina hissed through her teeth, her facial muscles draining her cheeks to purse her lips, and I remembered how, on our first afternoon, Regina had decided that this would be our secret sign: porch light on, sailors' delight, but porch light off, and sailors tack back to Somesville.

Tonight the light was on. Regina was waiting in a chair with a magazine, wearing a kimono. She greeted me with a yawn, her breath vinegary from liquor. I sat on the bed and removed my shoes. I didn't know what to say. It seemed impossible to say anything without meaning too much.

A shawl had been tossed over her desk lamp. She put a record on the portable turntable I'd bought her, and a piano led off "A Pretty Girl Is Like a Melody." Regina held her robe closed and started twirling figure eights, her show of feints and teases. I told myself to relax. A minute later, the record stopped. Regina jolted awake, the robe's hem still swinging above her knees when she froze.

"Aren't you going to fix it?"

I jumped up, but I couldn't get the arm to work again. Regina kicked off her heels and walked out, a little wobbly, her flat feet slapping on the floor.

"Someone is getting laid when I come back," she said from the hall. "Let that be known."

Regina returned and pushed me backward, intently focused on one thing. As for me, I was thinking of Russell laughing by the fire. I fumbled with her bra. I kissed her nipples but I couldn't remember if she liked that. When she said in my ear, "Let's do it doggie-style," I froze. I swung Regina around and threw her down, playacting the aggressor, seeing the will working through her face as she struggled to believe that here was Victor, confident, manhandling, while a voice in my head repeated the words softly, *doggie-style*, remembering how Sara had always hated that phrase. What would Sara have done with "wife beater"? Like a bus of kids driving back and forth between my ears, overjoyed with new slang: *dogs fucking doggie-style*.

A few moments of mutual, unsuccessful coaxing before Regina, unable to hide the disappointment any longer, rolled away and made herself come. Two minutes. Three minutes. Rap music exploded through the woods, a dog started barking. Regina returned with one hand on the mattress, propping herself up, one hand on my chest.

"*Chéri*, what's going on?"

"I'd rather not."

"Now don't be bothered."

"Regina, please?"

A minute later, rather testy: "Well, I'd like to be here for you, you know. But first you need to let me be here at all."

"Can we just not talk?"

"Sure. Great." She pulled down the scarf and covered her face. My mind drove through a whiteout. A minute later: "You're like miles away anyway."

"Look, I'm sorry. I'm sorry. I have two grants on the wire."

"Well, don't feel the need to apologize." She sat up. "You don't need my forgiveness."

I didn't know if I was being accused or encouraged.

"I said I'm sorry."

Regina fell back on the pillows. When I leaned over, her lips drew down. "I don't want any favors," she said.

She rolled away.

"I don't know what to say."

"Whatever, you were horny, I was horny," she said a moment later. "Fantastic."

I broke the world record for fastest-dressed. I closed the front door and marched out, snapping branches underfoot, kicking up gravel. Regina's room glowed with her lamp in the window. Then Otter Creek disappeared. Seal Harbor disappeared. I let the Audi coast home in neutral down the hills.

On the phone one midnight, the evening after our third encounter:

"I got a letter from my brother today."

"I didn't know you had a brother."

"You never asked. He has problems. I don't really talk about him."

"So people still write letters?"

"I get one every week. I mean, he doesn't have anyone else to talk to, I don't think. He doesn't communicate with my parents. They have to ask through me how he's doing."

"What's he say?"

"Oh, you know, the average digressions of someone who's been abandoned by their family, trying to make it as Detroit's next White Stripe." Regina laughed and didn't say anything for a moment. "Okay, he's clinically depressed, though not that my parents ever knew. They saw a happy kid who just started disappearing. The soccer star who quit all activities and listened to Norwegian death metal. Running away. Around fifteen, he installed this big deadbolt on his bedroom door and wouldn't come out. I had to bring him meals on a tray. I mean, I was reading *Wuthering Heights*, it was a bit too parallel. But my parents were like, so this is how their generation rebels against the man, so whatever. They wouldn't really listen to him. They thought they lacked the vocabulary, or he did. They wouldn't even listen to me if I tried explaining what I thought was wrong with Eric, my brother's name is Eric, since it wasn't him informing them. Indirectly they understood Eric needed help, but they required a direct plea."

"They wanted to participate."

"My parents don't so much communicate as signal their thoughts. Like Eric telling me he's splitting apart inside, no small comment, but my father rolled his eyes when I told him, and slammed a door. You have to understand, my parents used to be hard-core. Part of the movement, and depression was something conformists suffered, the malaise of the bourgeoisie, et cetera. But to Eric, you know, he actually *was* splitting apart. As far as he knew, there was all of us in the real world, me, my parents, the animals, the neighbors, the kids in school, the people on TV, and then there was him, alone inside his head. I mean, he trusted me, I was the conduit. But then he found out what I'd told our father. I mean, I had to, he was sick, he had this need. But my dad got angry about it, he'd banged on the door until the deadbolt slid and confronted Eric. See, he thought by repeating to Eric this confidence he'd buy his own access, then Eric could cut the quote-unquote bullshit that way, the stuff he was feeding me, and they'd just talk straight, man to man. And of course that shut Eric up. Shut me out, too. I mean, eventually Eric understood why I'd told them, he came around two weeks later, to the idea it was me saying, 'I'm worried about you, I want to help you.' But part of him still blamed me when my parents weren't able to fix anything. So he's seventeen, I'm fourteen, he goes to school and actually does okay, otherwise he's in his room with his headphones on, no hair, he's a skinhead by that point—"

"Like a Nazi?"

"Well, you had skinheads, you had gangbangers, straight-edge, the crunchy kids, the dirtbags. Whatever, it was about music, not politics. Not that my parents saw that, either. He was just trying to belong to something, to attach himself. So they prayed harder. I told you my parents are Christian Scientist? This is after the Communism period."

"No."

"Right, well, pseudo at least, in a Whole Foods kind of way."

"Organically."

"One time they got a healer who hooked Eric up to a car battery. Anyway, they don't trust doctors, the government, public works. So my mother now was convinced by TV that his school was at fault, the influence of his social group, so she should start homeschooling Eric. Great, well, then came the overdose. On Tylenol. My mother found him, she called the ambulance, they got him to the hospital, he came out okay. But now my parents were terrified, we all were. Eric especially. He called me into his room one night. He was really skinny by that point, and pale, like I could see through his arm. And he was so angry, but embarrassed more than anything. He tried to explain to me how he carried this burden not only of failing in life, but now with the suicide attempt, he'd failed at being a failure, so there was a double humiliation. Now he was nobody. We listened to Radiohead; he fell asleep with his head in my lap. So we started talking three times a day. I'd call him from the pay phone at the school gym. At night we smoked pot and watched Frank Capra movies. But nothing was improving. Then my parents decided Eric needed to go away, on their terms.

"They used me as bait, basically," said Regina.

"What does that mean?"

"I was the only person in Eric's world, besides Thom Yorke, he believed was on his side. They found this home outside Chicago where he was supposed to go stay for a year, a psych ward with nice landscaping, like a schizophrenic summer camp. First they had to get him there, though, so my parents pitched a trip: we would take a family vacation to the Art Institute."

"In Chicago."

"I'd been pleading for months how I badly wanted to see this Viennese show they'd just opened, but we had to go as a family, they said. Eric couldn't stay home alone. So I worked on my brother: needling him, goading him. It took every chit I had, but one morning we got in the van and drove to Illinois, even stayed the night in a schmancy hotel near Michigan Avenue, which definitely was not our style. I mean, my parents don't even like beds. But the next morning, I'm twitching I'm so thrilled, and my brother has caught my excitement; they had this big breakfast buffet at the hotel with salmon and bagels and an omelet bar. Then we come out on the sidewalk, and there's these two big dudes and some woman, the three of them are talking to my parents, and Eric and I are only just at that point sensing something's up when the guys appear, take up either side of my brother, carry him into a Suburban and Eric's screaming, staring at me, yelling at me to help him, stop them, so then I start screaming, but then they're gone. The Suburban drives away. Everyone's crying, my parents included, my dad later thanks me 'for playing my part.' He says this, you know, for playing the role I would never have agreed to perform had I been apprised of the plan, as I'm sure they knew. That was our last family vacation. My brother stayed eighteen months, got on phenelzine, now he's a reasonably functioning mattress salesman and proto-rocker. He doesn't speak to my parents, though, and I don't have much reason to, either. They tried taking me to the museum that afternoon as a reward."

I fell asleep listening to Radu Lupu play Schubert. In my dream, Regina was a projection dancing far away in a forest. I shouted at her to leave me alone. A fog came up from the ground, so I couldn't see where I was going, and I ran straight into a tree, sticking up in the middle of a highway. The tree was coated with tar. I couldn't move. Headlights from a car pinpointed me and flashed Morse code. Then the forest became a desert in New Mexico: infinite yellow sand, infinite black sky. But no stars. The driver in the car was a girl I'd dreamed about going down on when I was in the eleventh grade. I could see her face above the steering wheel, and I imagined her vagina as I used to in class, trapped between her legs, yearning to be exposed and kissed.

I was filled with the certainty that she'd run me over with her car and keep driving, leaving me to die.

The girl spoke through ESP. She informed me she'd crash into me soon, and then go after Regina, Regina who was starring in a drive-in movie projected onto the side of a mesa. But there's a condition, the ghost said.

"Victor, you're an awful boy."

"I can't say how sorry I am."

The windows dripped with rain. Her voice crackling: "A nuisance. A *pain* to me."

"Betsy, I am very sorry."

"And you'll never do it again, say that, Victor."

"I'll never do it again," I said, coddling the phone.

"That's right, you'll never stand me up again. Why, Joel has never been so *awful*, Victor, leaving a woman stranded when it was freezing wet last night, you remember? And I cooked both steaks, and not cheap, mind you. The potatoes the way you like. I made a pound cake for dessert, I baked an extra so you could have something nice around that empty house of yours, but now it's *dry*, Victor, in the trash.

You know how much they charge for filet these days at Pine Tree? Do you?"

Sara would have pointed out that this was very true to Betsy's character, to call early in the morning to own the slight.

"How can I make it up to you?"

"Too late, I'm going out to Cranberry."

"Betsy—"

"Next Friday, you'll take me to dinner."

"There we go. Of course."

"Well, don't sit too comfortable," Betsy snapped. "You pick up the check. And no whining about what I drink."

"Dear, I am truthfully very sorry."

"And we'll go to Blue Sea."

There was a second's pause and I could hear her considering how I would react. Blue Sea was her son Joel's restaurant, in Southwest Harbor. It was the island's best restaurant, not inexpensive but worth the price. It was also open year-round, a rarity come January. Everyone raved about Joel and his cooking. *Gourmet* had published an article the previous year about contemporary cuisine in New England, singling out Joel in a sidebar: "Organic Prophet Hidden in Tourists' Mecca." I found the clipping one day buried inside a book on Betsy's coffee table, though I don't think she'd ever set foot in the restaurant.

In the breezeway came a bang from the door. Russell appeared wearing running shorts and sneakers. He opened the refrigerator and finished off the orange juice.

"All right, Blue Sea, sounds good," I said.

"You eat there all the time, as though I don't know. They must have something I can stomach. Is there a smoking section?"

"Next Friday, seven o'clock. I'll get a reservation, okay?"

"In fact," she said, dawdling, "I've wondered if I wouldn't rather begin seeing Joel more often. Make it six-thirty. And that's right, you *will* pick me up, and if you don't then forget it, Victor, you'll never see me again."

At eleven years old, Joel had been shipped off to Uncle Bill's prep school alma mater in Massachusetts. During the summers, they enrolled him at a boys' camp in Vermont. Joel had told me about it one evening at the Blue Sea bar: that if his parents ever did see him as a boy, it had been at Christmastime, when Cape Near would be full of people, adults banging on the piano and philandering, a party every night. No wonder, I thought, Joel set fire to his dormitory. A great big burning plea for attention. Then he ran away and disappeared for two years. The Pinkertons and FBI were enlisted, to no avail.

Betsy once told me she and Bill were devastated at the time, feeling betrayed. "And just when I was becoming interested in him," she'd said.

She chirped, "Ta, Victor dear," before slamming down the phone.

I remembered Sara's play going up on Broadway. I remembered opening night on Forty-sixth Street, applauding from backstage amid the support staff. I remembered how proud I felt. I remembered the conversation backstage: "What did you think?" "Best I ever saw. Best you ever wrote." We kissed and she said under my nose, "Next time I'm doing a musical, how's that?" And then, without missing a beat, we both started humming, "Some Enchanted Evening." It was one of our old tricks.

The memory was vivid, remaining centered, but that had been Sara's doing. She'd retold the story innumerable times at dinner parties, how the two of us hummed the same song. She was always her own favorite subject, and we by proxy, but all that subsequent retrieval, telling the story one more time, had reinforced the synapses for both of us, molding our recall, our marriage.

By that point, most of my memories were probably more Sara's doing, neurologically speaking, than my own.

And apparently this absence of mine, in her critical career moment, had been pivotal, or so she remembered. It was my neglect that had been the impetus for the play. *The hunched shoulders, the earlier morning exits and later returns at night.* And yet I didn't remember feeling excluded, never mind upset. *He'll say I've got it wrong. He'll say my remembering is incorrect, that I'm over-emphasizing, under-analyzing, the typical dramatist's approach: emoting.*

Our bodies weren't more than habitats, was my take. How different were people anyway except for the memories we carried? At some level, weren't Sara and Victor the same, wasn't that marriage's implicit guarantee?

Outside, the clouds were parting, and the sun broke through; the ferns and trees were bright green.

"What I call Connie eggs," said Russell. He was stirring sausage around a pan with onions.

"I thought Cornelia was a vegetarian."

"Vegan. Raw foods only. I tell her it's that tofu bacon she likes, she never notices the difference anyway." He looked up. "I'm kidding."

"So how is Cornelia?"

"Misguided. Shitty peer group, all kinds of bad advice. Too much time on the phone with her mother, mainly. But I try not to meddle. That she even talks to me is a gold star. Oh, she told me to say, 'What's up.'"

"What's up."

"I'll let her know."

"I'm going to change."

"Maybe we discuss later why you're sleeping in your stereo chamber these days?" he called after me.

Russell toweled off the picnic table and set out breakfast. I watched him from the bedroom window. The place mats and napkins he put out, Sara had bought them during our trip to Puerto Rico. It rained day and night for a week. Sara bought a rain jacket and would go exploring after breakfast, past the beer and fried-seafood shacks, down the alleys, while I stayed in bed and read mystery novels.

One napkin would have a purple stain along the trim, I wanted to call out to Russell. Sara had used it to clean up a wine spill once, back in Manhattan. "That'll stain." "We'll wash it." "It's red wine, it won't come out unless you rinse it out now," I'd said. She announced, "It's a napkin, Victor." Then I burst out, "Why don't you ever think about anything besides yourself?"

This was when *Woman Hits Forty* was a month into its Broadway run, when I'd made my big change to be a better, more devoted husband.

"Well, it's about time," she'd said a moment later.

"So you think they have a corking fee?" Russell asked.

"Blue Sea?" We were planning to go there for dinner that evening. "I doubt it."

"Look, I don't want to offend local management, not if there's a deal to be done." Russell dunked his toast in his coffee. "You know," he said, "last night, I heard you."

"What?"

"Three in the morning, suddenly Beethoven was performing at Carnegie Hall."

"Sorry, I didn't realize."

"The dancing queen?"

"Look, not over breakfast."

"What I don't understand is why you don't just end it, if it's such a pain, unless it's the pussy?"

He was staring at me, my psychologist, my interrogator. Soon he'd ask about the cards in my shirt pocket.

"It's not that simple," I said.

"Pussy's always simple."

When we finished, Russell cleared the dishes like a waiter, stacking them on his forearm. He looked back at me from the door. "You know, we're supposed to be talking about me here, concerning romance."

I dropped Russell off at Jordan Pond on the way to work. His plan was to climb the Bubble mountains, then jog the five miles back to the house, on top of the five-mile run he had done earlier that morning. He was training, he said, this was nothing.

In New York, Sara had invented a game called "Who's Russell Sleeping with Now?" The game would proceed by our guessing the new woman's occupation, generation, and figure, and only once we got all three right would Russell tell us her name.

She set him up, twice, with friends of hers, but he cheated on both of them.

Russell hopped out of the car and ran off, his shorts barely covering his hamstrings, his back pocket stuffed with energy gel packets.

"Don't go too hard," he shouted, waving good-bye. "It's Saturday, remember."

In Boston, I was in the right place at the right time: I was one of several researchers connecting Alzheimer's disease with its molecular correlates, and our success became the foundation for my career. Afterward, though, I didn't know where to turn. For the first time in my working experience, after years of application, I was burned out. I had little interest in doing anything. I'd sit up at night, turning pages in a book without grasping a sentence. I was certain I wanted to continue research on AD, I knew I wanted to make a greater, more individual mark, but how, exactly?

During the evenings I took to walking around Cambridge, I went back to Mrs. Gill, to her butterflies and her lectures on Darwin, out near the utility sheds on a trail behind the school baseball field. *He's not telling us what it's like to be an ant. He shows us what it's like to be a human.* One of those evenings, a damp Boston dusk, I picked up a student edition of *The Origin of Species* and reread it in a sequence of coffee shops. Boiled down, what struck me was Darwin's key early insight: that species changed. Rare for his time, he understood that species weren't deposited on the earth finished by a higher hand, unchanging. Species evolved, though at first Darwin couldn't say how exactly.

A mentor of mine, Dr. Ernst Schranz, phoned one evening from Manhattan, just as I was hanging up my coat. He sounded as if his mouth were full of washcloths, but he was customarily curt: *Victor, why have you not called, you should be here in New York, Boston is for beans.* I could picture him in a bow tie, sitting with one of his dachshunds on his lap. He'd recently landed at NYU after an era in Chicago, apparently someone had found a mattress stuffed with money to establish a center on aging and had picked Schranz to lead. *If you are looking for direction, may I suggest to you south.* When Sara got home, once I mentioned Ernst's invitation, she started jumping up and down, but I needed more time. It was like when we were courting, I hadn't known I wanted to marry Sara until I worked it out on paper. One afternoon, going through Central Park on a long walk uptown from her apartment, I was so brimming over I had to sit down and decipher my feelings, and on the back of an old concert ticket I wrote a list to parse my thoughts, headed "About Sara." Item one: *"She is endlessly interesting."* Item two: *"I am happiest when I'm around her."* Item three, which was a surprise to me as soon as the pen stopped: *"Get married."* Two weeks later, I proposed.

So over a long week, I walked the river and snuck around Cambridge and made notes, like a homeless poet. There was a pragmatic side, I figured out, lacking in my work to that point. Human genetic research was an austere, cloistered discipline. From further phone conversations, I had the voices of Ernst and his wife, Trude, in my ear, imploring me in their Austrian accents to follow my instincts, yes, my gut, yes, but also to ground that hard thinking not only in the service of my career and science, but suffering, the human experience. *You will remember there are unique rewards from therapeutic angles.* And Ernst was right: most times, scientific labor was monotonous seed-counting, a series of such tasks as putting auto parts together, accomplished amid the din of refrigerator banks. But to believe that during the waiting, throughout the long night, the work might someday connect from lab to life, that it was more than factory procedures, meant a lot.

The molecular mechanisms we'd uncovered at Harvard provided specific targets to take aim at. Accepting that amyloid beta (Abeta) was the main component in the plaques in our sufferers' brains, there had seemed to me three solutions during those walks. I wrote them down one afternoon on a bar napkin: one, to immunize the brain against Abeta, so that the body could mount a defense; two, to stifle the production of Abeta in the first place; or three, to work at protecting neurons and their synaptic connections from Abeta, to repair or regenerate neurons under attack. It was the third tactic that appealed the most to me, realizing my childhood science-fiction fascinations: the idea that there was a way to lodge into a brain some neuroprotective assistance. Not to interfere, but to boost. To collaborate and shield. Soon after, I returned Ernst's phone call, and Sara and I went out to celebrate over cheeseburgers at a grim diner in Davis Square, our haunt, toasting with a red wine that tasted like sherry.

Both Ernst and his wife died the year Sara and I left for Bar Harbor, within weeks of each other. At the time, dragged down by liver disease, Ernst had been pushing me to leave NYU. *You're gifted, Victor, but you are no good at getting out of a rut.* Still to that day, a Saturday morning spent thinking about him and our work together was far more pleasurable than running ten miles around a park.

But I didn't have a succinct way to explain all that to Russell.

While my houseguest got his exercise, I reviewed the updates on a few of our running experiments. But my mind wandered. I'd stop work, and there was Regina amid the CD towers, inside the telephone cradle. While I stared at charts with my glasses perched on my forehead, my mind crafted lists of how remarkable she was, and how I'd let her down.

How she deserved a man who would take her out, not one she ordered in.

When my computer crashed, I got up and paced the hall that lapped our rooms. I listened to air conditioners and sizzling fluorescent bulbs, and the chattering of fingers on old keyboards. I stared out a window and thought about driving home and opening Sara's office again, unlocking the file cabinet, reading those other cards.

I still couldn't remember what movie we'd seen the night we met.

I decided on a drive downtown. I needed new swim goggles anyway.

The clerk at the sports store was a teenage giant with acne on both cheeks. I took my time testing out different pairs of goggles. I turned away, trying out the darkest lenses, and stared out the front window, and then there was Regina, blue-green Regina through the goggles, walking down the street.

She was wearing a tank top and black jeans. Her curly hair was held back with two butterfly clips. It was her cheeks that got me—bright, round, and high. Lindsay, the green-haired roommate, hung back a step, saying something loudly with a slanted mouth. They disappeared.

What would Hercule Poirot do? What would Darwin? I darted out and slipped into the crowd. Regina and the roommate had crossed the street and were going into a coffee shop. I watched them from a restaurant window's reflection.

You once had front-row seats, said one voice in a Viennese accent.

Now you are spying? said another.

A minute later the girls left the shop carrying iced coffees, and hugged and parted ways: Regina down an alley, the roommate heading straight for my spot.

I walked into the first open door, a native crafts shop. A woman was buying a poster of a wolf kissing a dolphin in outer space. The roommate walked past outside without seeing me, and after a minute, I jogged down toward the harbor, looking along the side streets. I stopped after three blocks and caught my breath.

Regina was gone.

And what I would have done if I'd actually caught up with her, I had no idea! I started laughing. I sat down on a stone wall, outside a video-rental store, and had to cover my mouth with my hand. People were staring. I stood up and faced the shop to avoid attention. A sun-faded cardboard figure was propped up in the window: Bruce Willis from *The Fifth Element*, with bleached-blond hair, wearing an orange rubber wife-beater, staring down at me.

I wiped my eyes and caught my breath, and focused on tamping down.

Be steadfast for once, said Bruce. *Act your age.*

Down the road was a drugstore with a working soda fountain. It was where Aunt Betsy would go as a girl, she'd said, to buy watermelon slices or blueberry pie. I sat at the counter, ordered a tuna melt and coffee, and ate lunch over the *Bar Harbor Times.*

On the cover, under the headline "Exclusive Investigation," was a picture of large dredging equipment being installed in Bass Harbor, and an inset picture of Betsy's famous fashion designer. She'd beaten the press once again. In her honor, I turned to the police report.

Report: An elderly man in Town Hill called 911 to report the vice president whispering obscenities through his mail slot. Report: A married couple in West Tremont was arrested for selling crystal methamphetamine. Report: In Northeast Harbor, there'd been two driving-while-intoxicated arrests after a fund-raiser for the local repertory theater. Report: A woman in Bernard had been fined for housing exotic animals, specifically a tiger cub, without proper permits.

I stared at the sandwich in my hand. I couldn't place the last time I'd ordered a tuna melt. I'd given them up one day after Lucy pointed out how I'd eaten a tuna melt sandwich for lunch every day two seasons running after Sara's accident.

The door jangled behind me and a group of retirees walked in wearing stiff new Harley-Davidson vests. I turned back to the crime reports, to the island the tourists didn't see: a flotilla of abundance and diversity still evolving, of burlesque acts and rare jungle animals. Another part of America where there were crystals to foretell and methamphetamine to forget, and nothing stayed the same for very long. Where ordinary people were trying to get by without superpowered rubber wife-beaters while the White House snooped through their mail.

I got up and paid the bill. Regina's green-haired roommate walked in and slipped onto my stool. She glanced at me, then picked up the newspaper, unfolded it, found the Sudoku puzzle inside, and started filling in the numbers.

"You really have nothing?"

"I'm sorry, sir, we're completely booked."

"Can I speak to Joel, please," I said. "This is Victor Aaron calling."

"I'm sorry, but Chef is out today."

"Will he be in tonight?"

"I don't know," said the hostess, "I don't think so."

Russell wanted to find out who was selling Joel his wine, and said he didn't mind mixing business with pleasure. I'd been looking forward to seeing Joel, particularly since Aunt Betsy wouldn't be present.

Joel and Sara and I had gone out for coffee a few times when he was setting up Blue Sea. He'd been getting sober at the time and had needed company with non-addicts. Sara even went to an AA meeting with him once. After the accident, though, when I started spending my Friday evenings with Betsy, I felt out of place when Joel was around. Previously, we'd talked as equals. We were two small-business owners who'd reached a dependable level of success, and we could commiserate over management headaches or how tough it was to find good people. Labs, restaurants, orchestras, sports teams, they all relied on the transmission of command: a small team focused on seeing a director's vision tested and checked and retuned prior to display. But with Betsy calling me at work to supply gossip reports or ask about her prescriptions, the kinship between Joel and me was trumped. I couldn't help seeing him as she would portray us: Joel the outcast prince, and me supplying a surrogate.

Russell fixed martinis and drank two. He puffed himself up before getting out of the car. The restaurant was jammed. Hovering around the hostess podium were at least ten people hoping to sit down. Russell pinched my elbow. Two places were opening at the bar, and we slid in. The bartender was a college-age kid wearing a black clip-on bow tie. Around his neck was a hemp necklace with a starfish knotted at the bottom.

"Is Joel in tonight?"

"Nope. He's over visiting family on Cranberry."

"Hey, that's your girlfriend, right?" Russell clapped me on the arm and laughed loudly. He was wearing a tight-fitting black sport jacket. A cigar case in his breast pocket was like an organ pressing up through the skin. "Listen," Russell said to the bartender, "for now, how about we get some glasses and a corkscrew?"

He poured the wine. "To Maine."

"To Maine."

"To us."

"To us."

"To Ben Lemery," Russell said.

"What?"

I left my glass on the bar.

"What's the worry?"

"You're an asshole," I said, and got up and went to the bathroom.

Sara had referred to it on her first index card, the secret I'd divulged the night we met: that a week before he killed himself, Ben had explained to me his plan. He'd shown me the gun, his father's .38 Special, and I didn't tell anyone. Surely another of his stunts, I'd thought at the time. Then, on the appointed night, he called me, asking for help with his homework, and I hung up. Besides Sara, Russell was the only person who knew about Ben's call.

"Look, I'm sorry—"

I sat back down. "How about we drop it."

"See, I was thinking, you're how old now?"

"Hold on," I said, and I took his glass out of his hand and clinked it against mine. "Do me a favor. You remove the nine-eleven sticker from your windshield, then we'll talk."

"Hey, fuck you, all right?" A second later he laughed, then stopped short. "Fine, I'll do it. For you, right when I get back."

"Stick it in an envelope. Send it to me."

"You'll let that shit go?"

"Swear to it?"

"Done."

"Fantastic," I said wearily, and we both laughed. Already I was wondering if I could put him on a midnight plane. "Tell me more about Cornelia."

Russell slugged back his wine. "Well, we have a problem. She's searching. You're not going to believe this. Of all things."

"What?"

"She wants to cook."

"So what's the problem?"

Russell cupped my neck with his hand, like he was back to wrestling. "Have you ever seen," he said, leaning in, "what their lives are like? Half ex-cons, the rest are from Guatemala. There's not a one who's not on drugs, and this is where my daughter, my only child, Victor, she wants to work like a servant so rich fucks can eat foie gras?"

His eyes fell to the remaining wine in the bottle.

"Hey, so *The Hook-Up*, that's still paying out?"

So what *was* it, I was about to say, about my wife's proportions?

"Now, see, that's where Connie was going for a long time. Screen-writing. Movies somehow. Connie idolized Sara, you know that."

What I knew was that I wanted to be home eating a sandwich, watching a DVD of Jeremy Brett playing Sherlock Holmes.

"You remember that premiere they went to at the Ziegfeld? Connie still talks about it. Best night of her life." Russell's hand was on my forearm. His face was flushed. "We miss her, Victor. You know that."

"You're drunk."

He shook his head: maybe yes, maybe no. "One time Sara told me this story, three guys in Los Angeles are trying to take a piece off her contract. They ambush her with the news over lunch. All smiles. Apparently, Sara picks up one guy's Perrier and dumps it in his salad bowl."

I laughed. "You're making that up."

"Fuck you. It was that fall, she told me herself."

"What fall? What?"

Russell wasn't listening anymore. An attractive woman our age had sidled in, wearing a low-cut top. "Great memory, you know," he continued, eyes glued elsewhere. "That was the thing about Sara. Soup to nuts, she could retell any conversation. Something you said a year earlier, she could still go word for word."

"Seriously," I said, grabbing his elbow. "Which fall are you talking about?"

"What? In California."

"You and Sara talked on the phone?"

"Jesus." Russell laughed, and turned back to me. He wiped his mouth with his napkin and folded it along the seam. "She just called, you know. Old friends. One time or something, when she was stuck."

"Stuck," I said. I was going blind.

"Her writer's block. What's the big deal?" He pecked his fork around the plate. "I don't remember what it was called anyway."

"What's that?"

"The movie. *The Perfect Husband*, that's it. Christ, this bottle's gone. Outstanding, though, you'll admit. You want I should order?"

"No," I said truthfully. I dumped the wine I hadn't drunk into Russell's glass and asked to see a menu.

The main movie theater in Bar Harbor was called the Criterion, a white flat-top on Cottage Street. Sara and I used to go there twice a week. Competitive research, she called it, when we'd meet after work and sit up in the balcony for the eleven-twenty show and watch whatever had come to town, but it was more than that: we were happy. We were movie people, we'd watch anything, all it took was Junior Mints to set the mood. Outside afterward, we'd listen to the manager in his suspenders talk business, about how surely this would be the year he up and moved to Arizona with his sister. Then we'd go home. And if we still weren't tired we'd pull a DVD down off the shelf.

The September before the accident, before California, Sara went four times in one week to see the same film. A festival was in town, and they were screening a movie by some Scandinavian director called *The Perfect Human*. The print came up twice in the schedule, but Sara got the Criterion's manager to run it two more times in private. She invited me to join her late one weeknight, a midnight special. It was a weird little movie, without a plot I could put into words—as if one of Sara's old art buddies had filmed one of his flashbacks. There's a main character and presumably his girlfriend. Mostly we're with the guy, always in a white room where our character exhibits his perfection.

A voice-over tells us again and again, "This is the perfect human. Look at the perfect human dance. See the perfect human eat." And he dances, he eats, he goes through daily rituals, but we don't know why. He wears black tie, but he doesn't go anywhere. For the most part he's alone. He lacks everything, but wants for nothing, existing in oblivion. "See the perfect human shave."

The total running time was about fifteen minutes. To Sara it may as well have been *Casablanca*.

"Because it's a perfect movie," Sara explained afterward, at home in the kitchen. Her voice was young with excitement. "The only perfect thing I've ever seen."

I didn't know what to say. I'd found it pompous and silly, but didn't want to say so. I said I wouldn't have predicted her liking it. That perhaps it was a little pretentious.

"No, you're not seeing it," she said. "The thing is, it's anti-pretentious. Because it's so clear. There's nothing to 'understand.'"

"Now *you* sound pretentious," I joked, but it didn't reach her. Sara was looking out the window over the sink. I was reminded of Sara back in her early days, transfixed by some idea she'd overheard at a party. But this was different. I couldn't help sensing that she was deceiving me for some reason.

"The director is putting everything on the line," she said to herself. "He's saying there's no one you can pin down. Even the perfect ones we can't know completely."

"Well, it was way over my head, obviously," I said.

Due to a recent incident at a party where I'd embarrassed her, we hadn't spoken in several days, and this was our first attempt at extended conversation. We'd been sleeping apart, a first for us, and I was loath to upset her. Part of me, though, was annoyed. Confused at the very least. I didn't see where all the pain on her part came from.

Maybe Sara thought I was pandering.

She dropped her head. She looked exhausted.

"What is it?"

"I want that faith."

"You want what?"

Her voice was the flattest plane: "Whatever is inside him. Whatever makes him create films, Victor, this is what it looks like. That movie. What permits him to work."

"I don't get it."

"No," she said, "I know." She finally turned around. "So I was coming out of yoga this afternoon, I thought, perhaps I'm overreacting. Maybe I'm making too big a deal out of things. Maybe Dr. Carrellas has it wrong."

Sara had been seeing Carrellas since the previous year, when she couldn't work. Couldn't write. For her follow-up to the blockbuster, she'd caught a writer's block she couldn't break through.

"Well, maybe you shouldn't see her anymore."

"See, you don't even hear what I'm saying." Sara was looking at me so hard now I glanced away. "It's like as soon as we begin talking, we're standing in separate rooms."

Dumbly, I looked around. Everything about the house was new. I hated new things. I preferred to buy my clothing at secondhand shops, at least when Sara wasn't looking. In the new house, all of our old furniture seemed out of place, and the new chairs and tables we'd bought felt like loaners, waiting to be returned.

I was staring at one of them. "You know how sorry I am."

"Yes, you've said."

Sara left for California two days later, for six weeks without contact. I didn't know when she was coming back, if she was coming back. I bought a ticket to Los Angeles but never used it. I worked and swam my laps. At night, in the house my wife had built, I dreamed about divorce papers fluttering around the hallways like trapped birds.

I wondered, wasn't the house enough to call her back?

Wasn't I?

Russell sat beside me in the Criterion in the dark. We watched a new action movie and digested our dinners. At home, Russell went right to sleep, bear-hugging me on the way to brush his teeth.

So she'd been writing, I thought. I remembered how, a week after the funeral, Sara's agent, Mark, had called, asking if I knew anything about a new script. He thought maybe she'd begun one in California, but he hadn't been informed, barely a word those six weeks.

"Could you look around?" he asked. "Check her laptop, it's probably in a folder somewhere."

Problem was, I didn't know the password to her computer. As far as I knew, Sara never wrote it down. The tech guys at Soborg said the best they could do was reinstall the system software, but probably that would erase the hard drive. I stalled. The next time Mark called, I told him the IT department had gone through her computer with a fine-tooth comb. Nothing found.

The next morning we drove to the airport in silence, except for the sounds of Russell checking his BlackBerry. Under the land bridge, low tide made the channel into a mud flat drying in the sun, an airstrip for piping plovers.

We said quick good-byes in the parking lot, promising to see each other when I came to New York.

"Look, man, thanks for the distractions," Russell said. "I needed a little R-and-R, get my head straight about that girl."

"Which girl?"

"The PR woman. The one we talked about." He laughed. "You really are a charity case."

"Well, give my love to Cornelia," I said.

"And mine to the dancer."

Russell squeezed my arm and gave me a light hug. While he strode toward the airport, compact and hustling, his suit bag like a shadow on his back, I thought, I don't care if I never see him again.

Days zipped by and the world shrank back to our lab's small proportions. I didn't think about Russell or Sara or Regina, there was only me and Lucy and the rest of the team arriving each morning for meetings and conference calls, shouting down the hallways, and eating candy by the bucketful. One morning it was someone's birthday, Lucy remembered, and she brought in doughnuts spiked with candles. We had the tempo of an umbrella factory. Of course there was also my anxiety about our grant under review and the next ones I needed to write to patch some funding holes, but that was normal. As Darwin had pointed out, anxiety was paramount for survival, it signaled a threat. An adapted response was required. A typical grant was only about seventy-five pages long, but I'd write at least fifteen drafts and sweat every punctuation mark. And then add to everything the constant locomotive rhythm beneath my thoughts—*keep it coming in, keep it coming in*—with dollar signs floating around my vision.

Work was everything as it was in the beginning, now and forever. One evening, flipping through my calendar, I figured out I'd taken less than ten nights off in the previous two years.

The big New York conference was approaching. I needed to look good and talk pretty. It was a sales conference and I was peddling the latest appliance to a crowd I knew personally. I'd sat with them in

lecture halls from Greece to Colorado, but I couldn't rest on my lau-
rels. Some of them might be judging my grants, and they needed to be
brought up to speed with some razzle-dazzle.

Dr. Low, aka Toad, Soborg's president, left me a voice mail at three
in the morning one night, saying he wished he was still burning the
midnight oil on something other than his digestive tract. He sounded
like a ghost trapped between walls: a mind still sharp and flexible, and
a body falling apart.

Sixteen-hour days became pleasurable. We were hunting again,
closing in, until a miniature crisis turned up: Lucy figured out that in
several databases, columns of figures had been accidentally swapped
sometime in the winter, invalidating an entire chain of results. Human
error, but error nonetheless, and one that had gone unreported for
months. Conclusions, previously solid, were in the wind. A lot of work
would need to be reanalyzed before it could be made public.

Panic swept through the team. Late one night, dizzy from exhaustion, I couldn't remember how Alzheimer's was spelled, and when I
asked one of my M.D. fellows to see if she could find a *Webster's* dic-
tionary, she told me to use my computer's spell-check tool. I nearly
threw an "Institute for Brain Aging" mug at her head.

But come the following Friday, when our new data charts should
have distracted me, I still clicked CHECK MAIL—every five minutes,
every minute, every thirty seconds.

Regina as I remembered her from the beginning, coy and funny
and new.

I forced myself up to take a walk. The quad was full of students sitting in clusters, draping their arms over one another, so that I couldn't
tell which ones were couples, which were friends. One boy wore eye
makeup and a white ruffled shirt over a black dress. A girl dancing reminded me of Cornelia, Russell's Cornelia, twirling around barefoot in

a skirt made from corduroy patches. But who was I to judge? She was probably an M.D./Ph.D. candidate with an IQ of 140. The boy would be the next Nobel Prize winner in applied mathematics, doing his best work with a cell phone.

On the phone a few weeks earlier, after she was done complaining about her roommate, Regina had asked me, "So when did you know?"

"Know what?"

"That you wanted to be a scientist."

"No idea, really."

"It just fell into place."

"Same story as everybody else, a great teacher. She showed me that people actually got paid to do this stuff. Weren't your parents biologists?"

Regina laughed. "Christian biologists. I really don't want to talk about my family right now."

I said, "Well, how did you pick up burlesque?"

"Oh, okay." She paused. "For fun, I guess. Glamour of the femme fatale. Don't you think I could be a community theater star someday? I don't know. Don't you have things you like to keep a mystery?"

"Scientist, dancer, actress, poet."

"A lady doesn't reveal too much. See, you should inquire more, there's a lot you don't know."

"And you me," I said.

"Well, exactly. God, who says that? 'And you me.'"

"I apologize."

"Accepted. Let's play a game, three questions each. Only truth."

"Only truth."

"How many women have you slept with?"

Both stenographer and judge, poised to record prior to verdict.

"Four," I said.

"Four as in three plus one?"

"How many am I supposed to have slept with?"

"So that makes me—"

"Two in college. Then Sara. Then you."

"No, I mean, sorry, I guess? I'm just surprised."

"It wasn't sexy, you know, in those days to be passionate about molecular biology. What about you?"

"Is that one of your questions?"

"Sure."

"Fifteen."

"Fifteen?"

"*Chéri*, I'm twenty-five. These days? It's not like I'm not careful."

"Is that what people worry about, being careful? For my generation, it was getting a girl pregnant, then the pill came along."

"Sounds like you didn't have *that* much to worry about."

"This was your idea."

"Fine. Sure, it's out there. But we've been schooled. My gym teacher was very clear about showing us how to put a condom on a banana."

"That's a joke."

"Seriously? Okay, sure, sex is different. Frankly, you want to know the major difference? It's that men these days, the dudes, watch so much pornography, there is no sex anymore, it's just fucking. I mean, pardon my French, but it's truly frightening. Men think women are puppets, and women go out and get surgery to look like blow-up dolls. I'm serious, men don't realize women grow pubic hair. That we're not fuck pillows. It's outrageous, what's on the Internet. There's prank pornography, rape rooms. I mean, forget worrying about waterboarding, this is humiliation on campuses nationwide. And it's not just visual. There are manuals on how to pick up women by insulting them. Handbooks on precisely what to say to trick women into sleeping with you. As though we're to be used and then discarded. And of course it convinces some girls," Regina said, and snorted. "I'm sure they love it, and why not? The brainwashing starts so early, it's amazing we resist. We're told by the overlords to primp, to shave, to slim down. It's safeguarded by other women, *for* other women, so how *should* our boyfriends behave when it comes to what they want, and in which position? Why shouldn't we give in to their rights? The older generation is caught up trying to get a woman elected president, and women my age refuse to be called feminists. So why burlesque? Because it's the personal empowerment revue. It's not about sex, it's about luster, it's about control. It's an ego steam bath. If the audience gets off, what do I care?"

"Is all that true?"

"That's your third question. But yes. So, my turn. Why do you accept?"

"Accept?"

"I want to know, why you reply when I e-mail," she said after a second.

"I was going to ask you why you invite me."

"But you're out of questions."

It took me a moment. "Because I want to," I said. "I look forward to it all week. Being in the audience, so to speak."

"Why?"

"Because it's so different."

A pause. "Fine," said Regina, "what's different?"

"Just from what I know. Regina, I'm nearly sixty, it's nothing I would have expected. What you do, is all."

Another pause. "Well, that's about the least passionate thing I've ever heard."

"Regina, I meant—"

"So what, I'm like your sideshow?"

"Now, that's not what I said."

"This isn't, you know, the variety show," she stammered, "where you get to go tell the boys in the locker room about us afterward."

"Regina, calm down."

"Don't tell me to calm down."

"Believe me, I have told no one."

"Why should I believe that?"

"Listen to me: I covet our time together. Do you understand?"

I was the desperate older man, the moneybags seeing his ward run off.

She said a moment later, "When I think about you—"

I said quickly, "And I you."

"Well, okay, exactly," she said. "Exactly."

"Regina—"

"What do you want?"

She caught me off guard. "Us," I said.

"No, you don't."

"Well, what *do* I want?"

Regina laughed but it was overwrought. "Why, darling, what everyone wants." The tremors fell off her voice a few seconds later. "Just tell me this isn't some fuck-buddy thing for you."

"Some what?"

"Yeah, exactly." She laughed. "No, you wouldn't."

A party game that Sara once invented: Reduce a famous movie plot to three bones, and elaborate only if the other players aren't able to guess the title.

Southern lawyer has a way with kids. Can't get an innocent off the hook. Boo.

Vito shouldn't buy fruit. Michael won't talk business. Diane Keaton?

Men embark on spaceship. Spaceship disembarks men. Sorry, Dave.

We got to the point, though, where Sara wouldn't play it with me unless other guests were around. I had a hard time coming up with the titles.

"Audi is part of Volkswagen, don't forget," Betsy said, "who may as well have been the Nazis' personal automaker. Besides, Victor, what's wrong with a Saab? Convertibles kill, *dear*."

"If you want me to scratch up your old hunk of junk instead," I said, "just hand over the keys."

Betsy was inside the hall, standing beside a bag full of gardening equipment, arranging wildflowers. Sunlight was pouring in. It could have been any summer Friday afternoon in the last two years, and I sensed a wild hope appear, one to run away with, that I'd never met Regina, that Betsy would allude to some faraway business trip I'd been on since April, one I forgot.

"Now take a look, dear," Betsy said, pointing me to the dining room, "those candlesticks on the table. They belonged to my great-great-uncle, the one I was telling you about, the banker. Take them when you go. Now I should get dressed."

Betsy trotted off and I remembered the banker: he'd warranted his own chapter in the family genealogy compiled by her father, the admiral. Ernest "The Boiler" Gardner, deceased 1884, made the newspapers a few weeks after he died when a secret chamber was found in his offices. Behind several locks, his daughter discovered a back room the solicitors hadn't touched, where inside were shelves of gleaming human skulls, cataloged with small cards. Letters she found in her father's files accounted for the exhibition: the heads were specimens collected for his amateur phrenology studies. He'd offered a price of one hundred dollars per head of "unknown peoples" to be boiled clean in his office, then measured and preserved. More than three dozen were on display from the Canary Islands to the Philippines, according to their cards. "The Boiler," said the *New-York Tribune*, had either ordered or condoned the murders of nineteen people. "Still people, no matter their religious beliefs, color of skin, or birthplace."

I put the candlesticks back in Betsy's kitchen cupboard and took a short nap on the living room couch. Half an hour later, Betsy was coming down the hallway, bejeweled and wearing a yellow tea-length skirt, a diamond pendant, and matching earrings. I knew she was dressing up for Joel. She'd changed from boat shoes to flats, though the beach hat remained.

"Where's my palanquin? Back off, you're too old. I'll have a martini, Victor—dry, with a twist." She checked herself in the mirror. "But you're driving, dear. You have tonic."

"Thanks, but I believe I can handle it."

"You're driving," she repeated.

Baht yur driving, de-ah. You have tah-nik. This from the generation that invented alcohol poisoning.

Joel had told me and Sara once how cooking had saved his life. At eighteen, he was living in Venice Beach, making ends meet by dealing marijuana. Then his supplier went to jail, and Joel took a short-order job in a diner. He discovered that he liked it: working, cooking, drawing a salary, plus the vagabond lifestyle of kitchen culture suited him—particularly the cocaine. After two years, Joel moved north and began ascending in the business, from a banquet hall in Fresno to a Sacramento members-only club. Finally to Berkeley, for an apprentice period, before returning East, this time to open his own place, a French bistro in Boston serving the latest fusions. He lasted four years. The reviews were good, but they were no match for Joel's addictions, and his investors dwindled to one, a car dealer's son Joel had known from California. That one disappeared with the chandeliers, auctioning off assets while Joel was away on a bender in New Orleans. By that point, Joel and Betsy were back on speaking terms over the phone, but he'd vowed never to return to Maine. Then Uncle Bill died. Joel came back for the funeral, found a job cooking surf and turf in Ellsworth, and decided to stay. He joined NA and AA and got sober, and thought about opening his own place again. One afternoon during a coffee visit, Sara gave him our lawyer's card, and Joel successfully sued his former partner, who'd turned up rich selling boats in Annapolis. Joel eventually received enough money from the judge to start Blue Sea.

The restaurant was crammed when Aunt Betsy and I arrived. The hostess fawned over Betsy and took her coat, complimented her hat, and followed us patiently while Betsy navigated the dining room with her cane.

"I'll have a martini," Betsy ordered as we sat down. "Dry, with a twist. Now, Victor, my lighter, please."

"I'm sorry, Mrs. Gardner," the hostess whispered, "there's a no-smoking policy."

"There used to be no-Jews policies, too, dear. Are they still in place?"

"Darling, wouldn't you like some wine," I said.

She glared at me but accepted the menu. I took off my jacket and hung it on the back of my chair. After a minute, Betsy pointed to a 2003 Montrachet, the most expensive bottle on the list.

"Let's start here," she said to the waitress, smiling. "Then we'll see where we end up."

The bill had begun at five hundred dollars.

Betsy appeared about to gloat when Joel walked up to the table in a baseball cap, chef's coat, and checkered pants. His name was stitched in blue thread over the restaurant logo. He'd shaved recently and seemed slimmer than I remembered, but was still ruddy in the cheeks. He was smirking, his eyes flittering around. Hands crossed behind his back, he was less the gym teacher, more the playful, reserved former athlete, aware when he'd been recognized. Heads turned. Joel bent down to kiss Betsy's cheek while I half rose from my chair.

"Joel, how are you?"

"Hey, Victor."

The waitress brought the wine and Joel took it, smiled at the label, and borrowed the waitress's corkscrew. Betsy said, "Why, boys, don't you look handsome. Men in uniform always get the girl. Joel dear, I don't see why they make you wear those awful pants."

"I make me, Mom," Joel said, laughing, rubbing his chin. Betsy reset her silverware and Joel poured the wine.

"So what's fresh?" I said.

"Well, there's good sea bass. I picked it out myself this morning. We do that with—"

"I'll take a steak, Joel," Betsy interrupted, picking up her wine-glass. "So will Victor. And some potatoes, not mashed. Victor's choles-terol can't stomach the cream."

I gave him a look, but Joel was gazing around the room, grinning.

After a moment, he laughed and glanced at me while he kissed Betsy on the top of the head.

Betsy soon finished her first glass and frowned for a few minutes, her lips squeezed tightly together. I remembered a dinner party at our house in Somesville while it was still under construction: Betsy and Sara and I had been eating in the unfinished living room when Betsy started to cry because of all the lumber sitting around—it reminded her of Uncle Bill. Bill had been an amateur furniture maker.

And I was helpless but to think of Regina, seeing the couples out on dates: bonding over appetizers, leaning toward each other. I was split over a gap, cleft in two: part of me longing for Regina, almost wrenching me from my chair, and part wanting to make up for my mistakes, to storm out and fly over to her house and make her promise to never see me again, to find someone younger, some boy more her speed. Betsy explained to me a recent doctor's diagnosis while I knocked back two glasses of the wine, ignoring how good it was, ignoring everyone.

I was too busy wondering, Why hadn't Regina e-mailed? What was happening at La Loulou's anyway?

I could have told Betsy everything right then. She didn't notice, just went on drinking.

The restaurant filled up and became twice as loud. Perhaps it was the wine, but I felt seasick. My mind had a peephole through which I saw the room, my vision shrinking until I needed to focus on a small, single thing, a lady's ear, a candle, or else I'd fall over.

When the steaks arrived, I was drunk. I heard Betsy calling me across the table.

"Dammit, will you listen?"

"What?" I said. I felt tears springing up. I wanted to erase everyone. Remembrances struck of Sara a few years earlier in Blue Sea holding court to a group of my colleagues, the center of bewitched attention as she revealed Hollywood gossip.

"What I said about Sara, what she was working on," said Betsy. Her beach hat had become a fedora by tipping forward.

"Sara what?"

The table behind us started in on "Happy Birthday." The waitstaff arrived singing, surrounding them in a huddle.

"Say that again?"

"You're drunk," Betsy said. "You're supposed to be driving!"

"Please, about Sara—"

The restaurant burst into applause. Betsy shoved away from the table, wobbled off to the kitchen, and poked open the swinging doors. I went to the bathroom, returned, and ordered and drank an espresso alone. Betsy and Joel came out, comrades-in-arm, fifteen minutes later, and Joel escorted us outside and got a cigarette off his mother. The two of them stood under the restaurant's front awning, speaking quietly between themselves. I could have sworn when Joel looked at me he was gloating. He didn't let me pay, not even for the wine.

Faking drunkenness, I didn't say good-bye. I didn't want to re-member that evening ever again. Wipe the synapses clean with some scotch and a hard sleep. When I dropped her off, Betsy gave me hell for driving tipsy, and also for not taking home the candlesticks. I left her waving them at me from the front porch.

The next morning I drove to the pond, swam ten laps back and forth, and walked up the road to the beach. White, green, and blue sailboats bobbed on the ocean like ducks, like elaborate wedding hats flung out to sea. I waded in to my hips. No junior, but not so ancient, either. Half a mile out, a tiny island marked where the open water began; people said the island belonged to the Rockefellers. For a moment I thought about swimming that far, just to take a look, but it gave me the shivers even to think about the open ocean.

I couldn't figure out why I'd gotten so wound up. I was fine.

I spent the rest of the day in the lab with Lucy and our postdocs, editing and re-editing the grant application. That night, I caught the late show at the Criterion, but by then I was too tired to pay much attention, something about terrorists in the future. Mostly I replayed my *Die Hard* moment in my head. "So what's your focus, doc?" That's what Bruce Willis had asked me the night we met, and I'd barely been able to respond. We'd been wandering around a rooftop party in Manhattan overlooking the Hudson River, me, Sara, and her agent. The roof was a block long and fully landscaped, and a teenager in a black tie played jazz standards on a grand piano—a grand piano on the roof—while waiters filled our glasses with champagne that matched the color of the lanterns in the trees. It was like something out of a movie. We were there because one of *The Hook-Up*'s backers owned the top floor, and it was his wife's thirtieth-birthday party. She'd greeted me silently, holding up her palms and pressing them against mine for a full five seconds, in the Persian tradition, she said. We were wandering around making small talk when Bruce Willis joined us. He seemed to materialize from out of the lemon trees. "So what's your focus, doc?" he asked me once we were introduced. "Your wife didn't have time to fill me in earlier."

He and Sara had met over lunch that afternoon, as arranged by their respective agents. At that point, *The Hook-Up* was starting to be screened privately, and the previous weekend Bruce had seen it at his financial manager's estate in East Hampton. By Monday, he'd ordered his agent to arrange a meeting. He was looking for someone to write him something funny and smart, to help him quit the aliens/terrorists scene.

So what's your focus, doc? Amyloid beta wasn't an easy party topic, and I said something vague about genetics, but not what was on my tongue: that, pardon my work as a scientist, sir, but you are Bruce Willis. You are John McClane. Were it not for you, our planet might have been destroyed by a comet, the Federal Reserve could have been plundered. If not for you, Cybill Shepherd would be remembered for sitting on a diving board because Peter Bogdanovich liked her breasts. And on and on.

But I didn't want to embarrass anyone. Mark and I wandered away to the roof's edge and let them talk. Not that I liked Sara being alone with Bruce Willis, or knowing they'd shared a bottle of wine at lunch. Bruce Willis must get jealous sometimes, I remembered thinking. What were superheroes anyway? Half divine, but also half mortal. Able to halt a speeding train, but still expected to pay taxes. Superhuman was never meant to mean *supra*human.

Classically, the type stayed consistent: Wagner knew if you stabbed in the right spot, down fell mighty Siegfried.

Which explained Willis's endurance, I thought, staring at him, as opposed to those on the big screen with no Kryptonite to fear. Willises were never perfect. They paid child support, but grudgingly. They drank too much, they wore rubber tank tops. McClane in *Die Hard* may have run across broken glass, but his feet bled like everyone else's.

What is a perfect human? Who is he? What does he look like?

Does he look like Bruce Willis, oozing charm and self-confidence, he who possesses himself so completely?

The Perfect Husband, I remembered, was the title that Russell had suggested at dinner.

At home after the movies, I went straight to Sara's office and flipped through her Rolodex until I found Mark's card. There was a single number, scribbled next to "cell." I called twice. Both times a computer voice said the number was disconnected. I dialed information in Los Angeles, but the closest Mark Koster they had was in Healdsburg, and when I called, I got a woman who said she'd take a message, since her father was at the YMCA for his water aerobics. I called information again and got the number instead for Mark's old agency. A voice message said the office was closed, but I could press zero for a directory. They no longer had any listing for Koster.

I searched on the Internet. A few mentions in newspapers and magazines, citing Mark at his old agency again, but nothing leading me to a phone number or where he was working currently.

I spun the Rolodex by the wheels. I couldn't think of anyone else Sara had worked with closely, not by full name.

I riffled the papers on her desk. Finally, I sat down. The chair, an extinct species Sara had carted up from New York, grated against the floor. I turned on her laptop. I'd tried this before and failed, shortly after the accident, but maybe I missed something. The password-entry screen appeared and I punched in her birthday. I tried her name, my name, my birthday. I tried "hook up," I tried "Betsy." I tried "password." Eventually the screen said I'd made too many attempts, that it would now shut down, and if I had any further questions, I could contact a network administrator.

Remarkable how loud a silent house sounds.

I remained sitting through a crying episode. The other index cards were in the filing cabinet where I'd left them. I picked them up and for a moment held them in both hands, and dropped them back inside.

A week later, two days before my New York trip, I should have been exhausted. I hadn't slept more than a few hours a night in two weeks. None of us could see clearly anymore. Three in the morning, I was just home from the lab, and a heavy rain fell outside. The ferns below my window, hit by the rain, made me think it was hailing.

The phone ringing cut right through the noise.

Regina sounded drunk. She launched into a story about her uncle Mitch, her father's brother. How Mitch was a stutterer, a published poet, a university librarian in California who grew his own marijuana. Apparently he'd FedExed Regina some new books in the mail that afternoon, accompanied by a film canister containing some illegal reading assistance.

She recited to me from Mitch's gifts of underlined Rimbaud ("Our bodies are invested with an amorous new body"), Sylvia Plath ("To make up for the honey I've taken"), Jean Valentine ("Anyone else may leave you, I will never leave you, fugitive"), Frank O'Hara ("You were the best of all my days"). It was Mitch, she explained, who had first inspired her to write poetry, the one trustworthy, decent adult in her life who showed her that being older than seventeen could be cool.

"You should hear how he uses poetry, it's how he escapes his stutter. I mean it's amazing how useful it is to him," said Regina. "Like lithium for the autodidact. You know what I'm saying?"

"Not really," I said resignedly.

"So he'll be in a conversation with someone and there will be a moment when his stutter is about to strike. And he senses it, that he's about to run out of options, but then right in that opening where his tongue should trip, out pops something he's read, like 'riotocracy.'"

"Riotocracy?"

"Or 'masticates.' He's written them down for me. 'Tatterdemalion.' Some word that's so oldfangled, yet it saves him, it lets his tongue relax and then he can speak normally again. You know? Check this out, 'dendroglyphs.' I mean, these are lifelines. Imagine if words meant that much to you or me, to be a saving grace."

Just do it already, I told myself.

"I mean, because what's left afterward," Regina went on, "except what we've written down? This is fascinating to me: how the body decomposes, they stop the clocks, but if you can find means to get something recorded first, if you make your consciousness into words written down somewhere and preserved, well, that's the imperative. That's the fucking imperative. Otherwise we are, what, just mute animals, kneeling before the victor."

"Are you still there?" she said a second later.

Kneeling before the victor. I wondered if that last part came from one of her poems. Regina had never shown me any of her poetry, not that I would have known what to do with it. Poetry was one of those things I'd never understood. Sara's province, not mine.

Try again. Write this. Dear La Loulou.

And I thought of Regina's brother trapped inside his head, writing his sister's address on an envelope with the simple trust that she'd receive it, read it, and understand not only what he'd said, but what he meant.

I thought of Sara, a discussion we'd had one time about people who talk to themselves, Sara saying, "I don't see why it should be a sign you're psychotic, talking to yourself. I talk to myself all the time. Fine, it implies two, not one. Speaker and audience, therefore the unified self divided, schizophrenic, okay. But we don't say the same thing about people who keep diaries, right? Look, as someone who works alone, whose job it is to work out what she's thinking, to bring my thoughts out and see what they mean and then follow them through, is it so wrong to keep oneself company? Don't you do it in the lab? Isn't it less isolating, less *lonely*, to live with your thoughts aloud rather than keep them trapped inside your head? Don't you ever sing in the car?"

Regina hung up.

The island was foggy the next morning, Thursday, fog so thick the backyard was a cold gray moor. When I left the house, there were deer in the driveway, snacking on my blueberry scrub. They stared at me for a moment, then popped away into the mist.

The phone was ringing when I walked into my office.

"Buddy, I have a computer filled with God knows what," Russell said. "Manure, probably. The whole thing just crashed because I forgot my password."

"Trust me, I'm familiar with the idea."

"So I call some number, now there's a kid in a blue uniform on his hands and knees under my desk. Like he's the new class of plumber, except he's got a Ph.D. Seriously, he's probably buying a Porsche with my credit card as we speak. So look, I'll see you Saturday night."

"For dinner, right. Sorry, I'm under the gun here."

Did I really want to see Russell? Maybe to see Cornelia, but that was it.

"I won't keep you. I've got a new Italian place I've been working with, you'll love it. Lower East Side, it's happening. I'll ring up for the royal treatment. Hey, I wanted to mention, Connie wants to see you for coffee."

"Ah, great, I'd love to."

"She says she wants career advice."

I laughed. "She wants to be a scientist now?"

"Tell me about it. No, it's a direction thing, she says. Get this, now she wants to go to cooking school. The Cordon Bleu. Paris. This is two days ago. I tell the daughter who will barely look her father in the face, one, you don't speak French, two, you try working in a kitchen first, see how hell on earth compares to *Iron Chef*, then maybe you can say 'Paris' in my house. But Connie pouts. What do I know? My daughter, who smokes cigarettes in my living room, screaming how she doesn't want my connections, she loves her mother more than me, loves Fucknut the most, and that's it, either Paris or she's out of my life. Buddy, those are my negotiation skills I taught her, now she turns them on me? Then she says, out of the blue, good old Uncle Victor, how come we never see him anymore?"

Russell exhaled a thick sigh. "So do me the favor, talk to her. As long as it's not going north to grow Christmas trees, I'll give you top honors."

"Sure," I said, "sounds fine."

"First Connie wanted you to text her. I explained, Uncle Victor doesn't text."

"Well, I'll call you Saturday."

"Hey, Vic," Russell said before hanging up, "so how are things with tiny dancer working out?"

After my seventieth PowerPoint slide, I wanted to throw my laptop out the window. Outside, the fog was moving in, starting to shroud cars, a plaque turning each car gray and shapeless, indistinguishable from the rest.

I thought of Sara's first card, about our swapping confidences the night we met.

I wondered if by that night I'd been waiting for the right person to confide in, to confess to. Perhaps that's what love was, when finally a secret found its rest. But didn't that imply it could have been anyone, that Sara was simply in the right place at the right time?

The afternoon Ben Lemery showed me his father's gun was about a week before he died. We'd just come in from the pool, a Saturday afternoon in September. Both of us were dripping wet and freezing cold, our teeth were chattering, but we didn't know where to stand. The newness of the house set the protocol. The fruit in a bowl on the counter, apples and oranges, was made of wax. It was warm to the touch. The Lemerys' house was a sparkling white set piece built to spec, flanked by empty homes, the first to be purchased in a new development near the interstate. It had taken me fifteen minutes to walk over from my parents' house, through what I'd always considered the bad part of town: run-down, the lawns wild.

Rumor was, when Ben's parents divorced, his mother gassed herself in the garage, back where they'd lived, outside Philadelphia. But no one knew. We'd only seen Ben's father, a big quiet fat man who wore granny glasses, who never said a word. Passing by one day running errands, weeks before the incident, my mother let me know she found the Lemerys' house unseemly: designed for people too blind to know their position or decent taste. I'd rolled up the window and decided to gradually lose Ben as a friend. That Saturday was the last straw. Above the garage, Ben was holding the gun in his lap, explaining his plan in boastful tones, as though I'd be impressed. He dared me to say he wouldn't do it. I made up an excuse and walked home a few minutes later.

Ben became my charge the day he arrived at Roosevelt High School. A teacher asked me to mentor him, to help Ben adjust, and I invited him to sit at lunch at the table for the overachieving and underappreciated. Quickly, though, none of us liked him. It seemed a great insult to be saddled with Ben Lemery, as though in the Roosevelt social world, as we watched him drop from one social pool to the next, falling closer to ours, we had to admit when he reached us there'd be nowhere lower he could go. But he wasn't one of us. He broke into the school at night and stole things from teachers' desks. Once in the parking lot, he picked up dog shit with his bare hands on a dare. But he'd latched on to me. He smirked if we passed in the hallway, would whisper conspiratorially at lunch about schemes he'd engineered to prank the faculty. A week after the gun episode, I convinced myself he was joking. Ben Lemery couldn't be that crazy. Then he called. I was watching *Men into Space*. Would I come over to help him with his math homework? Ben was the best student in trigonometry. I said no to a fifteen-minute walk in the dark, no to the vibrato in his voice that scared and embarrassed me into staying put. I hung up first. In the kitchen, my mother was listening to opera, preparing dinner, frying green peppers in butter.

We'd never had anyone in our school kill himself, and no one knew the drill the next morning in homeroom when the intercom clicked and the principal asked for a moment of silence. He said, "Ben Lemery was a boy we will always remember in a special place in our hearts," and someone snickered. A girl in flared trousers started crying and I was on the verge. A refrain sank in, one that would reaffirm itself for years afterward, that I could have done something.

"This is becoming ridiculous," Lucy said, striding in. Her laptop was in her arms, along with a coffee mug the size of a thermos, a rock climber's carabiner clipped to its handle. "I keep discovering another section, there's a technology part, a biomarkers clinical kind of thing— and exactly how am I supposed to manage people who won't admit to making mistakes?"

She put her laptop down on my desk. "I'm sorry, but I cannot troubleshoot problems downstream that I'm given two weeks late, when the crucial intervention moment was at least ten days ago."

"Lucy, breathe," I said.

Lucy stared at the wall behind my head.

"I was the one who messed up those reports," she said. "This is my fault."

"It would be no one's fault but mine. Do I look upset?"

"You're asking me that."

"Why don't you tell me what's wrong."

"Are you even listening?"

Sometimes, I noticed, Lucy's age showed through her face: trembling where the skin stretched over her cheekbones. But she did look more wrung out than normal. Probably she'd been suggesting as much to me for weeks. Sara always said it was a hindrance of mine, that I expected people to tell me what they needed.

Lucy picked up her laptop.

"I just don't know what I'm doing anymore."

"You're being melodramatic."

"Who says we're on the right track, and not the guys at GSK? Why *not* the guys at GSK? Don't you ever think this could be a multimillion-dollar mistake?"

I laughed but regretted it. "Lucy, you'll get your drug. Most likely, the mice will turn out smarter afterward."

"I'm telling you, I just don't know anymore."

"Know what?"

Lucy twirled a hand around her head, indicting me, the lab, the air particles. "I am trying to explain that I am very, very tired." She was daring me to break away. She leaned forward and lowered her voice, "Listen to me."

"I'm listening."

"Take a nerve cell."

"A nerve cell."

"Take the membrane, the ion channels. Potassium goes out, sodium flows in. A little negative on the inside, a little positive on the outside."

"Right."

"So the potential remains reliable. Lively in public, a cynic on the interior, but pretty stable on the whole."

"Lucy, I get it—"

"Now, apply a charge in just the right place. Give a jolt. What happens?"

"The gates open."

"The gates *fly* open. All kinds of things get through. The balance goes out of whack."

I waited for part two.

"Remember park ranger Terry? Do you know what he said when he broke up with me this week?"

"I thought you weren't going to see him again."

"That part of me is missing. However I'm built, I lack something that everyone else has."

As if a film previously applied to her face had slipped off.

"Lucy, you can't listen to that. This creep doesn't know the first thing about you."

She stared at me for a moment. "I really need some girlfriends. I mean, forty-one. *Forty-one*. Where are my children? My mother asked me that on the phone last night, like I'd lost them recently."

We both laughed. I reached out my hand but she managed in getting up to duck her shoulder. Lucy left the door open on her way out and I watched her go: her shoulders flattening, her knobby hiking sneakers treading silently down the hall.

I sat very still for a moment, staring out the window. Fog was in the treetops. Two dead roaches lay on top of the radiator. Sitting on top of a stack of laboratory equipment catalogs was my lost address book. I weighed it in my hands like a fish.

I dialed Sara's only sibling, her sister, Miriam, in Kansas City. She picked up on the second ring. We exchanged pleasantries. After a few minutes I snuck in my question with a lie that Betsy was having memory lapses. We were bringing her in for some cognition tests and needed to confirm that we had the correct versions for some of her stories. How did Miriam remember the night Sara and their mother fought, the night Sara almost ran away?

Miriam backed up Betsy's account. It was the night of Sara's play at the high school, her starring role. Probably because she was nervous for Sara, their mother had drunk more than usual before going to the auditorium. During a quiet moment in the second act, she'd vomited in the front row. Back home, the fight was terrible. "Singed the wallpaper off, from what I remember." At the high point, Sara punched her mother in the mouth and ran out in tears, vowing never to return. She bought a bus ticket for California, in fact.

I asked if Miriam was sure. Hundred percent, she said. "Look at any family portrait afterward. Mother never smiled with her mouth open again. She needed two front teeth replaced."

We made conversation a few more minutes, because yes it had been too long, particularly for family. And didn't I remember those nice vacations we'd taken together, the one that winter to Baja. And didn't I remember what fun we'd had. And didn't I remember. And perhaps if ever I was near Kansas City, I always had somewhere I could rest my feet.

Yes, I said, of course, of course I remembered.

———

Neurologically, though, it made perfect sense. Combining the degree of my knowledge of Sara's early life with, in this case, a lack of specific recollection (I hadn't been there, after all) made for a plausible case of misattribution. I could have told Miriam as much off the bat.

I'd learned early on with Sara that marriage wasn't science. Both evolved, both went through cycles. Science grew through fine-tuning, one scientist turning up with an idea about nature, then a little later someone else saying in fact it's like this, here's my data, and down through the line, fully documented in the literature. But a marriage had no literature. There was no microfiche for arguments. There was only he said, she said. A picture postcard of what happened.

My father gave me one piece of advice on my wedding day: to remember the wife's always right. I recalled telling Sara about it later in the beige hotel room, and how we laughed, both of us so happy, secure knowing that our marriage wouldn't be the norm, wouldn't be anything like the families we'd come from.

I drove back to Somesville just after midnight, packed my bag, and set the alarm clock for five a.m. My mind was dull and clouded when I fell asleep, nervous and clear when I woke. By morning, rainstorms had swept over the island and shoved the fog out to sea. Gulls cawed with the sunrise. I stopped for coffee in Seal Harbor, where the crowd at the gas station was mostly contractors, about a half-dozen guys with sunburned necks. The other neuroscientists probably purchased their soy chai lattes elsewhere, I figured.

There was an island legend people told about that gas station and a certain celebrity neighbor. Martha Stewart comes down one day to get gas, the story goes, and she asks the station clerk, can I use the phone? The clerk politely informs her there's a pay phone outside, that the house phone is for employees only. Stewart lives up the hill in the old Ford estate, to get home it's only a minute to her driveway, but Martha's not going anywhere. Martha says she's got no change and she really needs to make a call. The clerk tells her again about the difference between the house phone and the pay phone, that it's been store policy for more than thirty years. By now the line is backing up. Martha's upset. She's Martha Stewart. She's never been treated like this before. She says to the clerk: Do you know who I am? Do you realize who you're talking to?

At which point, an elderly gentleman steps out of line, taps Martha on the shoulder, and says, "Excuse me, but I'm David Rockefeller. And I use the pay phone, too."

And he hands her a quarter.

At seven in the morning, campus was empty, the lab deserted. I sat at my desk and did nothing. My thoughts were tied to others further back, and those bound to ones even deeper, stored under wraps in unused rooms. The sun filled my office with soft yellow light. I scowled at the parking lot. I closed the blinds and booted up my computer. The newest message in my in-box said it had been sent at four a.m.:

From: belletter@umich.edu
To: vaaron1118@yahoo.com
Subject: No shit

I won a contest. I'm having a chapbook published. I WILL BE A PUBLISHED AUTHOR. Bring champagne. No funny stuff.

When Lucy got in, I asked her to inform everyone I wasn't to be disturbed. For lunch, I grabbed two Diet Cokes and a bag of Fritos, and in a spree of work I conducted several conference calls, edited an article for Lucy, reviewed some résumés, and answered enough e-mail so that I'd be caught up when I returned from New York. At five-thirty, I left for the airport.

I was saying good-bye, hearing wishes of good luck, when I dashed back to my computer. I stared at the screen.

"Can't make it, going to New York for a conference, congratulations," I typed.

Rather than SEND, I clicked DELETE.

I jogged out of the lab, down the stairwell, through the quad, past the maintenance building to the parking lot with the sun on my back, my suit bag flapping on my arm.

"Sir, I need to look through your bag."

"Go ahead."

"Please lift it over the barrier, thank you. Now, I'm going to ask you several questions about your luggage. I need you to answer them to the best of your knowledge. In this bag, do you have any liquid—"

"No, no."

"Sir, I am required by federal airline safety regulations to ask you these questions."

"I know. All right."

"Do you have any liquid or perishable items in this bag?"

"No."

"Whose bag is this?"

"What?"

"Whose bag is this?"

"It's mine."

"Sir, who packed this bag?"

"I did."

"When was it packed?"

"This morning. Last night."

"When specifically was it packed, please?"

"Excuse me? Last night."

"Sir, I am required to ask these questions. If you cannot answer them to our satisfaction, we have the right to deny your boarding privileges."

"Deny my boarding privileges."

"Who packed this bag?"

"I said, I did. Last night."

"Has any person, strange or familiar, approached you since you packed this bag?"

"You realize what a ridiculous question that is."

"What do you mean, sir?"

"Forget it. No."

"No, you have not been approached by anyone?"

"Right. No one has approached me."

"Sir, has anyone offered you anything to bring on this flight?"

"No."

"Have you or anyone—sir, what is this?"

"That's a gift. Excuse me, what are you doing, that's for a friend of mine."

"Wrapped presents are forbidden. We are required by federal law to unwrap any wrapped items. In particular, when I asked you, do you have any liquids—"

"I said it's a gift. My friend's in the wine business, I'm bringing him a bottle of wine. I don't understand."

"Sir, may I remind you, when I asked if you had any liquids or perishables in this bag, you said no."

"Oh give me a break. It's a sealed bottle, I would need—you think I'll endanger the flight with Pinot Noir?"

"Sir, please, if you will lower your voice, I need you to calm down."

"Ma'am, I am calm."

"Right now I need you to lower your voice. If you will not lower your voice, we will conduct this interview elsewhere."

"Well, I can't believe this."

"Sir, are you going to calm down?"

"I am perfectly calm."

"Sir, will you calm down?"

"What do you want me to say? I am calm. Can I at least go put it in my car?"

"Put what?"

"The bottle. The wine."

"It will be confiscated here at the airport, but you may claim it upon your return with proof of receipt. Now, do you have any *other* liquid or perishable items in this bag?"

"No."

"Very good. Thank you, sir. Stan, can I get a wand check? Sir, if you will step out of line, we need you to remove your jacket, belt, and shoes."

The aging conference in New York was eight hundred strong, elite scientists from around the world presenting findings in brief slots and accepting awards, making speeches, picking from melon platters during breaks, and shaking hands. We were both priests and mongrels, musical prodigies with degrees in proteomics and chemists with Psy.D.'s, we cutthroat, graying Alzheimer's researchers, each of us guarding secrets we might sell someday to Big Pharma and use to buy vacation homes for ourselves and a board of executives. Really, it was more a gathering of old friends, folks from NYU who used to work down the hall, men and women I'd known my entire career and whose children were doing interesting things with biofuels to save the world, people who shared a common interest and the same lumps and frustrations and budget cuts, for whom it mattered on a deeply personal level what progress we made.

Saturday, we broke for lunch and blinked in the daylight. I joined a group going out to an Italian restaurant off Fifth Avenue, former colleagues and lab mates from NYU, and sat next to Georgia Rhodes, wife of Sandy Rhodes, who'd recently transferred to Duke. Georgia, who proceeded to drink too much wine and tell me she was sad she hadn't seen me in so long. "Now, how is Sara?" she asked. "Has she ever met that Colin Farrell? I swear, Victor Aaron, where are you keeping her?"

Sandy gave me a look and took one of his wife's hands. She said, "What'd I say, don't you apologize for me, why are you always apologizing when no one's done anything wrong?"

I gave my presentation in the late afternoon and caught up with people afterward until I needed to meet Russell for dinner, leaving my friends to their orange decaf carafes. I was sad to leave. The heat was hanging around Washington Square, snared under the trees. Everyone was sweating. Boys going by me wore white T-shirts to their knees, like communion dresses. My plan had been to walk to dinner for a little exercise, but after fifteen blocks my jacket was wet, plus I was lost where once I'd known every corner.

And was I really preferring to spend the evening with Russell?

Sara and I had expected to miss Manhattan when we left, but we both caught movers' amnesia. We fell in love with Maine and also with each other again, our older, more demure selves. We shared a feeling of being evacuated. It was a team effort. We didn't swap our leather jackets for parkas, but we invested in proper boots. "I like the winters," I told Sara one night in bed, the two of us staring at the ceiling, "how everyone waves on the road." "When you've got a couple hundred people trapped on an island, you get to know the faces." "Sure, and even if they don't recognize you, they still wave." "Who else but a neighbor would be on the island in January?"

It took me ten minutes to find a pay phone. Russell told me where to go. I passed the address to the cab driver, then asked him to roll up his window.

All those years schlepping to the lab as the doughnut guys hauled their carts into place, walking home at night past the drug dealers, I must have blocked out the smell.

Hoofer hits it big, but lacks the girl. Eventually gets his cake and eats it too. Donald O'Connor never got the credit he deserved.

For nearly two hours I didn't speak, just played Sara's game in my head. Russell ran the show once we were seated, somewhere below Houston Street, deep downtown, behind an unmarked door where a dining room had been decorated to look grimy, authentically though improbably a hundred years old. A brand-new artifact, though more like an English hunting lodge than a Tammany slum.

"If you believe this, she prefers it doggie style," Russell said, pushing himself away from the table, balling up his linen napkin. "She prefers it, she gets off on it. You think I say no when she insists?"

Russell had sufficiently recovered from the last girl to find a new one, a Ukrainian blond, Larysa, he said, with chipped teeth and breast implants, who worked as a hostess for one of his clients. After the coffee he was still focused on how she liked it, how she took it, he put it, going into details to show off his good fortune for discovering a woman who didn't mind facing away from him during sex.

"Look at me," he said, yawning, one hand up in the air behind his head, "here I am, thinking we need variety."

"Maybe she's lying," I said.

"What? Why would she do that?"

"So moneybags won't dump her, possibly?"

He gave me the finger. "So, Connie wants to see you tomorrow."

"Yeah? Where do I meet her?"

"How should I know?"

He pulled out a cell phone from his jacket and handed it to me.

"What now?" snapped a girl's voice a moment later.

"It's Uncle Victor. Are you always so rude?"

"Oh my God, Victor, how are you?"

Russell watched me, drumming his fingers.

"I heard you're buying me coffee tomorrow."

"Totally, oh thank you, but are you sure? I don't want to bother you at all."

"Honestly, it will be a treat," I said. "Where do I find you?"

Outside, Russell lit a cigar, and I was shocked by the tightness of his blue jeans. We watched young people go in and out of bars like so many fireflies. Next to them, we were artifacts, though probably not of a mold they'd ever grow into. Russell said he wanted another drink and led me to a wine bar. Afterward, he suggested a strip club near Wall Street. Half an hour later, I was staring through a fish tank behind rows of liquor bottles, behind which naked girls were bending over to touch their toes. Russell rented us a private room and we spent twenty minutes with a girl Regina's age wearing a rhinestone-encrusted thong, with a face like wet cement. I felt a crying episode coming on. Of all the places, I thought angrily, sitting on my fists.

The girl asked when she finished, would we like to have again, bik boyz? Behind her was a large ATM. Its green sign was the brightest thing in the room.

I caught a cab and Russell leaned in through the open window, jacket sleeves scrunching up on his forearms. The street smelled like urine and cabbage.

"This isn't for me," I said.

"It's not like we all have our own private dancers."

"Good night, Russell."

"You know what I mean?"

"Why don't you go home."

He looked up the street. He laughed. "I mean, a girl doesn't need a pole to know what she's doing."

"You don't know what the hell you're talking about. We're finished. Are you pleased? Is that enough?"

Fuck you, I said quietly. Fuck you.

"Look, look, I'm drunk," he said, pushing himself back from the car. "You're right about Larysa, she probably just wants to cuddle. Vic, call me tomorrow, I'm sorry. Hey, I've got something for you."

He slipped an envelope through the window. When the cab pulled away, Russell slapped the trunk like he was spanking it, hard enough so the whole car jolted. The cabbie hit the brakes, but Russell was already going back into the club.

"Asshole," the driver said under his breath.

We shot uptown. I opened the envelope. Inside was the sticker Russell had peeled off his windshield: an image of the twin towers smoking, with the words underneath, "We Will Never Forget."

Sara once claimed that if movies were eliminated, if cinema were wiped off the planet and then somehow, a hundred years later, film was discovered again, two styles would instantly reemerge: kung fu and pornography. The genre's cockroaches, but also in possession of its genetic code, the bonds of movies' base pairs: athleticism and sex, war and love. I said slapstick surely came next, with westerns in tow, but Sara disagreed. She wanted romantic comedy in third place, so that any descendants of ours could have a shot at claiming royalties.

Slapstick always beats romantic comedy, I thought, staring out the back of the cab. Not that we produced any descendants anyway. Going up Third Avenue, I counted three new multiplexes that hadn't been there when we were living in the Village. I stared at Russell's sticker, then peeled off the back and stuck it on the door.

At three a.m. the night was still muggy. The crying jag never struck. I watched people in the dark walk their dogs, pick up dog shit with plastic bags over their hands like mittens. At five in the morning, the garbage trucks appeared.

Too tired to sleep, I caught an hour at best. Most of the time I sat in a chair by the window and pictured Russell and the airport security guard crawling around like insects.

For the second time in a month, I caught a sunrise. I showered and shaved and watched CNN. As I was packing, I found a stray jar of moisturizer inside my bag. One of Sara's. It must have been from some trip ages before, when we shared a suitcase. The coincidence seemed overpowering—not a coincidence but a significant event with no correlative, the sudden appearance of this little pot.

I had an image of myself trekking and suddenly needing hand cream, and I'd reach into my backpack, and there would be a tube of Aveda, next to my water bottle.

We Will Never Forget. As though it was a syndrome, not a pledge.

Was this the bag Sara had taken to California?

I couldn't remember.

Then I had my big idea.

My goddaughter was dreadlocked as Russell had described, but her dreadlocks were blond and thin as twine, not the thick ones you'd see on a reggae album. Tied up in a bird's nest, they made her seem top-heavy, her neck was so long. Cornelia made for a very pretty Rastafarian. She'd always had a gaunt, masculine face, wide eyes with her father's heavy eyebrows, his turned-up nose. I found her sitting on a bench outside a coffee shop on West Eighth Street. She wore a billowing black skirt and black flip-flops, lots of jewelry, a rose-colored silk camisole, and glitter across her cheeks. The Cornelia I remembered had been an animal-rights activist, an A student, a smoker, and, of all things, a dedicated fan of *Singin' in the Rain*. She'd stayed with us for a long weekend the month she graduated from high school, and on Saturday night, we presented her with an early graduation present: Sara had arranged for a late, private showing of *Singin' in the Rain* at the Criterion. They even opened the candy counter.

Now she was a woman of twenty-two, alien to me. But there was something refreshing about her posing as an adult. For thirty minutes, Cornelia drank iced chai tea and filled me in on existence post-Cornell: the bar life with friends, sunbathing alone, some boy she had an eye on, an Internet animator she'd been hooking up with since graduation but now considered more, like, a friend with privileges, she said, perhaps. Cornelia's voice was permanently caught between registers, hoarse and cracked like an adolescent boy's. The last time I'd seen her was at Sara's funeral. Cornelia had been in her first year at college. The day was cloudy. She'd worn a baggy tan cotton dress puffing out like a spinnaker, like a portable tepee. I remembered her nose had been red from a piercing that had become infected.

The nose ring was gone. "Uncle Victor, you have to help me." She took one of my hands and started massaging my fingers. Cornelia's fingers were long and spindly, dry and cracked around the knuckles, covered in rings. She almost never dropped eye contact.

"Of course I will."

"What did my father tell you?"

"That you want to go to cooking school. That he wants you to work in a restaurant first."

"What an asshole," she said, then she laughed, kicked off her sandals, and slung her legs over my knees. "But please, I know, it's so sad, he's still paying for college, so who is Connie to ask for more. But I am so serious about this, Victor. Someone should make me an apprentice. I want to have a craft and pay rent and have a career, you know? This is my calling. If I felt called to be a monk, I'd ask for a ticket to Tibet, but I'm not a monk, I'm a cook. Russell got into business because he wanted to make money, but I don't care about money."

I said, "Maybe because it's his money we're talking about."

Cornelia yanked her feet down to punish me, and we watched a young man walk by wearing a tuxedo, pushing a big instrument case on wheels. What was he singing? Glancing away, I noticed Cornelia still didn't shave her legs, one of those things I'd always found admirable about her, if not pretty.

I'm never upset around her, I thought.

"Well, if you're so serious," I said, "then why not take him up on his offer?"

"What offer?"

"Setting you up in a kitchen in New York."

Cornelia snorted. "Please, excuse me, then he's the power broker and I'm indebted. I'll be the third-world country that can't export corn. Can you see me in his friend's restaurant, under, like, surveillance? Plus, how would I know if I was there on my own merits, or because someone owed him a favor?"

"That's just networking."

"I hate networking."

"Young people always hate networking. What if I had a friend who owned a restaurant?"

"What?"

Now or never, I thought.

"Why don't you come live up in Maine for the summer?"

She deliberately blinked twice in a row. "You are joking."

"You'll have your own room, your own bathroom. That house is too big for one person anyway."

"But why?"

"Because I'm your godfather, I'm supposed to do these things," I said gruffly. "People my age like feeling useful. Plus, I actually do know a guy, he owns a terrific restaurant. There's no guarantees, but I should at least be able to get you an interview."

"But, like, Uncle Victor," she said, "you're joking."

"But, like, I'm not."

And I wasn't. What I was was exhausted. I missed my routines. Somehow, I sensed, by bringing Cornelia up to Maine, I'd get them back.

Cornelia shrieked and nearly burned me with her cigarette. She kissed me several times on the cheeks. I told her we needed to make sure her parents approved, but that turned out to be a piece of cake: Russell phoned that evening to say he was surprised, but also supportive and grateful, and Cornelia's mother called the next morning to say how much she appreciated my cordoning off Cornelia from her ex-husband.

By Cornelia's age, I'd written encyclopedias inside myself on the ways of the universe and the gears of man. Now I contained about a pamphlet, mostly relating to rodent brains. I flew to Logan, bought a coffee, and waited for my connection to Bar Harbor. I knew I'd never swim a mile faster than thirty minutes. That I wasn't one for political buttons, country clubs, merchandise with logos, one cuisine over another, the latest trends.

That I wasn't any good as anyone's boyfriend, at least not yet.

I sat with my coffee in a rocking chair, feeling tired in every muscle group, staring at Boston across the water. Time to face facts: I wasn't ready. Between work and looking after Betsy and now Cornelia, I had more than enough to sustain me through the summer, at least another year.

I knew I should have replied to Regina and congratulated her about her poetry book, for courtesy's sake, but that otherwise we were through.

I boarded my connection.

The man next to me on the plane was a Texan businessman, employed by IBM, I gathered, based on the logo on his polo and his matching laptop bag. He brought up e-procurement channels. Sensing he wouldn't shut up, I asked him about his family, and he talked for an hour about his dog. He said when we landed, "You just don't meet people like you where I'm from anymore, people who will talk to a fellow passenger rather than pretend to be asleep.

"Must be Maine," he said.

A good modest Mainer, I didn't commit to more than "Perhaps."

three

Change of direction three. It's been a week since I wrote *those last cards, and here I am at my desk, on the daybed, back at the desk again. What to write? Where to start?*

Today, I played solitaire on my computer for forty-five minutes. I went outside and did yard work. Paid the phone bill, made lunch, went to yoga, and did e-mail after that. One message I got from Mark: "Four words: Move to Los Angeles. Maine is for lobsters. We miss you. Everyone does."

Yes, Mark, thank you, dear, but I'm still stuck, and surely I'd be stuck in California, too. Stuck: frozen while fulfilling the worst suspicions of myself as: a hack, an amateur, not good for much except: using colons.

Writer as lobster: she who grows into a shell of her own construction.

Even my own mother vomited at my work. Cheap shot, but true.

I just read again the last line from card set number two, what Victor said when Mark suggested I try writing screenplays, "What do you know about writing screenplays?" And now I can write. Now I'm ready to go shove these cards up his nose. Do something about it, as you and I've discussed, Doctor, rather than just complain and mull and weather (as my mother drank and starved and napped to survive her own marriage).

So I'm out the door and on my way to the lab, but actually I don't leave the chair. The idea of being even an ounce like my mother was enough to sit me still and fall back in love with Victor. I'm thinking: What good from confrontation? What would be gained? Victor is who he is, no matter who I've become, and why should he change? Who wants to change at our age anyway? Who says it's possible? I'll be sixty soon, almost twice the life expectancy of a century ago. Would those generations of women, suffering far worse, have contrived one-tenth of my complaints?

Victor would point out, the reason people didn't have Alzheimer's back then was that no one lived long enough for it to develop.

But sixty. Jesus.

After Woman Hits Forty, *I wrote four scripts in two years; none went anywhere and each was tougher than the last to finish. Victor came around. He saw room to maneuver. Since I was back to scratch, he was ready to coach: looming, notating, leaving Post-its on the fridge. We'd spend evenings together in our separate chairs studying movies and rehearsing dialogue and discussing character motivations (which cracks me up now, Victor The Unaware under the reading lamp twirling a pencil, wondering why people do what they do, but of course he was very good at it, better than me with people on paper: nailing cause and effect with no sympathy for mystery if it wasn't reasoned and strategic). And again, it was helpful, I knew as much, but I was also quite aware of what he was doing and what I wasn't, and I remembered the joy of writing* Woman *on my own.*

When Victor bought books on how to write screenplays, he always bought two copies, keeping one for himself to read on the subway. He over-participated right when I wanted back my sense of soloing. Was that so egotistic? Supposedly I was the artist in the house, he the scientist. What if I'd stayed up late reading Nature, *giving him tips?*

Do all scientists fancy deep down they're polymaths?

What Victor does believe, I've long suspected though never said, is that his work is fundamentally more important than mine. His for the dedicated, mine for the dabbler. And who's to say he's not right? What difference would it make if I never wrote another thing?

Or maybe I've just been conditioned over thirty years to think that way.

Or maybe I'm being unfair.

So bad news struck. Aunt Betsy got breast cancer. And Uncle Bill wasn't fit to look after her, he wasn't fit to look after himself by then. They needed help. I don't know where the idea came from, but one evening I was in the living room, drinking tea, talking to her on the phone, and out popped my revelation. Victor and I had discussed getting them a caretaker, and this was the conversation where I was supposed to suggest that idea, but then I blurted out, "Why don't I move up?" Betsy loved it, and a flood of rightness washed through me. I needed a break. A retreat from run-ins around the city with friends whose careers leaped from success to success. An escape from Victor's lingering. In Northeast Harbor, I could write half the day and shuttle Betsy to her X-ray appointments.

Victor was pleased. On the surface because Betsy needed help, but also because he and Lucy were preparing some big grant, and he could maintain his sixteen-hour days guilt free.

I flew up in June. In July, Betsy underwent surgery, a complete mastectomy of her left breast, and survived to smoke another day. And by the end of August, I had a rough draft, as easy as that. As though hatching from nature, out she came. And it had gone exactly as conceived, from an idea during the flight to Bangor through to the last typed pages: a hundred thirty pages word-processed in a stuffy yellow room overlooking the ocean: all mine, and my first reader, Betsy herself, calling it a smash.

And Mark sold it a month later.

When people asked me where I drew inspiration, I always wanted to say my Aunt Betsy. Her determination, her carnal will was so affecting, not only to get my own ass up and out of bed, but also for the character. Doctor, if you haven't seen The Hook-Up *(I realize how awful that sounds, but it seems as if everyone has seen it by now, if only on a plane, and after it came out I gave up on false modesty anyway. It's my baby and I'll be proud of it as long as there are DVDs on this planet), it's about redemption and revenge and a rather extreme May-December romance: the story of a washed-up movie star who makes a come-back at seventy-two, post-cancer, with the help of a young film director. Who knows why, America loved it. When Sony tested the movie, the most common comments were "sweet" and "light," and if that led certain critics to call it sappy, it still nearly paid in cash for the house in Somesville. Two months after the release, Mark set up an auction, and in a weekend he'd sold my four other screenplays. Didn't matter that they were crap. One alone bought me and Victor new cars.*

Oh, the cars, beautiful day! I remember thinking at the dealership, you're buying this out of guilt over the trappings of success, but also because you can. And you love that you can, that you're the one bankrolling lavish toys, not him.

Of course Victor protested. When he saw the car, the Audi he'd picked out from the catalog, there was evident shame I was buying it for him, and then embarrassment as the modern male about feeling ashamed of his wife's largesse. He left to pee when I was signing the final papers. Still managed to drive home with the top down, though.

But for the look on the dealer's face, when he learned it was the wife who'd be negotiating the sports cars.

But aside from cars, houses, investment accounts? Frankly, The Hook-Up *did nothing good for our marriage. Talk about a change of direction unforeseen. The more successful I became, the less Victor liked it. The less he respected me, was how it felt. And I'm sure he felt less loved. It really was something, that year, where here I was the toast of some midnight dinner in Tribeca, and Victor was home with the television. Some producer would pull me aside at a festival and tell me that this happened only once in a lifetime, that I should enjoy myself, and so I did: me with a suite for a week at the Chateau Marmont, being recog-*

nized at the gate, being driven here for a photo shoot, there for a panel discussion, and where was Victor? In the lab with his specimens. As though for a year I was constantly abandoning him for further trappings of (accidental? undeserved?) success, was how he saw it, and yet he never said a word, just went back to the microscope, and meanwhile I was flying to Vancouver, to a festival in Toulouse, lonely and sick with a cold and tired of traveling solo and imploring him to join me.

First-class tickets! A suite at the Four Seasons! Paid for by studio assholes! But Victor wouldn't budge.

My relentless seeker had turned reluctant.

After thirty-odd years, we are our furthest apart. Perhaps marriages shouldn't last so long. Perhaps by prolonging their span, we expose our relationships to diseases that would have remained dormant. Victor won't admit my success has driven him away (to his "music room," to the lab, inward, away from me), but I'm tired of trying to draw it out of him.

When The Hook-Up hit it big, the tables flipped. Victor wore all sorts of smiling faces, but obviously he was wounded. He was lost. Me? I was too happy to observe much, much less act on what he wouldn't confide. When I say the movie did nothing good for our marriage, do I mean I did nothing good by creating it? Or was it how Victor responded, how he continues to respond? I loved the limelight. It was one long, fizzy dream. If Victor had a memory—false, in any case—of what we once were like and he wanted to preserve it, fine, was my thinking at the time. Let him stand in place. Me, I was on a flight somewhere, probably to California, business class.

Two weeks after the conference in New York, my physician's office called, an automated voice recording saying I was due for a checkup. The night before my appointment, a storm brought down power lines, and I took it as a sign of doom. In the locker room at the pool, I eyed the other men closely, senior faculty in their sixties and early seventies with fluffy eyebrows and white spotted potbellies and fallen arches, losing balance, lacking motor skills, shuffling to avoid a fall. In the waiting room at the doctor's, one specimen gave me the fish-eye. He was probably eighty, gray-skinned with long brown fingernails, hooked up to an oxygen tank and a walker for ballast. Incontinent, I guessed, and probably vexed about that. During my appointment, I inquired how old he was. "Sixty-one," said my doctor. "Three years on you, but that's cancer for you. You don't smoke, correct?"

I told him about the insomnia, and he wrote me a refill for my sleeping pills. We went through tests and screenings: skin check, prostate, blood sampling. By the end I received congratulations. "Better than good," he said, and squeezed my arm. "You're a regular forty-seven-year-old if I've seen one."

People with Alzheimer's often saw a reverse process of aging as the disease progressed through its final stages. A terrifying sequence, as though one's life reel were spinning backward, a person would lose in reverse the skills they'd gained as an infant: intelligibility, language, motor skills, the ability to swallow.

The next morning, when the rain stopped and the sun broke through, I felt such contentment going outside that it drew my breath short. The diagnosis didn't say I was going backward toward being spoon-fed, but that I was going forward, I was advancing in advanced age. At the gym I hit the bench press, rolled up my T-shirt sleeves to the shoulders, and swung barbells in front of the mirror. I wanted more life, more breath, more nimble mornings! Around the gym, in the halls on campus, in town, July gave everyone a lift. We were in peak season, and wasn't this life as it should be? Strawberry fairs, summer chorals, fireworks over Frenchman's Bay?

What wonderful smells of cedar!

Not that I had much time to visit any roadside fairs, pancake breakfasts, "Whittle-a-Warbler" workshops. But I noted the signs on the telephone poles and daydreamed. Every moment since New York had been dedicated to assembling a fail-safe grant application in case our first one fell through. Finally, one Thursday twilight, Lucy and I drove to the Bar Harbor FedEx office just before closing and we watched the courier load our packet into her truck and drive away, and we drove away ourselves, out for burritos to celebrate. The team was exhausted, but triumphant. We'd pulled through right on time and done our best. After three margaritas, I tapped Lucy's shoulder—she was sitting next to me—and I said, "Lucy, why don't WASPs attend orgies?"

She said, "Do you know how many times you've told that joke?"

A minute later I took her hand. I told her how much I'd always appreciated our collaboration, how proud I was to have her by my side. Then, before she could respond, an episode swam up. I felt it in the corners of my eyes. I squeezed my fists and pushed away from the table and excused myself. Lucy rejoined the group conversation. When I returned, she shushed me right away, smiling, patting my hand under the table, and her smile was partially one of forgiveness, but mostly pity, and perhaps a little embarrassment on my behalf.

On the drive home I parked by Eagle Lake, hiked in through the dark, and pissed standing on a rock sticking out into the black water, the black mountains encircling me and a quarter-moon just rising. I don't know that I'd ever felt more alive.

For two weeks I hadn't heard from Regina or seen her around campus. There weren't any phone calls to confide poetry or discuss movies. Perhaps, separately, we'd come to the same conclusion. The first Monday after New York, I'd answered the e-mail about her book, citing the conference as why I hadn't congratulated her sooner, but I didn't receive a reply.

Was this how affairs ended in the digital age? The electronic circuit cut in two, the connection severed via BlackBerry at a Starbucks?

Early the next morning, despite a hangover, I shaved, clipped my hair, and drove to Seal Harbor for a swim. Trees along the road trapped sunlight in their branches, suspending it like pollen. Already the day was hot and the water temperature wasn't too terrible. I reached Rockefeller Island and I was in such good spirits afterward, I drove down to Bass Harbor and bought two bags of fresh lobsters and handed them out at work. Everyone deserved a day off, and I spent mine working on Sara's old garden, opening the windows so that Chopin could pour out of the music room: mazurkas hung across the sweet-smelling heat.

Then it struck me around three, while I massaged my knees, that I wouldn't be having many more days so peacefully alone.

Cornelia's plane was to land at eight-thirty.

I went inside and listened to a news program on the radio without changing out of my gardening shorts. Someone in the Middle East was shelling someone else. A senator had been caught with his hand in the till. My mood caught a fever. What had I been thinking, inviting Cornelia to come stay? How would I benefit from a loudmouth vegan around the house? Cornelia was wonderful in small doses, but she could also be intolerable: self-righteous, coarse, selfish, pampered her entire life. Once, back when Sara was alive, she'd stayed with us for a week and Sara almost murdered her, just for leaving the bathroom a mess.

I showered and read a little from Betsy's genealogy book, a section on one of the Gardner ancestors participating in the Civil War, part of Joshua Chamberlain's fighting volunteers. Driving over to Betsy's an hour later for dinner, I passed the Asticou Inn, an old hotel the Gardners had originally founded. I stopped and picked up a rate card and studied the numbers while the bellhop eyed me from his post near the pay-phone cabinet. It wouldn't be an inexpensive folly, I thought, if things with Cornelia didn't work out.

"I'm on the phone with Joel!" Aunt Betsy shouted when I pulled up. Somehow she'd stretched the cord outside from the dining room, so that she could converse from the swing. The light framed Betsy as though from Hollywood's best kliegs: for one thing, she was dressed up, wearing a blue skirt and a heather-yellow sweater. Her lips were a dark prune color, matching the scarf she wore in lieu of her hat. For another, she was smiling ear to ear. "And take off that tie, you're not eating," she snarled as I walked inside, and she went back to her conversation, laughing like a girl.

I waited in the living room under a Japanese painting of farmers, bordered in white birch. I wondered what Joel was saying that was so funny. Five minutes later, I was ordered upstairs, where I spent half an hour folding khaki trousers and faded cotton underwear.

On Sunday, she explained, Joel would escort her to Little Cranberry, where she'd decided to repair for the rest of the season. I lugged a battered trunk down the stairs and went back for several hampers and two sacks of linens. So Joel chauffeurs while I play butler, I thought. It wasn't much of a scenario for competition. I'd called Joel that afternoon, in fact, reaching him at the restaurant.

"Joel, hi, it's Victor. Victor Aaron."

"Victor, hey. How are things?"

"Good, you?"

"You know. So how's Mother?"

"Much the same. Smoking with her snorkel in."

"So, to what do I owe the pleasure?"

"Actually, I'm calling for a favor."

I explained about Cornelia, about her interests in cooking, the discussions she'd had with Russell, about looking to get her feet wet in the business.

"She's watched too much Food Network."

"Well, I think it's a genuine case," I said. "She's passionate. She's just a nice kid who loves to cook."

"Well, honestly, the trouble is, it's a cutthroat business. Even when we're booming, times are tough. Not that passion doesn't count, of course."

"Of course. I was thinking, maybe, if you needed some help."

"What's her résumé like?"

"In a restaurant setting?"

Joel turned away from the phone and shouted at someone in the background. A second later: "All right, hello? Tell you what, Victor, send her by and we'll chat, maybe I can talk her out of it. It's a pretty ugly business, for women, especially."

"Even if you just meet her, I think you'll be impressed."

"Have her come by lunch tomorrow. We'll see if she can pass a fiddlehead test."

"Joel, I appreciate it."

He laughed after a moment. "The question is, Does my mother know you've got a new girlfriend?"

With Betsy's last bag stowed, I slammed down the garage door. The sun was setting behind Cape Near, shooting light through a few rooms where the curtains weren't drawn. One of which, I knew from stories, was where Sara had written *The Hook-Up*, the yellow room with the slanted roof and the view of the bay.

I hadn't known exactly which room until Sara showed me, the last time we visited Betsy's together for Christmas, the December before the accident, when Sara had returned from California. A snowstorm enclosed the island. After the turkey, Betsy said she needed to put her feet up, and passed out on the couch. Sara took my hand and led me upstairs. The wind off the ocean beat against the house. It was the first time we'd made love in months, it was intimate and playful and slow, until we lay holding each other under an old orange quilt.

"Where did you go?" I remembered saying.

Betsy appeared on the porch. Or she could have been standing there a full minute, staring at me, shading her eyes. We walked through to the terrace.

"So when does the girl arrive?"

"Tonight."

"It's a bad idea. Are you sure?"

"What's the problem?"

"I'm just asking, have you thought about it, Victor?"

"Thought about what?"

"About *her*. You haven't had a woman in your house in ages. Trust me, I'd know."

"Well, don't tell me you're jealous."

"You listen to me, Dr. Aaron," she said, laying her cane across her knees. The flagstones radiated heat. "You've never had children, and this one's practically a teenager. These days they're feral. You've seen the television."

"She's an adult. She just graduated from college."

"She's a woman and you're a man." Betsy slapped her cane with both hands. "Do I have to spell it out for you? Pass me the goddamn cigarettes."

"She's my goddaughter."

"I don't care if she's Shirley Temple. You'll want to observe yourself, Victor."

"Well, you don't know her," I snapped. The wind came into me suddenly. "Now I'm a dirty old man? What have I done every weekend except attend to your needs?"

"Then tell me, why should I get to know her?"

"Maybe you are jealous," I said. I stood up and walked a little way down the lawn.

"Horse crap," Betsy shouted. "You're a fool. You watch she doesn't run you and that house in a week. I'll be a hundred if she doesn't."

The sunset was a B-movie star—cheap, pink, and gold. Over the hedge, Betsy's closest neighbors were visible through their living room windows, parents and three children facing a television. I heard the sounds of a voluble spokesman trying to sell them a car.

I had to hand it to Betsy, she could always get my mood back on track. So what if Cornelia was opinionated, if she was still forming her opinions? I'd spent too much time recently growing old.

"For the good, though, Victor, at least now I'll die knowing you'll have some companionship when I'm gone."

"You're not dying."

"We're all dying, you can take that to the bank. Now, I'm famished. See how I dressed up? And not one compliment. I bought steamers. Least you could've done was wear a tie."

"You're gorgeous," I said.

But Betsy was already clomping inside.

I must have stayed too long at dinner because the airport parking lot was empty when I arrived. The employees inside were going home. My interrogator, the federal marshal who'd confiscated my gift for Russell, was putting on her coat, still wearing her sunglasses.

Cornelia sat on the curb, her elbows between her knees, next to a tall purple backpack. She wore the same clothes as in New York: flip-flops, a billowing skirt, a silk tank top, and lots of necklaces and brace-lets and glitter. When I parked, she didn't look up from her book. On the cover were four women in tight jeans and high heels, giggling over cocktails.

"Is that what they call chick lit?" I said.

Cornelia jumped up and launched herself into my arms. My back ached when we embraced. A woman, I thought, not a girl.

"I'm sorry I'm late," I said.

"Hey, it's hard out there for a cook. You should have seen me explain why I needed to pack so many knives. You've got glitter on your face," Cornelia said, laughing, and brushed my cheeks with her fingers.

We joined a stream of cars and RVs heading over to the island through the dark. Cornelia lowered her window. Steam was rolling off big kettles set up outside the fish shacks serving dinner. The tide was out and the mud flats were exposed, so the air smelled of seaweed, muck, and salt water. Satisfied, Cornelia fell back in her seat, propped up her bare feet on the dashboard and retied a silver ribbon, threaded with cowry shells, that kept her dreadlocks off her neck.

I noticed she hadn't buckled her seat belt. She looked at me at the same moment and twisted around to pull it across her chest.

"Uncle Victor, I can't tell you, thank you so much."

"So I called my friend Joel," I said. "He says he'd be happy to talk to you tomorrow. If you can pass a fiddlehead test, maybe there's a job in the kitchen."

"Get the fuck out."

"I'm driving."

"But I am, like, a fiddlehead guru."

"I told him you were, like, a fiddlehead guru."

"Oh my God!" she squealed.

Right before my road, we passed a white tent set up in a church parking lot. In the summer months, the island supported dozens of stands selling berries, corn, and firewood, sometimes manure. (The manure stands always had signs saying "You Buy It, You Haul It.") The guy manning the tent wore an orange hunting cap and a New England Patriots jacket and was reading a newspaper, a night owl burning a halogen lamp off his truck battery to snare the day's last tourists. His table was cluttered with bones. The sign hanging off his tent said "ANTLERS, FRESH, 50 CLAMS."

I was reminded of the living room in Regina's house where a similar rack mounted over the fireplace wore a Michigan cap.

Cornelia stuck her hand out the window and gave him the finger.

I laughed. "Are you still wearing your PETA button?"

"Dude, whatever. But who wants to buy antlers anyway? It's, like, so fucking arrogant. Whoever is paying for that doesn't have the balls to hunt, they just get to hand over fifty bucks."

I drove slowly down the road past my neighbors: couples outside, gardening at twilight or grilling dinner, waving as we rolled past. At a neighborhood meeting the previous winter, we'd decided on a maximum speed limit of ten miles per hour. The breeze smelled of wood and charcoal smoke.

"Do you remember," I said, chuckling, "when you tried to set our neighbor's dog free?"

"It was chained to a tree!"

Cornelia pulled herself up and sat on her knees, facing me with an elbow propped on the headrest. She was smiling. "Okay, this from someone who actually tortures animals for a living?"

"Hold on. That's not true."

"I mean, maybe I could respect a hunter. But you breed mice just to kill them," she said, staring screws through my head. "You want to talk about man's arrogance?"

In high school, Cornelia had been a suffragist for lab rats. One of thousands, she participated in a letter-writing campaign that targeted prominent research scientists, including me. It ended up making headlines after one wacko, admittedly operating on his own, sent a letter bomb to a colleague of mine at Oregon State. Fortunately, the bomb didn't explode, but Cornelia and I didn't speak much that year.

"Look, I'm sorry," she said a moment later. "You're being so generous, I'm totally grateful. But you know me, if you're asking me to forsake my convictions—"

"Cornelia, let's get this straight." I paused to reinforce my authority. I couldn't let this go on all summer. "I don't torture animals. I never have. As an institution, in fact, we take extraordinary measures not to harm them."

"Like not setting them free?"

"We didn't trap them on the savannah, Cornelia. These are mice that were bred for this purpose. Simply by living, they save lives."

"Save human lives, you mean, which are more important than mice lives. A value we're entitled to impose?"

"Listen, Cornelia," I said, my voice rising, "this issue is a lot more complicated than we have time for right now."

"Yeah, complicated, deeper than I'd understand, okay, fine," she said, and that was that. She stared out the window. I sighed and parked in the driveway.

Back when Sara was having a bad day, and I'd ask how she was, she'd always say, "Fine. I'm fine. How are things? Oh, things are nice, they're fine, oh, thank you for asking."

Surely the Comfort Inn would be cheaper than the Asticou, I thought.

"Look, Cornelia, for the sake of the summer, why don't we just agree there are certain issues where we don't see eye-to-eye—"

"Okay, just stop. I'm totally low blood sugar, I haven't eaten since breakfast. I just need to snack on something, I promise, and I'll stop being a bitch."

Then I remembered my plan to grill steaks to celebrate her arrival. I'd neglected to remember Cornelia was a vegan. I didn't even have salad supplies.

There had to be a vegetarian restaurant open somewhere. This was Mount Desert Island, after all. The food would probably turn out to be made from hemp.

To get us back on easier ground, backing out of the driveway, I asked if I could touch her dreadlocks. Apparently this was a hilarious question.

To prepare for Cornelia's visit, I'd taken in Sara's old BMW for a checkup. It came out with new oil and a clean bill of health. The car hadn't been used in several years, though I drove it once a month around the neighborhood and it still ran fine, despite the accident. At the time, I'd felt compelled to have it repaired.

Before bed, I handed Cornelia the keys and gave her a Chamber of Commerce map of the island, showing her how to find Blue Sea. As I was leaving, I heard, "Victor, come back" in a little-girl voice. She pulled me down in a hug. Her sleep clothes consisted of black underwear, a flimsy wife-beater, and no bra. I avoided looking too closely. For the right boys her age she was probably intensely desired. The right boys being ones she could control, I thought, who'd relish being charged around.

There seemed to be a lot I hadn't considered to my big idea: soy milk, boyfriends. Would I be repelling hippie Romeos through August?

Normally I wore only underwear to bed, but that night I added an old T-shirt, a freebie from *The Hook-Up*'s opening night.

It always amazed me how sharp some memories remained, whittled to their most significant points. The literature was filled with Alzheimer's patients progressively losing grip on their address, their phone number, the names of their children, but they still could recall a girl from elementary school, as though they'd known her better than anyone.

In seventh grade, Claire Shore trapped me on the playground after

I scored the highest math grade too many times in a row. Flanked
by cohorts, she teased, "Victor, do you think you're perfect? Do your
parents call you Mr. Perfect?" Claire Shore with the pale gray eyes, later
to be the first in our class fully at ease with sex, the bored queen of us
all, the hit maker who shot "Mr. Perfect" up the charts and made
the other children believe I desired so badly to be ostracized that I'd
written the tune myself, as though I didn't have enough trouble as
Vicky, or Vicky Dicky, or plain Dick. So I flunked the next three tests
deliberately, semi-passively: I added extra numbers to the correct answers, or left fields blank. Not that it helped my social status. "Hey,
Perfect, what's happening?" survived until we transferred to high
school. But too many forties and fifties, instead of my normal ninety-
eights, caused my teacher to request a parent meeting, a fallout I hadn't
anticipated.

Sitting next to my mother after school, I told the truth, just not
all of it. Yes, I'd failed, I said, yes deliberately. But I refused to explain
why. They'll never get it out of me, I thought, and I stared out the
window to where a team of boys were running around in gray sweats.
First my mother thought it was a practical joke being played upon her
perfect little man, someone's idea of a prank. She drew her finger
across the teacher's grade book: indeed, her son had not been forging
his report cards, he did otherwise have perfect grades, so from the
pride of his father's and mother's hearts to this, without reason? No,
the disappointment would be too great. It was impossible her son
could conceive of such a thing, much less see it through. Where's the
motive? she wanted to know, playing homicide cop.

Like I don't have the balls to pull it off, I remembered thinking.

My teacher informed my mother that I was going through a stage.
There were hormones to consider. Boys will be boys. Then she half
stood from behind her desk to let us know there were other stu-

dents who didn't have the luxury of failing on purpose. My mother left school clutching her purse below her stomach. Three F's meant the path she had conscientiously, sacrificially prepared for her only child now was condemned.

Woman as mourner, I thought. Women who grieve as men don't know how, who are the ones left behind, like we'd learned about in our Civil War lessons. I followed with my head up, trying to feel proud, like the Union generals, but underneath my sweater I was sick. I was on the verge of willing it out of me, the idea was almost tingling, picturing myself upchucking on the school lawn. *Then she'll see what she's done.*

When my mother refused to speak to me, the uncertainty was torment. A few days later, after a loud fight with my father downstairs, my mother walked into my bedroom crying, dressed in high heels to go out, smelling of some overwhelming perfume, like burst-open hydrangeas. I was wretched. The last person I could imagine hurting was my mother, but I knew that I had, and also that I'd enjoyed this new power. The perfume crept up through my sinuses as a pressure inside my head. Did I know, my mother asked, kneeling by my bedside, that she'd once dreamed of becoming a doctor? When she was a girl, she told me, she'd wanted to be like the men her father worked with, her father who had also been a pharmacist, as my father was. But in those days, she said, women didn't become doctors. She'd learned this when she was about my age: that she could become a teacher or a nurse or a housewife, but never could she become one of the doctors who visited in their shiny black cars, the big men with the soft-hard voices. She said, "Did you fail those tests because you want to be a pharmacist? Nothing would hurt me worse, you becoming like your father." Her eyes were dry. Both our heads were inside the perfume. I stared at her earrings, blue drops on gold wires. I'd always thought it was exactly what she wanted, me to become a pharmacist like my dad, but now the man was faceless in the dark, dreamless, a nobody. At school the next week, I scored a ninety-nine on a quiz and received stars again by my name: a straight line of red and gold adhesive stars punctured by a three-star gap.

While Cornelia slept, I unlocked Sara's office and opened her filing cabinet. Read as many cards as I could stand, ran upstairs, and stuck the rest in the drawer of my bedside table.

If Victor had a memory—false, in any case—of what we once were like and wanted to preserve it, fine, was my thinking. Let him stand in place.

I called information and asked for Dr. Sylvia Carrellas, Bar Harbor. I got her answering machine. I left a message. I swallowed two Ambien and chased them with a scotch, which knocked me out cold before I'd gotten more than a few pages deeper into the Admiral's genealogy, into the history of one George "Starky" Gardner, Betsy's great-great-grandfather, the family black sheep by way of cowardice, but forgiven because he'd paid for it. Apparently Starky had tried to flee Gettysburg, the battle of Little Round Top, but was shot on his way off the battlefield.

Whether it was enemy or friendly fire that killed him wasn't noted. Either it was unknown or it didn't matter.

Saturday night, the sky was a scratched plum, purple over gold flesh. I got home around eight and found the outdoor lights on, making the woods in relief seem darker. I didn't remember leaving the lights on. Getting out of the car, I smelled smoke.

Behind the garage, there by the grill, was a faerie of the woods dancing, flicking a pair of tongs like castanets. Her siren song was playing from one of my three-thousand-dollar Reynaud speakers, terrifyingly jimmied halfway out an open window.

"Aren't the Grateful Dead dead already?" I said.

"I think Andy Rooney wants his joke back," Cornelia retorted, looking up, and then went back to nodding her head, her dreadlocks in a beehive bobbing up and down. She was wearing the same camisole as the day before, otherwise barefoot in jeans that were falling off her hips, with a kitchen towel tucked into the waistband. She lifted the top off the grill to show me two thick steaks, my uneaten tenderloins from the fridge, lying side by side.

"You're making me two?"

"Actually, one is for me."

"You have got to be kidding."

"In about seven minutes, give or take," she said, "I'll be off the wagon."

I stood there with my hands on my hips while Cornelia disappeared inside the house. She came skipping back with a bottle of champagne I'd kept for years in the vegetable crisper. Foam spilled over her arm after the pop. "See, apparently there's no point," she said excitedly, "working in a kitchen that serves everything if you can't taste half the menu. At least that's what Chef says—"

"You mean Joel?"

"And since it's local, you know, the ducks are from his friend's farm, the pigs are from a woman somewhere nearby, then at least it's the best possible scenario, you know, morally I just need to accept that the majority of people eat this way, and if I'm truly to understand as a cook all the varieties of flavors, I mean, Victor, I got the job!"

Cornelia's hug spilled my wine. I probably had bruises from all the hugs I'd received in the last two days. I wondered what would happen if Betsy and her cane met my new houseguest. One of them could end up with a broken arm.

"And it's such a beautiful restaurant. Chef is like *amazing*, they cooked this big staff lunch, and I swear he's doing exactly what I want to do someday, just very Alice Waters, totally in sync seasonally. I mean, you should have seen his baby greens, I'm not joking, I could have died."

"With baby greens."

"Actually? They're called mâche."

Stars appeared in a few small clusters, but it was too early to pick out constellations. Cornelia lit citronella torches and spiked them in the grass. Eating dinner at the picnic table while she jabbered on about "Chef's" charms as a teacher and sage, I couldn't get a word in edgewise. I sank into myself, staring up at the heavens and nodding at appropriate moments, but I was gone in the star patch, to remote bodies whipped through the universe. To Regina, La Loulou.

My stomach became a bowl of microbes. A soup of bitter baby greens.

What I could have taught Cornelia was that people are plastic mysteries. Unknowable and in flux, our cells constantly dying and being replaced. Samsara on the molecular plane. What Newton knew: "I can calculate the motion of heavenly bodies, but not the madness of people."

We the people, we the results of handed-down mistakes and chance, we the equationless, bristling organisms, ignorant of time aside from when's lunch.

Not palimpsests, but coal.

Most likely, I thought, Regina read my belated congratulations about her book as the final straw, a kiss-off "let's be friends, shall we?" And wasn't that what I'd wanted? Wasn't it what I wanted still?

Cornelia wouldn't stop moving: tapping her fingers, pulling on her bottom lip. She tucked her bare feet underneath her ass on the bench and hunched forward, craning over her elbows, her camisole falling off her left shoulder as she operated the wine bottle like a derrick and told me about organic farming.

"Will you stop fidgeting, please?"

"Whatever. You want more wine?"

How much better never to want again!

"Hello? More champagne?"

"Look, I think I'm going to call it a night," I said.

"What? But this is my celebration dinner!" She'd just pulled the champagne bottle out of the ice bucket. I laughed and gave her a kiss on the forehead and said good night.

From my window in the dark, I watched Cornelia smoke and finish off the champagne, drinking straight from the bottle. I reread Sara's cards about *The Hook-Up* and replaced them in the drawer.

Cornelia came inside. I listened to her clean. When she went to her bedroom to watch television, I crept outside and lay down in the grass. I stared at the blue light of Cornelia's TV through her window. Between cricket songs, I could hear dialogue and gunshots. I stared at the fragile constellations, thousands of stars ghost white, white like crystals' cores. Memories rose on two flanks and erected their battle flags, fled back to their supply column, and re-entrenched. I found a rock in my right hand and tried squeezing it hard enough to make it crack.

Picture entering the brain with the smallest of tweezers, picking out the correct dendrites and giving them a twist.

I need you. I can't get you out of my mind.

Regina must have been on the computer because she responded right away.

WTF? Whatever. Tomorrow, make it three.

The next day, I worked at home. When I left, Cornelia was out tanning in the backyard, reading fashion magazines and wearing a yellow bikini. She'd shown up for breakfast refusing to speak to me, but when I made pancakes she wolfed them down.

"How do you not have wireless around here?" she asked.

I sped to Otter Creek through the forest, up the gravel hill. I ignored every inclination to hold back. I called out from the foyer. A sweet smell of marijuana hung in the air. I stood in the bedroom door, seeing Regina in bed in sweats. No makeup, no costume, no music playing. "Did La Loulou retire?" She didn't answer, just stared at me. I stooped down to kiss her. She smiled slightly and lay back, avoiding my lips. I sat on the side of the mattress and arranged my shoes. The bed creaked as I lay down beside her, wondering if some password was required, some sign someone younger would have known.

"Are you okay? What happened?"

I touched her arm. Light streamed in through the windowpanes, framing her cheeks.

"Show's canceled," Regina said. She looked at me with her eyes wide open.

"Okay."

"So, you *need* me," she said, sitting up, her cheek against one shoulder. "Define this need."

"What is this?"

She notched her eyebrows and said it flatly. "What you see is what you get."

"I don't get it."

"Exactly. It's not what you get, it's not what you want." She lay down again and stared at the ceiling.

"Why does it feel every time you come here that it may as well be our first time together?"

"Regina, I had to see you. I care about you."

"Right now you do. At this moment. At your convenience."

She covered her face with a pillow. We lay there a couple minutes, the seconds piling up one on top of another. I felt my head fill with pressure. I couldn't stand it. Regina pulled herself up to a sitting position and whipped a blanket over her legs.

A moment later my focus broke, like a cable splitting. "What do you want from me?" I put on my shoes. "What do you want me to do?" But the shouting just made her more placid, watching me unravel. I stared at the poster of the Japanese singer and scraped it off the wall, actually digging up wallpaper under a fingernail.

A voice came through the door, "Hey, are you okay in there?"

I went out past the green-haired roommate, lost for a moment. From the doorway, before rushing in, the roommate stared back at me, watching me out.

See Regina crying in bed.

See Victor in his car, driving down the gravel.

See Victor parking in a public campground, crying at the steering wheel.

See the perfect human hiking. See the perfect human hiking Pemetic Mountain at a steady pace. He never tires. He is comfortable in the woods, a man with long legs good for hiking, an experienced boy scout.

He is always prepared. He doesn't fail. He doesn't ask for much.

He has a pleasant appearance. You would trust him.

See the perfect human reach the top of the mountain. He doesn't pause for the view. He proceeds back down the trail, carefully following the markers back to his car.

The perfect human never considers why he climbed the mountain.

He is neither thirsty nor hungry. The perfect human wants for nothing.

He does not want at all.

Wednesday afternoon at the lab. Outside, the sky looked scraped clean but for clouds in oatmeal clumps. Inside we had nothing but gray. An ecosystem for artificial, modified life, the lives of Lucy's mice with genetic code the earth had never before seen.

We'd been checking frequently online for our grant's priority score, the number that would determine its status. Normally we would've gotten the skinny through back channels by that point, but no one had heard anything. Then that afternoon it appeared: a 110, a golden ticket on the grading scale. We'd receive our $2.5 million. We could breathe again. Lucy went out and bought champagne. Word got around and colleagues stopped by with congratulations. Toad, Dr. Low, Soborg's president, called at the end of the day. "Not easy when purse strings are tight. A job well done, all of you. Now I glanced over the application," he said, and paused for air. "Wasn't bad. What I'll do is stop by this week, I thought perhaps I spotted a few things you may want to consider."

"You just let me know," I said, and hung up. I pictured him in his office, reading Viagra offers in his junk mail. Toad was famous around campus for still putting in a regular workweek at age ninety, but he also had horrendous eyesight. He worked at a special computer monitor that made each word the size of a candy bar.

The team celebrated that night at a fancy Italian restaurant in Bar Harbor, my treat. Lucy kept glancing at me from her end of the table, concerned about something, but I didn't find out what. I picked up the check and went home.

Early Thursday morning, I woke to the sound of breaking glass. At first I thought it was a dream. I looked around in the dark. Then I ran to Cornelia's room. She was dead asleep, with a fan blowing loudly beside the bed. The sun was just rising. I grabbed a tennis racket from a closet and crept downstairs. The house seemed empty. No sounds. All the windows looked intact.

The Audi's windshield was resting in two solid pieces on the front seats, held together by some internal glue. Sticking out was a rack of antlers, like conjoined hands of bone. I stood staring at them for half a minute, then wrenched them out and squeezed them into the trunk. I found work gloves and extracted the windshield fragments, stowing them under a tarp in the garage, and brought out the vacuum cleaner.

Half an hour later, I left early, dropped the car off at a garage in Bar Harbor, and walked up to Soborg. The town was just coming to life. Dogs were being walked, squatting to pee.

Kneel, mute animal, I thought, walking up the hill to campus. I felt especially earthbound all the way to my desk.

Two hours later, I shouted for Lucy and pointed out some mistakes I'd found in a paper we were to publish soon in *Nature*. If she'd been the last person on the edit, I said, why were these errors still slipping through? There was such a thing as lab blindness, I reminded her, where the vision goes dark to what it doesn't want to see. How many times did we need to go through this?

Lucy didn't disguise the hurt on her face, but said nothing, took my highlighted pages down from the windows, and walked out, and what I saw in her glance I ignored. I knew her technicians had been going through hell recently with their design experiments, and I could see she was hoarding their anxiety, trying to preserve a calm atmosphere and project confidence.

Lucy wasn't the best writer on the team, maybe I'd been too harsh.

That afternoon, I went back down into town, picked up my car with its new windshield, drove to Seal Harbor, swam out to Rockefeller Island, came back, then did it again, carving through the water. I dived at the end to see how long I could hold my breath. Not long.

After my second slog, lying on my back, drip-drying on the swimming dock, it occurred to me: Sara wanted me to find those cards.

She'd left them behind as clues.

And yes, I had been hurt, I could admit, when success struck in New York. To be left behind in the apartment, home alone without her in my bed or in my life, right when I was striving to be a better partner. It was no fun, being abandoned at parties where I knew nobody, except I knew who everybody was, because everybody there except me was well known. Sara would say, "Don't mope, go introduce yourself, look that's so-and-so from such-and-such." Of course it wounded me when she no longer sought my counsel, when I was edited out of her creative life. When Mark, and not me, was the one who read her first drafts. When someone else saw her photograph in a magazine before I did, since I hadn't been told. To be unsure what good I was, and in what capacity as a husband?

And why, when the one job I'd thought I'd done best, better than anyone, was taken away from me, why wasn't I informed?

Secrecy before discovery. Ambition rather than collaboration.

The summer when Jimmy Carter said in *Playboy* how he'd committed "adultery in my heart," Sara was deeply disappointed. It was August '76. We'd rented a cabin for a week in Connecticut on a lake,

me and Sara, two mountains of books, a screened-in porch, an antique black-and-white TV, and two ceiling fans that spun only slightly.
We were young, we were dopey with love, we even brought the Kama
Sutra, but we never cracked it. The heat was too intense, the humidity
oppressive. The only solution was to drink rosé with ice cubes (a
French friend of Sara's said that's how it was done) and swim as much
as possible. Most nights, I'd cook dinner, while Sara narrated the evening news, pronouncing her own judgments on world affairs. For a
liberal from the avant-garde, Sara often surprised people with some of
her more inflexible positions. She took public events personally, especially when loyalty was involved. She was reading in a wicker chair the
night that Cronkite gave his report, sounding more stern than usual:
adultery in his heart many times. I was in the kitchen, doing something
in a wok. Politics were never my thing, but Sara was a junkie. She was
among the fallen faithful. The indignation she'd felt after Ford's pardon for Nixon burned her wick until Clinton took office, and then she
was outraged all over again. She longed for honor, for Eagle Scouts.
She'd been raised on her mother's and Betsy's stories of the Roosevelts
coming to dinner in Northeast Harbor and taking the girls out sailing. Bobby Kennedy had been a big hero of Sara's. She always kept a
photograph of him sitting at his desk, in a pewter frame next to her
hairbrush, his face half in shadow, seemingly injured. Around the time
we got married, as an update to *Goodnight, Icarus*, she wrote a political
one-act envisioning Bobby as the boy with wings, undone by the sun
and his father's second-rate engineering, anything that excluded his
own culpability.

"I've never done that," Sara said that night at the lake, referring
to Carter's secret infidelities. I remembered looking up from the stove,
not sure I'd heard her correctly.

"What?" I said.

"Looked at someone else that way. I haven't," she insisted, and put her book down on her knee. "Have you?"

I remembered there were sounds of the neighbor's children fighting: shrieking geese two cabins over sounding bloodthirsty. Sara was wearing one of my shirts, open three buttons from the top, and cut-off jean shorts. Her hair was in a single, long braid. It was probably her loveliest period, I thought, very easy and natural. Very easy to love.

Never was there anyone else for me.

"No," I said, "but men look. They're coded to reproduce. It's not a wolf whistle."

"I can't be married to you if you're like that."

I laughed. "Like what, the president? Normal?"

Sara glared at me and turned back to the television, to some soap commercial.

The children next door had been silent for a minute.

"I'm sorry," I said. "Come on."

"I won't have a normal relationship. That's not who I am."

"Of course not."

"I won't be dragged down to what other people do."

"That's not us, you know that."

I had my arms around her, but she wouldn't look at me. Both of us were sweating through our clothes. "Swear to God," she said, "if you're just saying that." We went straight to bed.

More important than children, more important than our careers to Sara was the singularity of our relationship, never compromised. Always growing, never-ending. Its own species, one that didn't need millennia to evolve.

An unreasonable, unrealistic aspiration that I learned to share.

At home, I composed an e-mail to Regina, apologizing for our last afternoon together, for all the previous afternoons. *Jesus, don't apologize. You're always apologizing.* I deleted the text. "Kneeling," I wrote in the subject box, then left the message area empty and clicked SEND.

An e-mail from the Toad appeared in my in-box, to all Soborg employees, congratulating my group on our grant. "Research thrives on challenge and risk. Victor Aaron, Lucy Sejung Park, and their team continue to be a model for how Soborg can participate in, even lead, the global fight against a vicious disease."

But what difference did it make that *we* were leading? Lucy might have said. If not us, some other lab on a different campus could develop the same ligands, could offset amyloid-related degeneration, could reach our conclusions by the same paths of reason and late-night insights, and probably pretty quickly. I shut down the computer. I locked up. I turned on the radio, took two sleeping pills with a scotch, and closed my eyes.

None of us was special, I fell asleep thinking. Everyone performed as programmed, leering and wanting as intended by nature. Progress was time's measure, not effort's. The only surprise was when the unknown got bigger, just when we thought we'd reduced it some.

Friday night, I got home from work around ten-thirty. Because Betsy was out on Little Cranberry, we spoke on the phone in lieu of our regular date. She and Joel had spent the day fishing with a friend of his, a commercial fisherman whose son had recently been arrested for drunk driving. Betsy had promised to get her lawyers on the case.

"It's going to cost you. You don't know the guy."

"Who asked you? Mike Wallace, you know, did a brilliant piece last week on methamphetamine, did you catch it? Trouble, Victor, and not just for the addict. We're not talking cherry soda. If that girl's mixed up in this, she'll burn your house down."

"Is that right?"

"Why don't you call me more often?"

"Darling—"

"I had a dream last night," she said. "You were working on my roof, the roof caved in, and you broke your legs."

"Charming. Did I make it out okay?"

"Don't make me regret you, Victor," Betsy said, and clicked off.

The house was empty. Cornelia was done with her training at Blue Sea and had begun working the dinner service six nights a week, fixing salads. In my home office, there was a new message from Regina, though not addressed to me. I'd been included in a group e-mail sent to all Soborg employees, an invitation to a poetry reading that she was giving in two weeks for her new book.

The title of the book, I read, was *Fair Merman*.

I went out for a night swim. The dark was ravenous, swallowing up the road. At that hour, Long Pond was black and silver and grooved with ripples. No one was around, so I swam naked, a habit I'd picked up that summer years ago in Connecticut, when Jimmy Carter upset Sara and the nation with his betrayal.

No one ever told you that you could measure progress in a marriage by language. Say the two of you are in bed late one night. She's engrossed in a biography and you're reading a detective novel. She belches and you say as a joke, "You begin to interest me, vaguely." Later, you employ it randomly and it becomes something fine and cute, part of a marriage's filigree. *You begin to interest me, vaguely*. Then one day you drop it. For no good reason, it's passé. Thirty years go by, other phrases come and go, but one night, a late-summer evening in Maine with the bedroom window open, with the air full of honeysuckle and pine needles, you're both watching an old movie in bed, *The Big Sleep*, when Humphrey Bogart walks into a bookstore and a girl says to him that exact same phrase, the pet phrase you used to say to your wife, and the bookstore girl says it exactly the same way.

You begin to interest me, vaguely.

And you stare at the side of your wife's face, the same you've known, though now framed by short hair, touched attractively by crow's-feet. And she says without turning, "You didn't realize that's where it's from?" And you think, all those years, it was just a reference in her mind, a synapse, a junction between two points, whereas for you it was something the two of you had made up from scratch, not just a step, but a path you'd forged together.

I dried off and drove down to the beach in my towel. The parking lot was empty, dark except for the one-tone glare from a streetlight. In the bay, dozens of masts gleamed like pins stuck in the water. There was a couple on the beach, over the dune, I could see them screwing, the man on top until he paused, turned the woman's body around, and she backed into his thrust. Or maybe it was another man, Sara's gay lovers grown up. It was hard to tell by the shapes involved. Either way, under the towel, I wasn't hard.

I thought, watching, in a marriage you're like two ships, two tankers crossing trade lanes in the dark, never knowing what cargo the other carries.

I watched the couple until they finished, donned their clothes, and walked out of sight. One moment I knew they were gay or straight, and the next I couldn't remember. I didn't trust my memory. I couldn't turn the ignition or tune the radio. After a few more minutes, I called information from a cell phone I kept in the glove compartment for emergencies. Information gave me the number for Dr. Carrellas. I got voice mail again.

Lucy caught me in the kitchenette, crouching in front of a vending machine. I was trying to decide between chips and yogurt for lunch.

"Hey, I'm taking the rest of the day off."

"It's Saturday, Lucy. Good idea."

"I've forwarded my calls to my cell phone. I just need a couple of hours."

"Lucy, what's going on?"

She sighed through her nose, like a bull. "Promise me, you can't tell anyone."

"Is something wrong?"

"I'm serious, if you tell anyone," she said, digging into her pocket, "so help me God, Victor."

The flyer said that evening's performance would take place at an art gallery in Bar Harbor. Lucy shoved me when I laughed. As far back as New York, where she'd played violin with a highly competent quartet of other amateurs from NYU, Lucy always got a bad case of upset stomach on performance days.

I called Cornelia from my office.

"What are you doing?"

"Sunbathing. As though you're not completely jealous."

"What do you know about Shostakovich?"

"Sounds like a supermodel," she said.

"You've got the night off, right?"

At seven on the dot, Cornelia posed in the doorway. I was shocked to see her dressed up, wearing a strapless ruby red dress that stopped at the knee. Gold dangling earrings matched the color of her dreadlocks, worn long down over her shoulders. But what really threw me were the brown leather work boots that came up to her knees, as though she were prepared for an evening of mucking stalls.

"You're pretty for a farm lass," I said as she got in the car.

Even furry, she had very nice legs. Cornelia wrinkled her nose.

"Who says lass? It's not my fault you don't keep up with fashion." She flipped the visor down to inspect her hair. "I assume this is a concert?"

"Well, you look terrific," I said.

Cornelia widened her eyes and stared away from me. "Whatever, you're forgiven. So," she said, ducking her head and putting up her hair, with a hair band in her teeth, "I listened to some of Shostakovich. *Shostakovich.* So, I mean, it wasn't mind-blowing." She finished with her hair and fell back against the car door. "Can we go? I'm seriously starving."

We ate dinner at a Cuban restaurant. Near the bar was a three-piece band: a piano player, a drummer, and an overweight woman who sang in Spanish. During an interlude, the piano player said into the microphone, "My wife, ladies and gentlemen, she sings these sad songs because she is married to me. She says she would be selling me up the river tomorrow if she could."

Everyone laughed and Cornelia whispered, "I am feeling so *cultured* right now."

When the waitress took our orders, Cornelia insisted on tequila shots.

I asked Cornelia about work, and if she'd made any new friends. I focused on remembering their names, though mainly I noticed how terrible her posture was. I finally had to do something. I went around and straightened her shoulders, pulling her back against the chair.

"You're like Russell to a T," she said when I sat down. I noticed, though, she didn't slump again before we left.

The gallery was a short walk away under the streetlamps through downtown Bar Harbor, past knife and taffy shops and crowded outdoor restaurants, and a buckboard hammered from copper. I could tell we both were a little drunk. We passed a Native American museum, and I explained to Cornelia how, before the Europeans showed up, Bangor's Abnaki Indians would camp out on Mount Desert Island's shores during the summer months. How the common upper-crust use of "summer" as a verb probably had a longer history than we realized. Cornelia feigned interest, slung her arm through mine, and clomped forward in her boots. People stared at us, probably mistaking us for some May-December couple.

The art gallery was built like a chapel with a glass ceiling. Everyone was pale and overfed or pink and over-exercised, in bow ties or yellow shawls, boat shoes or lime-green flip-flops. Lucy was nowhere to be seen. The other musicians were mingling and shaking hands. I seated Cornelia in the back row and left for the men's room, nodding to a few colleagues on the way out. More than one glanced back at my date, who at that moment was applying lip gloss from a pink tube.

A minute later, at a urinal, reeling from the alcohol at dinner, I heard quiet sobs through an air vent just above my head, cries I recognized.

"Lucy?"

A moment later: "Victor?"

I waited in the hall for three minutes before she came out, patting her face with a paper towel. Lucy was wearing a red dress similar to Cornelia's, but with shoulder straps, and high heels rather than farm boots. Her cheeks were damp.

"Can I get you anything?"

"Just my pregame ritual. Now it's ruined, along with my mascara. Thank you. Enjoy the show," she said, and waved and started to walk away. Perhaps it was the tequila, but I was overcome with tenderness. I reached out and grabbed Lucy's arm and, when she let me, hugged her tightly. She resisted, but relaxed a little.

"This won't improve my makeup."

"Break a leg," I whispered.

"Hey, that's me, Miss Invulnerable."

Back in the gallery, Cornelia snapped around in her seat so I wouldn't see that she'd been watching for me to return. Her program was folded on her lap into an origami crane. A hush went through the crowd when the musicians sat down and tuned their instruments. A few latecomers arrived, going up the center aisle and squeezing themselves past people's legs, greeting their friends with whispers and small embraces.

I glanced up from my program just as Regina walked by, straight to the front where she took an aisle seat, sat down, and placed her program on her knees.

A Russian folk piece started. After a few minutes, Cornelia sighed loudly through her nose. I forced myself to look away, to look anywhere but at Regina, fearing that by some intuition she'd realize I was staring at her neck. Those shoulders. Those ears. Absolutely it was her. I'd known it when her ankles went past. I knew it from the cascade of her hair.

My Regina, or at least her ghost, but what was she doing there? Had she followed me, was it because of my e-mail? Had Regina heard about Cornelia somehow?

After fifteen minutes, Cornelia pretended her program had come alive as a paper bird, and flapped it around in circles. She leaned into

my lap and whispered, "It's like so *cultural* in here." I shushed her and
tried to concentrate on the music and ignore my stomach. By then,
Lucy's group had engaged with the score, they were leaning in and
sliding back and forth over dynamics. I had half a mind to call Cornelia a taxi, half a heart to save her seat and invite Regina to sit down.

The group concluded for a brief intermission. Cornelia and I both
quickly stood up. I followed her outside, daring a look back from the
entrance. Regina was talking animatedly with the cello player, a man
my age.

Then I remembered: Richard Cajal, senior scientist in the lab where
Regina worked, married with triplet teenaged sons. Cancer survivor,
very tame. Doubtful.

Cornelia had disappeared. I found her around the side of the
building, smoking under some trees, leaning against a bronze sculpture of a seal.

"So can we leave yet?"

"You know that will kill you," I said quietly, pointing to the cigarette. A few other people had come out to smoke, one man with a cala-
bash pipe.

"Victor, whatever," Cornelia said, supporting her elbow on her hip.
"Seriously, do they at least serve wine during intermission?"

I tried to remember what I'd told her about the concert, but my
mind was unavailable to external control; it had found a panic loop
and was cycling, picking up speed. "You really should give it a chance,"
I prattled. "There's an interesting backstory. Now *Time* magazine, actually they put Shostakovich on the cover smack-dab in 1942, which of
course—"

"Fine," she said. "I get it. So you're staying."

"What?" I paused. "What?"

"No, obviously." Cornelia turned in a circle on one toe. "You know, you don't have to wait with me out here."

"I want to wait with you," I said dully. She didn't respond or look at me. I stood there waiting until she finished, then followed her in, trailing by five feet.

Regina was nowhere to be seen. Cornelia seemed calmer, though. Perhaps nicotine was good for something. The musicians resumed. Someone, an older woman in a lemon-colored pantsuit, took the aisle seat near the front, where Regina had been sitting. She must have left at the intermission, I thought. Probably she had somewhere to go, someone to see. Performances of her own to enact with gratitude for an audience who met her halfway.

Looking centered and happy, Lucy was lost in the music, smiling at certain phrases, moving her upper body in time. During the seventh part there were several fast, aggressive sections, and the group attacked them in unison, taking the turns together, as if on the hunt.

Cornelia bucked in her seat, leaned over, whispered, "Victor, I need to go."

"What are you talking about?"

"Don't worry, I'll see you at home."

The music entered a gentle passage. Lucy closed her eyes. Cornelia placed her paper crane on the floor and squeezed past my knees. My heart sank. A moment later, quietly as possible, I went after her, seeing in the last row, on the aisle, Regina slightly smiling, noticing us leave, blankly registering us pass, her face otherwise a mask.

Cornelia was plodding down the sidewalk.

"Cornelia!"

She looked back. "You don't have to come with me."

"Really." I caught up and grabbed her elbow. "What do you call that little performance?"

"Don't yell at me, I didn't ask you to leave."

"How in hell did you plan on getting home?"

"Stop shouting at me!"

We stopped in place. Cornelia was enraged, huffing and rigid.

"They have taxis around here, don't they? I mean, they have *Shostakovich.*"

We drove home in silence. I was furious. My mind was divvied up between four horses pulling separate chariots, sprinting to the compass points. Halfway home, Cornelia fiddled with the radio.

"God, Maine has shit radio." She said a minute later, "Okay, I'm sorry."

"Sorry for what?"

She sighed. "For leaving?"

"No, you're not."

"Okay, whatever."

She stared out her window. I felt like booking her on the next flight to New York, Montpelier, wherever she liked. Ten minutes later, we reached the turnoff and Cornelia put her head on my shoulder, her dreadlocks uncoiling like yellow vines into my lap.

"You're still mad at me."

"Yes, Cornelia—"

"I'm a brat, I know. I'm sorry. Seriously. You were just trying to show me something new, and I ruined it, didn't I? I just don't think when I'm drinking—oh, I'm terrible, say it."

"You're terrible."

"See? I drank too much and you wanted to stay. But why did you leave?"

"I don't know."

"Well, that's your bad."

I sighed. "Fine."

"I totally could have gotten a taxi. But you were playing the good godfather, I know, oh you must hate me now."

I shrugged her off my shoulder, but not brusquely.

"I don't hate you," I said, and unrolled my window. "I'm sorry I yelled."

"You strongly dislike me."

"No, Cornelia, but—"

"You would like to be selling me up the river?"

I snorted. She'd caught me off guard. Cornelia patted my shoulder and put her cheek down again.

I returned to regular hours at the lab. I may as well have been on vacation. The big grant we'd received would fund, for the moment, research already under way, so my role was mainly administration and attending status meetings and clearing paperwork, fielding phone calls and avoiding department politics, receiving updates from Lucy, who kept tabs on everyone else. Mostly I looked after my exercise and the garden. I took off two full afternoons to dig boulders out of the ground, rocks that had been undisturbed since the last ice age.

Aunt Betsy and I spoke on the phone occasionally, mostly about a new BBC detective series they were broadcasting on public television. I'd take the phone out into the backyard, hear the birds, and listen while Betsy analyzed plots for inconsistencies. And when we hung up, when the chickadees stopped, when the crickets and tree frogs and dragonflies stopped, and when silence settled in on those evenings, I wished it wasn't so quiet.

Cornelia and I were ships in the night. She didn't have to be at Blue Sea until lunch, but she wouldn't return home until two in the morning, some nights later. Occasionally, if I'd stayed late at the lab and the timing was right, we'd have a beer together on the back deck. One evening she said she'd seen a deer in the yard and named him Bananas. I said I thought Bananas was a ridiculous name for a deer. A few nights later, I saw a deer skipping along the perimeter of Soborg's parking lot and wondered if it had been sent by Cornelia to check up on me.

Then life changed dramatically. Lucy surprised me with a gift, an iPod, her old one, because she'd upgraded to a newer model. I threw it in my briefcase and forgot about it, but curiosity struck when I was home alone one evening. I connected it to my computer, buying five albums to download into its little white stomach. The next morning, gardening with my headphones in, I was transformed. I'd owned portable music players before, but this was different. After lunch I drove to work with my headphones in place. For the entire afternoon, I browsed around the online store and spent seven hundred dollars, half of it on music I'd never heard before. I went for a walk downtown, letting the iPod randomly choose songs, and noticed I wasn't alone: we were a tribe, the iPod nation, recognized by small white buds we'd pierced through our ears.

Lucy threatened to get me a BlackBerry next.

Cornelia had already owned three iPods, she said, because she kept losing them. She caught me shoveling rocks one Saturday morning, trying to build a flower bed and singing along to George Harrison. She said she was proud of me for "dusting myself off." That afternoon, running errands, I noticed a window display of Hawaiian swim trunks at the sporting goods store, particularly a pair of sky-blue shorts covered in large white flowers. I wore them to Long Pond for a swim that evening. They went past my knees. As I was toweling off near the boathouse, a young couple appeared with a pair of Labrador retrievers, and the boy was wearing the same shorts. He caught my eye, smiling, and chucked his chin.

A big storm that night knocked out power on half of the island. The next morning, I found a note from Cornelia saying that she had the day off because the restaurant had closed due to the blackout.

Meet me at seven at Hunter's. It's my thank-you present. xxxooo, C.

Under the note, she'd left an island map with the trailhead for Hunter's Beach circled in blue ink. Next, I thought, she'll be taking sailing classes.

To reach Hunter's, you parked in a small pull-off above Seal Harbor and hiked down a remote trail through the woods. Who'd told Cornelia? The beach was a locals' secret, known for its pink rocks shaped like dinosaur eggs. As I drove there, my hands felt young, taking turns quickly, passing slower cars.

The first time Sara brought me to Hunter's, on a vacation one summer when we still lived in New York, she'd walked me down with her hands over my eyes to preserve the secret, to present it like a gift. The next time we visited, after the move, I reminded her of that, her blindfolding me with her hands, and she said, "I did? Are you sure?" "Absolutely," I said. "I almost broke my ankle, don't you remember?" She said, "Well, it sounds awfully romantic. Sounds more like how you would have wanted me to do it, know what I mean?"

Cornelia was standing over a steaming pile of seaweed. Wearing a long skirt and an enormous hooded sweatshirt that flapped in the wind, she resembled an apprentice monk. She stood with her back to me while she fussed with the fire. I sneaked up and pinched her sides, and she screamed.

"Jesus, what the fuck?"

"Cornelia, sorry, I'm sorry," I said, pulling her away from the fire. "It was a joke."

The corners of her mouth trembled.

"Don't you ever do that to me again."

"Hey, I'm sorry." I lowered my voice. "It was just a joke."

"Well, it wasn't funny."

"I'm sorry," I said, and squeezed her shoulder.

We had the beach to ourselves. A clambake gave off the smell of an ocean boiling. Cornelia cleared off the top sheaf of seaweed, and a great cloud flew up around her legs. Underneath were three lobsters, still blue, a scattering of clams, and four ears of corn.

"They need fifteen minutes."

"Cornelia," I said, chuckling, "how long have you lived here?"

She smiled finally, biting one of her dreadlocks between her teeth. "Dan and I did one over there," she said, pointing from inside her sleeve down the rocks. She said abruptly, "He's a friend from the restaurant. You haven't met him."

I wondered if it was Dan's sweatshirt she was wearing

A few minutes later, we toasted our beer bottles to the sunset, to my grant and her new career. Only three weeks in, Cornelia was full of stories about the names of obscure North Atlantic fish, her new French cooking techniques, about the South American line cooks who proposed marriage to her every night. I was reminded of Sara's initial set visit when *The Hook-Up* was being shot, when she returned and proudly described to me the set rituals and the crew guys' gross-out stories, the catering trunk's menus, and the obscure production terms.

Cornelia leaned over at one point and wiped her fingers on my khakis. Our hands were covered in lobster. She asked me about Joel and Betsy, and I explained the backstory, in greater detail than she probably was entitled to know, considering that Joel was her boss. But it felt good to talk.

"So how is he as a boss?"

"Well, you know," she said, "he's tough. He demands a lot. But he lets you know what he's thinking. I mean, you can tell he cares. He puts way more pressure on himself than anybody else, so you kind of want to live up to that. Like you, you know?"

"Me?"

"Or not. Whatever, what are you looking at?"

The rim of the horizon was black by the time we finished. We walked down the beach. A stream ran out of the forest and Cornelia leaped over to the other side, her skirt getting wet. She said something, but the wind caught it and blew it away. Like that scene in *La Dolce Vita*. We climbed down, back to our picnic site. Cornelia bagged the trash while I rebuilt the fire, hauling driftwood and dry brush down from the woods. Cornelia sat with her sweatshirt stretched over her knees. She looked like a small blue boulder. I put my jacket around her shoulders and poked the fire.

What did I want with that big, empty house? A tent, an iPod, a small food supply, a tide pool for a lab—Hunter's could be all I needed.

"Your father and I used to sit like this."

"Oh, yeah?"

"When we were scouts, with the other boys."

"That's so gay."

"We went to Alaska once, backpacking for two weeks."

Cornelia laughed and looked at me. "Russell? Backpacking?"

"Actually, he was quite the outdoorsman."

She shivered, shaking out her dreadlocks so they fell down around her neck.

"Hey, I didn't tell you," she said, "I took a psychology elective last year, we actually studied a lot of brain stuff. Did you ever hear about that guy, H.M.?"

"Of course," I said, "wonderful, what did you think?"

H.M. was a well-known case study in neuroscience, one frequently taught to undergraduates to whet their interest. As a boy, H.M. had been hit by someone on a bicycle. His head injury led to epilepsy, and he suffered from blackouts and seizures that grew so terrible, the knife was the only option. It was 1953 when a surgeon removed H.M.'s hippocampus and parts of his medial temporal lobe. As a result, re-markably, the seizures went away, and H.M. remained a smart young man, but he lost the ability to form new memories. After a few min-utes, any event would be forgotten.

No one had ever seen anything like him. A person for whom the present existed only in the present, to which we said, then did it exist at all? What value did it hold until we could measure it? Judge it, as-sign it feelings, assess its worth? Names, faces, tests, H.M. remem-bered nothing new.

The scientist who worked with H.M. visited him every month for thirty years, and each time she walked through the door she had to reintroduce herself.

"Like he's just stuck in the 'now,' right? It was pretty wild."

"I can recommend some good books if you're interested."

"Victor, I'm kind of freezing. Can we go home?"

Maybe you shouldn't have worn flip-flops, I thought.

"You don't want to stay?"

She looked at me sideways. "Uncle Victor, my lips are blue."

Sara and I used to swim at Hunter's before work. We'd wade out nude, two soapstone figurines, and when it was deep enough we'd push off and zoom out into the water. One time, Sara exited earlier than me, bundled up, and sat on the rocks to read the newspaper. Then a biology class appeared and I had to remain in the water while they collected samples. Sara almost choked laughing. Meanwhile I nearly caught hypothermia.

Back in the parking lot, I noticed the BMW wasn't there.

"Dan dropped me off," Cornelia said, her teeth chattering.

I turned on the stereo in the car. Cornelia dialed up her seat heater.

"Victor, I've been thinking, maybe you need some time off."

"Because?"

"When was the last time you took a vacation?"

I couldn't remember. "Not in some time," I said.

"And didn't you just win that grant? Why don't you take off a week?"

"What do I tell people?"

Cornelia scoffed. "Um, that you have a guest? You tell them it's for courtesy's sake. Plus it's true, Joel pushed me to part-time for a week, I'm in need of hosting. It's simple. We'll go hiking, you show me the island, the rest of the time you garden." She looked at me and looked back out the window. "Seriously, you are, like, way tense."

"Interesting," I said a moment later.

The house seemed darker that evening, as though the forest had gotten inside. I parked and we listened to the engine hum.

"I could always check my e-mail at night," I said.

"See? You already sound better."

There was a single message waiting on the answering machine inside: "Dr. Aaron, Victor, hi, this is Sylvia, Dr. Carrellas. I'm sorry I'm only now getting back to you, my husband and I just returned from vacation. I would be happy to see you if you'd like to call and set up—"

"So I don't sound well," I said, erasing the message. "I seem impaired." Cornelia didn't respond. "Tell you what," I said, "this is a terrific idea."

"Yeah!"

Cornelia made me give her a high five.

"How about we start tonight," I said. "I'll grab some wine from the basement and we'll watch your movie."

She tucked in her jaw. "What's my movie?"

"*Singin' in the Rain*."

"Oh, please," Cornelia said, laughing, kicking off her flip-flops. "You used to make me and Sara watch it, and we were both, like, uh, can we go to bed now?"

Cornelia ran up the stairs two at a time.

And she was right, I realized. I'd been the one who had arranged that night at the Criterion all those years ago. It had been my idea, my initiative.

But then, what was wrong with me? What senescent state had I entered? Of course I'd been the one who asked the manager to open the candy counter. Of course I remembered writing the check out to the Criterion, the manager joking I was welcome to rent it anytime.

Of course I remembered how both Sara and Cornelia had thought the whole idea was corny, a night at the movies with Gene Kelly, but they played along, humoring me, as though I wouldn't notice.

The phone rang at midnight but I didn't answer. I was awake, apraxic, unable to doze off or even move from my position, performing every mental exercise I could remember to fall asleep. No messages when I checked forty minutes later. I passed Cornelia's room. She was snoring loudly. We'd split a bottle of wine and watched *Die Hard 2*. It was the one with the catchphrase "Die Harder," which Sara used to whisper if we passed old men on the street.

It seemed that if the house were not a living thing, then someone had walked through touching the pottery, making everything quiver. Perhaps I was drunk. I closed up the music room and walked around shutting doors and double-checking window locks. I went into Sara's office and opened her filing cabinet, pulled out her laptop, and set it on her desk.

I left it alone and instead read through the final batch of index cards, the fourth set. Apparently she never got around to number five.

How disappointed Dr. Carrellas must have been.

I fed them, all of them, into the shredder next to Sara's desk.

Not a shred of reluctance to hold me back.

At two in the morning, I walked laps along the property line. The night was quiet and brittle, then down near the southeast corner it snapped. I heard a loud smacking noise. In an envelope of yellow light a quarter-mile away, out past the marsh, a shadow leaped around. The sound repeated itself, finishing as soon as it started, like someone being slapped, but it was louder, like a gunshot.

Another one. Then another.

During college I would dream about Ben, the worst nightmares of my life. They'd have me waking shivering, some nights spastically. In the dream, he'd walk me through each step, holding my hand, showing me what he was doing while loading the gun and putting it into his mouth. He'd explain to me what he planned to do next, but I wouldn't be able to understand him. "You've got a gun in your mouth," I said. I woke up after he fired.

My roommate eventually insisted I visit the health clinic; he was sick of waking up with me screaming.

"Where do you think they come from?" the counselor asked.

I didn't have an answer. "I want to know how it happened," I said.

"You'll never get that," he said. "The good news is, that's not what you're really looking for."

"What am I looking for?"

He looked surprised. "You want to know the reason why he killed himself."

On the fourth shot, I jerked around, then I was able to place it: just someone playing basketball.

four

And here, number four, if I don't know where to start, should I begin? Is it a change of direction this time, or just another step in the way we're headed?

Or perhaps is this THE ONE change of direction, is what I'm really thinking. And if it is THE ONE, is it too big for these cards? These aids that help me return to bed and say everything is all right, go back to sleep?

I can't be in the same bed with him. I feel betrayed. Humiliated.

You're a fluke, always have been, Victor said in so many words.

I don't know where to start. But sure, start with the story, start with the get-up-and-go. Change of direction number four, and it's only just occurred.

"I did not mean to start a fight," he said. "Now, please sit down. You're being hysterical."

"I can assure you, this is not hysterical," I said.

"He" in this instance was not Victor, he was "Toad," hosting us this evening for dinner. "Obviously people have lied to you," said Toad, grinning at me. "Victor has lied to you."

I tried to work today. I fiddled with some half-baked drafts for two hours, some touch-up work I've taken on recently for the hell of it, until once again I realized it was soulless flab. I sent and received e-mails. I was called in for my thoughts about new digital features for a Blu-Ray release of The Hook-Up's DVD. I went to yoga, I watched an old episode of Moonlighting. On the kitchen calendar was penned, "Dinner with Toad, 83 Sargent Drive, Northeast." Toad being Dr. Low, Victor's boss.

They call him Toad because he's fat with a hunchback and has bumpy eyes. Some federal committee Victor wants to join is in Dr. Low's hands, in terms of handing out appointments, and Victor's worried, believing Toad has it in for him. We've met before at faculty functions, me and the Toad, back when Victor was being recruited to Soborg, but he never remembers my name. Personally I find him charming. Victor warned me I would, perhaps was afraid that I would. He reminds me of Uncle Bill. Each time we meet, I think, Ah, yes, the gentleman sailor with a gin problem.

Victor was already standing there in the foyer under a Tiffany chandelier. His face was tight, but he relaxed when he saw me. At crucial moments, I thought, I'm a good crutch for him.

"Just be yourself," Victor said.

When he's nervous, his voice is far-flung, emerging from a cave.

"It's going to be fine," I said, rubbing his arm. "You'll get the appointment."

"Not tonight." He looked over my head down the hall. "Tonight he wants Hollywood. You're the reason he invited us. He told me on the phone."

"That's why we're here?"

"Practically speaking, I may as well go home."

"Oh, come on," I said, "I'll do the floor show, maybe afterward he'll give you that chair." Then I tried to move him down the hallway, but Victor was stuck. He paused before a mirror and fixed his shirt. I noticed the scuffed hems on his khakis, thinking, I should replace those tomorrow. Realizing those pants are ten years old. He hasn't changed an inch. The same man I met in Macy's, my own Jimmy Stewart, and I'm complaining he never altered, never grew?

Who ever wanted Jimmy Stewart to change one bit?

So you see, I began the evening in good humor.

Toad was sitting in a white, book-lined parlor by a fireplace, surrounded by ferns and orchids. I thought, They got the nickname wrong, he looks like a garden turtle, shrunk into its house.

"Now, I don't see why they call you Toad at all," I said when we were shaking hands.

"What? Victor, is that true?" Toad's head swiveled on his shell, and poor Victor didn't know where to look. Toad scowled for a moment, then started laughing. "Oh, look at Victor," he said to me, chuckling. "God, man, have a drink. Now, I like you," he said, taking my hand, "not many gals have guts. You know, there's still a prince here waiting for the right girl."

"We've met before, actually."

"Is that right? I'm sure I'd remember you."

The room could have been a greenhouse. Victor excused himself, removed his jacket, and went to the sideboard to make drinks. Toad motioned toward a chair for me. He was still clutching my fingers.

So pause there while we're holding hands, Victor rolling up his sleeves, already sweating, rummaging around with tongs in an ice bucket, and let me get this right, but with the smallest preamble. This season has been pretty shitty. I want to say this up front, that I'm among the culpable here, right up to the moment I parked in the cul-de-sac. That it's me whom we should keep an eye on. For weeks this fall I've played the bitch, instigated arguments about nothing. Fights over toothpaste rolls. Something Victor's done for ages suddenly becomes too much one evening (how he splatters water on the mirror when he brushes his teeth, or how he loads the dishwasher like it's a gym bag), and I explode. Now I know the cause on my end—this endless block is finally coming to a head—but when Victor doesn't fight back, it's so much worse, when a fight's exactly what I crave. When I wish he'd clamp me down, scream how much he can't take me anymore, and instead he does nothing or says he's sorry, and once again I'm the only one who's pissed off. Feeling guilty for being angry, as though being mad is a sign of madness, of anti-wellness among those of us who don't swim our laps every morning.

No, all this new Victor wants is to retreat. To put further distance between us when already we're far apart. To apologize when he's done nothing wrong so he can be mighty and take more weight upon his shoulders—as though he's been carrying me these thirty years, so it seems—and abscond. The new remote, reluctant Victor, scuttling back to his desk like a crab, his shell forming since around the time Woman Hits Forty *went onstage and slowly hardening ever since.*

I remember, before I was successful, at least Victor would tell me what to do. Be a man as I desired a man. When we moved down to New York from Cambridge, when he was nervous but so inflamed, how I loved that sight of him, risk-taking, hoping to make a difference. And there was hope once again when we moved up to Bar Harbor and Victor got his own lab; we re-fell in love, and there was that active, old yearning. But it faded away. Now he demurely remains hands-off. Should I mention sex? Like I'm a special artistic case to be accommodated. To be indulged, petted, cared for by its handler.

And would I have my old Victor back in this late chapter? Would I, my controlling, didactic Svengali? Would I?

The Toad bore a head of white straw, two black button eyes, and a tie from the Pot & Kettle Club. Uncle Bill in a nutshell. Toad also appeared to have a big appetite for Entertainment Tonight *when every time I tried to steer the conversation toward Soborg or federal research committees, he took us right back to film. For an hour in the steam room he quizzed me about all the gossip. He was a movie buff and we breezed right through the checkpoints, Hawks and Hitchcock and* Some Like It Hot. *Victor, meanwhile, sweated through his shirt, watching us talk and drinking whiskey.*

"Now, tell me about your family, Sara," Toad said on our way into dinner. "You're saying Betsy Gardner is your aunt?"

A cold breeze blew through the dining room. A window was open somewhere.

We ate a roast served by Toad's housekeeper and discussed local news. After
dinner, beckoned back, we returned to the sitting room for cordials. We'd drunk
quite a bit by that point. I was tired and wanted to go home, I think Victor did,
too, but Toad wasn't having it.

"So you wrote The Hook-Up," *he said, passing around tiny glasses of co-*
gnac. I threw back mine and requested another, seeing where this was going.

"My wife, the celebrity," said Victor, and winked. He was fiddling with the
stereo, trying to spike an LP on the record player.

"Did you see it?" I asked Toad.

"Just recently. Didn't like it much, I'm afraid." Toad laughed, so we all
laughed. "No, not very much. Probably it wasn't my style, as they say."

I gave him my rich smile. "Darling, let's adopt him," I said, "for those nights
when I need a quick boost of confidence."

"See, here is my question," said Toad, "my line of thinking all night. Can and
should. What's the real role of cinema? Now, those are two separate questions."

"Try me," I said. I was thinking, Will he put Victor on the goddamned com-
mittee if I play along?

Toad twirled one of his eyebrows between his fingers. "Well, cinema shouldn't
be waste, to start. Obviously it can be, obviously it's very easy for movies to be
terrible, the sewage we accept based on the classics that came first. The studio
pieces, the million-dollar monsters."

"Does The Hook-Up *qualify?"*

"Well, probably. Why not?" He smiled. "It was a bit of a monster, wasn't it?
But I apologize. I shouldn't say monster."

"A fluke," Victor piped up, staring down at a record jacket.

"What?"

Honestly I thought I'd misheard him. Victor looked at me and rolled his eyes.

"Now, by 'monster,' I mean at the box office, of course. You see the grosses
right there in the paper these days." Toad removed his glasses and rubbed his eyes.
"But as to quality, well, it was perfectly watchable, which perhaps is what all

movies should aspire to. It's ninety-five percent of the industry. For example, take Greed. Entertaining, of course, but that doesn't equal great."

"Darling, I just meant," Victor said, "it's not like we anticipated that kind of success."

"Aha," I said.

"It was 'the little movie that could.' You said so yourself. Tell him how many others you wrote."

"But you said fluke," I said. The Toad was watching us, he appeared peeved to be excluded. "Like it wasn't deserved."

Then Victor gave me a look that said I'd drunk too much, which was true, though so had he, and I threw the look back, extra-strength.

"That's not what I meant. We were very, very lucky—"

"You mean I was very lucky."

Part of me was cold. Most of me was thinking, Finally, let's do this, who cares if it's in your boss's sitting room.

Victor paused. "Fine. You were lucky."

"And aside from luck?"

"Will someone tell me what you both are talking about?" asked Toad.

Victor spun on his toes. He didn't know where to look. "Dr. Low, I apologize. If you'll excuse us—"

"I'll excuse nothing. I am not in need of pampering, thank you. I believe your wife asked you a question."

"Yes, Victor," I said, "about this luck."

Victor squeezed his nostrils and closed his eyes. It's the same look when he's on the phone with customer-service people. "For argument's sake, then, no, probably there wasn't much going on besides luck if—and it's an essential if—we're going by ticket sales alone, and nothing else. I'm only relating here what you've said before, Sara, many times. That commercial success never relates to what's written down. Now those are your words. That it's the director's and the editor's vision, the studio's plan—never mind whatever the audience wants, which nobody knows!"

Victor laughed and glanced at his boss, and rubbed a hole through the mois-
ture on the window with his sleeve. "Think about it," Victor said, peering out.
"Going by tickets sold, you really want to be compared to Moonstruck*?"*

"Ha!" yelped Toad. "Olympia Dukakis." He fixed his glasses. "And that
singer, too."

"Cher," Victor said.

I was about to speak, then I lost my train of thought. "Now, let me remem-
ber," Toad said. "Your movie, Sara, is about an actress, once upon a time a star.
In the present day, though, she's a has-been. An old amphibian like me."

He dropped his glasses. He bent forward and wiggled his piggy fingers. I
jerked out of my seat to pick them up.

"Thank you. Then she falls in love with a young film director. I saw it
on television recently, that's why you're here, of course. I thought the next morn-
ing, I must invite that woman to dinner. Sara, tell us, what did you set out
to create?"

"It's a romantic comedy," I said.

"A comedy," said Toad after a moment.

"You didn't laugh, I take it."

"Oh, I'm sorry, my dear." He laughed now.

"It's an homage to Billy Wilder," Victor said, as though he'd said this a thou-
sand times before; it was the first time I'd heard it. "A pastiche."

"Is that right?" I said.

Victor tilted back his head.

"Exactly!" snorted Toad. "But then all art is homage, isn't it? It can't help
itself. Don't tell me that you didn't set out, Sara, at least unconsciously, to pay
tribute to Sunset Boulevard*. That's Wilder, isn't it? I knew it the moment the*
credits rolled."

"Well, not pay tribute," said Victor. He was staring at some picture book he'd
taken out from the bookcase, with a lighthouse on the cover.

"Rewrite. No, I don't mean rewrite," Toad said. "Improve upon. As in

research, for example, we take what's put forth, then search for improvements. It's not the best film anyway."

"Sunset Boulevard," *Victor mused.*

"Without the pool."

"Right, Sunset Boulevard *without the pool," Victor said, laughing.*

"Can I get a word in here sometime?"

Then silence. As if I'd wandered into the men's room.

"Oh, Sara," said Toad, flapping toward Victor, "my dear, excuse us."

"So a Wilder homage. Minus the pool."

"Sara, he's only joking—"

"Well, if you look to the masters you'll find—" started Toad, but I inter-rupted him: "So if I did anything here, it was to repackage a classic, is what you're saying? The success wasn't really mine. It probably had more to do with Wilder, or some marketing person at Sony, is that right?"

"There's nothing wrong, per se, with Sunset Boulevard," *said Toad.*

"Sara, be reasonable," Victor said.

Now it wasn't humid anymore. Toad was blindly smiling, staring at me with blotto eyes.

"I think I'm ready to go," I said, getting up.

"What?"

"Unless there are other flukes to cover. Woman Hits Forty. *My meno-pausal masses. My career of chance."*

"Sara, my dear, slow down," said Toad. "We are but simple scientists. We spend our lives chipping away at a stone. How one prepares for luck, how hard one works for it, we don't appreciate. You see, we don't understand how to give it credit."

Victor was exasperated, fidgeting by the window as if he wanted to grab me, hug me, scream at me. He did none of the these things. "Come on, tell him," Victor said, losing his hands in his pockets, "how many screenplays you wrote before The Hook-Up. *I mean, why weren't they picked up?"*

"Well, they weren't any good," I said, pausing.

"What?"

"Weren't good," I said.

"Sure they were."

"My dear, my dear," Toad said, now all the way out on the edge of his chair, "I did not mean to start a fight. Please sit down, you're being hysterical."

Finally I could laugh.

"I can assure you, this is not hysterical," I said when I had my breath back, though honestly, I did feel hysterical, but only for that second. Then everything was hardening to a single sharp prow.

"Sara, I see you believe what you say. Obviously people have lied to you. Victor has lied to you. However, I do not lie. And I will tell you, I didn't like your movie much, but I'm sure its success was hard earned and hard fought."

The housekeeper appeared. If no one needed anything else, she'd excuse herself. We saw ourselves out. The Toad moved chairs around and peered at us through the window. In the driveway between our cars, Victor said, "Look, you lost me back there."

"You're right." It was the quietest thing I'd said all evening.

"What do you mean?"

I met his eye. "Really, you don't know?"

Truly, I don't think he did. I was the first one down the driveway. I wondered, driving home with Victor's headlights in my mirror, perhaps our longevity is a fluke, too. An accident three-decades running.

Right now I can't write any more.

UPDATE: This is not to change what I've written. Rather, it's to say I have seen the most wonderful movie, and it's connected to all this, I don't know how. For the moment. I've just come in the front door, here I am clanging around inside. I have to get this down.

The university started a film festival on the island a couple years ago. This year they asked me to chair a panel on screenplays. Fine. It was held under a tent on the square downtown, and there were exactly thirty people and they had two questions at the end: what type of software do I use, and do I know any agents who read unsolicited manuscripts. Afterward they held a panel on short films, and they opened with something I'd never seen before. The Perfect Human. Released 1967. In Danish: Det perfekle menneske. Black and white, about ten minutes long. But revolutionary. Like I'd never seen a movie before. The smallest, most perfect thing.

And the whole time I'm watching, I'm thinking, God, why can't I write this? I made a note on the back of a dry-cleaning tag: WHY CAN'T I WRITE SOMETHING SO SIMPLE AND SHARP? I don't know if I've ever seen anything better.

We have discussed this, Doctor, you and me, the pressure post–Hook-Up for more success. The load I bore alone, partnerless, once Victor decided to ward himself off. The offers afterward, the proposals for collaborations from strangers, rewrites, adaptations of novels I hadn't read since high school. Money out the wazoo, but for what? A thousand too many options, and all of them spooking away any original ideas, aside from the house.

So I built a house.

But, for this afternoon. This moment.

First time in forever, I'm inspired, I remember what it feels like, and all because of one little movie. Here's something, I thought, that reminds me I once made somethings, too.

UPDATE: Victor and I haven't slept in the same room since that dinner at Toad's. That was three nights ago. Not that we've discussed this as The Deliberate Next Step of Whatever Is Happening. It's never happened before. The first night, I closed the door when I came home, and Victor slept in the music room. That's the way it's been since.

Both of us suave, sophisticated adults, purposefully avoiding each other in the bathroom. But I'm still too upset to behave differently, and Victor's on tiptoes. He thinks I'm still upset about the other night. He's in the business of being unaware, looking to turn a profit. Both inside and out, I'm incredibly fatigued. I act pissed off when I'm not, and then I'm upset all over again, angry again, crying over the laundry.

Finally, have we put too much distance between us? I don't know that I want to breach it. I'm haunted by that ringing superior tone in Victor's voice: the absence of respect.

Got the Criterion's manager to play The Perfect Human *for me again. Afterward, he burned me a DVD. At least someone understands my mania. He agrees, for its ambitions it's a flawless film. Like* Meet Me in St. Louis. *Like* Charade. *He says he can get me the original poster on eBay. I told him to order two, one for each of us.*

I've watched it three times at home, with a notepad.

And it's just the littlest film. But you can tell, whatever compels the director inside to create, this is what it looks like exposed to air.

The Perfect Essence, *it should be called.*

What would that look like for me?

What do I have left in me anyway?

Here I am, fifty-eight, losing my marriage.

Here I am, forty-four, thirty-five, losing my parents.

Here I am, twenty-nine, losing my baby.

Here I am, seventeen, punching my mother in the mouth.

A life beholden to insecurity.

Really I am just tired of all of this.

UPDATE: Took Victor to see The Perfect Human. *Why not? I thought it could help. Perhaps communicate something to him I can't express. But in conversation afterward, it was clear, no progress made. No connection. He heard all the dialogue, but nothing said.*

What I've been thinking all along, I've decided to put into action. It's only now that I can say this: I must go. For how long I don't know, but for our sake, I should leave.

Vámonos. Vamoose.

"Deke telephoned last night. He wanted to know if I wanted to hang out. I said, 'Hang out'? 'Play video games,' he said. Victor, this is an established M.D., forty-four years old, he proposed marriage to me six months ago, now he's inviting me over to play Mario Kart. When did modern man give up on shame?"

Lucy was tossing a football she'd picked up somewhere. In a sleeveless shirt, she looked tanner than normal. Darker and also more muscular. I wondered if she'd added weight lifting to her rock-climbing workouts.

"I explained that I didn't have time this week to play Nintendo, but now I feel bad about the whole exchange. No man wants to be called an adolescent, he just wants to preserve the right to act like one, am I right?"

"Yeah."

"Yeah," said Lucy. She held out the football. "Hey, are we at thirty thousand feet?"

I had already sent a notice about my vacation to the team, but I'd stopped by campus to write some e-mails.

"What?" I looked up from my computer. "Sorry, Lucy, try me again."

"I am posing the question to you: Why men this exact way? You know, I have better things to do."

"Are you saying I'm a poor receptor?"

She hunched forward, as though schooling a toddler. "Take the neuron."

I looked up again from the monitor. "That's your theory? Men are neurotic?"

"Know what? Forget it."

"No, I'm here, man as neuron. Please continue."

"Feign interest, go ahead."

"Lucy—"

"So connections aren't made aimlessly. We know this."

"Between neurons."

"Circuits occurring between certain cells and not others. Signals traveling in predictable patterns."

"Well, not always."

"Not always, there are special cases, yes, and that's my point." She pointed one end of the football at my nose. "So what if I'm not seeing the synapses for a ball of string? What if I'm wrong about Deke? What if it wasn't a conviction about him so much as an uncertainty about me?"

"I don't follow."

"Me valuing myself enough as one who could end up with someone like that. Didn't you see him at the recital?"

"At your concert?"

Her eyes were frozen.

"I did not see him," I said.

"Well, I am not unseeing. I didn't even tell him about it. Yes, I am aware of my tendency to catch and release. What I don't get is how easy it is for some people, how someone wakes up to the stimuli and says yes, yes, I'll take that one, I mean, how do they know?"

"How do they know what?" I snapped. This time I really hadn't been listening. I was trying to understand an e-mail sent by a colleague about some new federal report. Lucy smashed the football down on my desk. She left it there, her hand pinning it next to my computer.

"This deafness, Victor? Your blindness to those of us still sticking around?"

Lucy walked out. I shut down my computer.

I stood up and gazed at the football.

I hurried outside, remembering Cornelia sitting in my car.

Cornelia had never seen Thuya Gardens before, so we drove there first, then hiked to the top of Day Mountain. In the afternoon, I gardened while Cornelia suntanned. With seventy-five dollars and a quick trip to Walmart, she'd equipped my house with wireless Internet access, and was soon able to instant-message outside while Web-surfing while e-mailing while watching a DVD of some TV show she liked okay.

Around four, I offered to tour Cornelia through my record collection. Part of me didn't want to play her any music, instead I wanted her to see how merely possessing all those albums was its own satisfaction, to know that they were there. The collector's joy. There'd been a time when I knew every recording of every piece, the sign of a specialist who understands very little. But now to gaze upon the sleeves, to *not* play them. To be in awe. I wanted her to use silence to appreciate that, in comparison, the experience of listening was a lot more personal and complicated: how it depended on the day's mood, the temperature of the air, what clothes you were wearing and how they felt, what you'd eaten for lunch, and then of course the equipment and the tones it produced and at what volume, and every associated emotion and memory brought by the listener. Never mind the music. The experience of music was so different for each individual, it wasn't even worth discussing. As soon as I pressed PLAY, we may as well have existed in separate dimensions.

But Cornelia said, "So what have you got?"

I let her choose at random. She plucked out Sibelius, Barber, Dvořák. I explained, here's how I thought of Dvořák, particularly the violin sonata she'd chosen, because she liked the cover: that this was music Emma Darwin might have enjoyed, if the technology had been available, while composing letters to her husband. The romance matched, but more important, there was wretchedness underneath: Emma's terror about her husband's lack of faith, not because an angry God might strike him down but because someday she'd be alone in heaven.

"You've got like a serious boner for Darwin," said Cornelia.

"Do you hear the sadness?"

"I mean, it sounds jaunty to me."

I pulled down Steve Reich's *Music for 18 Musicians*, which I figured would appeal to Cornelia's drum-circle side. It was a trip, she said. Afterward, we went out for a cheap dinner in Bar Harbor and caught a documentary at the Criterion.

The second day, we hiked around Eagle Lake, where Cornelia said we should take random turns and I was the idiot who agreed. After an hour, my knees ached and my lower back was in knots. It was hot under the dense tree cover and there wasn't any breeze. We were lost.

But Cornelia kept running ahead around the trail's next bend, her dreadlocks wobbling like a swami's basket, her wife beater sticking to her ribs. I was stunned when we came out half an hour later at my car. Cornelia gloated that she'd known the way the whole time. She said she'd been there before with Dan, the boy from the restaurant.

"So what's this Dan like?"

"What?" Cornelia looked up from her cell phone and pulled her feet down from the window. "Oh, he's cool. I mean, there's lots of kids working here for the summer, in the restaurants. The bartenders know us, so they comp us drinks."

"How does Dan know the island so well?"

"He likes the woods. It's a mind-set."

"A mind-set," I repeated.

There were several messages on the answering machine when we got home. "Hi, Victor, this is Dr. Carrellas again, I just wanted to touch base and see—" I pressed DELETE. The phone rang.

"Victor, it's Betsy."

"Oh—"

"Why haven't you returned my messages?"

"We've been out."

"You and Trixie. Well, should I stop by Pepcin's or not? They had terrific cod last week, they give me a good deal, you know."

"Do we have a dinner scheduled?"

"Victor, what good is an answering machine if you don't use it?!" Cornelia turned at the noise. "I said, I've come over to Southwest for the afternoon, and it would be nice to meet the little courtesan. You don't have *plans* tonight, do you?"

"No."

"Is that Aunt Betsy?" Cornelia was sitting on a stool, kicking her legs.

"So how's six? Pepcin's got the best, I don't know why you don't shop there."

"Fine, dinner, bring the fish."

"Lovely," Betsy chirped. "Ta, dear."

Tar, de-ah.

Cornelia and I cleaned up the living room. I was pouring myself a glass of white wine when Cornelia came downstairs wearing a floral skirt and a plain white T-shirt and actual shoes, her hair tied back in a ponytail. I was thinking up a compliment when we heard the sound of gravel being kicked up in the driveway.

Betsy remained in the driver's seat, smoking. She was wearing a showy necklace for the occasion, a diamond pendant worth thousands.

"Well, aren't you sparkling," I said.

"Aren't you desperate, dear," she replied, grasping my hand through the window with no intention of getting out, pretending no one was standing there beside me.

"That's a beautiful necklace, Aunt Betsy," Cornelia said.

I thought I saw a deer near the woodpile, but it was only the wind blowing leaves around. We moved slowly to the porch as a threesome: me with groceries, Cornelia politely asking after Betsy's health, and Betsy, deaf to inquiry, telling me about running into one of the Rockefeller boys at Pepcin's, so she wasn't too sure anymore about the fish if they let just anyone shop there.

Cornelia fixed drinks while I went inside to prepare dinner. Cornelia had suggested I cook "so we ladies can have girl talk." When I came back out, Cornelia was lighting a cigarette, hunched forward in a chair opposite Betsy's.

"Ah, Victor. She smokes, then?"

Betsy herself had a cigarette in one hand, ashing on the armrest.

"It hasn't killed me yet," said Cornelia.

"But it will, dear. You must know that. When I was a girl, why, everyone smoked, at least all the men, and any girls who had guts. Now we were raised believing it was healthy, but you, dear, I'd think anyone your age who started smoking would be a nincompoop."

"Betsy, can I get you a glass of water?"

"I'm trying to quit," Cornelia said. "I started when I was thirteen."

"No, thank you, Victor," said Betsy. "Dear, what was your name again?"

"Cornelia Caratti."

"How about we call you Connie? Victor tells me you're working with my son, is that right?"

"Oh, Mrs. Gardner, Joel is awesome. You must be so proud of him. He's totally become my inspiration."

Betsy scoffed. "Well, I didn't raise him to cook, so much good it did. I can't cook in the slightest, that was always Bill's métier. They say a lot of drugs float around restaurants. Now, when Victor told me about your career, I must say we never thought our struggle as feminists all those years would end up putting women back into the kitchen."

"How about we play nice," I called over from the grill.

"I don't know that that's true," Cornelia said. "I don't think it's really a struggle anymore."

"Don't bullshit a bullshitter, dear."

"I'm doing what I want, I made that choice. I'm paid, aren't I?"

Betsy scrunched her nose.

I went inside and brought out a bowl of tomatoes Cornelia had roasted the day before. "Betsy," I said, holding them out, "wouldn't you like a snack before dinner? Cornelia made these yesterday—"

"No, thank you, too rich for me. But aren't they scrumptious. So, Connie, you just graduated from college. Cornell, was it?"

Cornelia nodded.

"Cornelia Caratti, Cornell graduate. Marvelously alliterative. Now, I want to know, do the news reports have it right, your 'hooking up'? Truly, I wish you to be honest with us, help us old people understand, was a lot of hooking up done while you were in school?"

"I think I'm going to go get some wine," Cornelia said.

When she'd gone inside, Betsy hoarsely whispered, "Why, she's wonderful, Victor. You found yourself a partner in prudery."

"Maybe the elderly shouldn't drink at breakfast," I said. I closed the top of the grill and stood in front of her.

"I may be tipsy," Betsy said, "but the girl still needs a shampoo."

I took her wine and her cigarettes. I began sliding the cigarettes out, one by one, and snapping them in half.

"Well, aren't you man of the house."

"It's a mind-set," I said.

"What does that mean?"

"That I'm about to drive you home."

"Well, I don't know that I've seen you so resolute before. Why the urgency, I wonder? Now, give me those back."

"First you play nice."

Betsy struggled to get up, but the chair was too deep. Her hair flopped down into her glasses and the veins bulged in her arms. "Quit playing dirty. Oh, fine, fine, you win, now give me those back!"

I threw the pack in her lap and put the wineglass on the ground, six inches from her reach. Maybe it was the heat from the grill, but my shirt was spotted with sweat marks. The sun had disappeared below the treetops. When Cornelia slid open the door, Betsy was back to smiling, a cigarette in her lips, once again reclined.

"Cornelia," I said, "did you know that Aunt Betsy—"

"Dear, I apologize if in any way I offended you earlier," Betsy said. "Now, do you have a boyfriend?"

"I'm sorry?"

"Or a girlfriend? It's all right, darling, I know how the world works,
I think it's wonderful. Victor, look at her, signs of love are palpable."

Cornelia mooned at me for a moment and laughed.

"See? Obviously she has someone special, don't you, dear?"

"I wouldn't say I have him," she said.

"Deductive reasoning, you see."

"I didn't know you were dating anyone," I said.

"Why, how *mossy* of you, Victor. So how did you two meet?"

"He works at the restaurant. But it's not like we're, whatever,
dating."

"Ah, he's one of Joel's. Well, hooking up, would you say?"

"So what was it like when you were young?" asked Cornelia. "It's
not like we're discussing anything revolutionary."

"Oh, but the world was different, you know. It was very important to maintain appearances. No, of course, there were cars to drive
in, movies to see. If there weren't chaperones, you could explore the
rumble seat afterward."

"Did kids have sex when you were in high school?"

Betsy didn't blink an eye.

"No, dear, no," she said, adjusting her glasses with both hands.
"Well, I'm sure some *did*, but it wouldn't be something you'd hear
about, unless a girl went away for a short time. But there were ways,
ways if a boy liked you—"

"So did you go all the way? I mean, before you were married?"

They both laughed and Betsy shook her head. "Now, not that I'm
necessarily proud about that. In those days one saved oneself, you
see. What a funny thing to say now. For what, one wonders. Not that
I wasn't tempted, mind you. We had dances in the summers, you'd
curl your hair. But you wanted to maintain dignity, always dignity.

Remember, darling," Betsy said, whispering and leaning forward, "there's still a lot of ground to cover when you're running around the bases."

They both fell back in their chairs laughing. Dinner was eaten outside on our laps. Cornelia lit the citronella torches and quizzed Betsy about Uncle Bill and how they'd met, what their courtship was like, what it had been like to live in Japan after the war.

"You know, I did almost have an affair."

"What?" I said.

Both women looked at me.

"What are you two talking about? I'm sorry, with who?"

Betsy laughed and turned in her seat toward Cornelia and took one of her hands, sliding the rings up and down her fingers as though on an abacus. "Bill, bless him," Betsy said to Cornelia, ignoring me, "took on junior engineers in the summer. One year we had a Princeton boy named Ford. Fordie Wheeler, family from Virginia, I think. Anyway, delightful young man, smart, and very tall. Sort of a young Bill Holden. At the time, boys stayed at the house, that way Bill could work them around the clock and make sure they didn't get into trouble. Well, Fordie was a good guest, very polite. A little too well trained. He'd eat dinner with us, help me with the housework, and always interesting, you know, telling stories about the fraternity, and could he play the piano! Well, one week Bill had to fly on business and it was just the two of us."

Betsy sighed. "The remarkable thing," she said a moment later, her head up, "I don't think he ever would have laid a hand on me. And I was a looker, you know. But Fordie was soft, you see, he read too much poetry, he had *ideas*. Me on the other hand, I'd thought about it all summer. I was dying to be his ruin. It's terrible to remember, I would go to bed dreaming. I couldn't take my eyes off him at the club. Why, the legs on that boy." She paused for a long moment. "This was a few years after Joel had disappeared. He'd resurfaced once or twice. We'd be relieved, of course, not for long, though. I was sending him money secretly, then he wrote these vile letters from Sacramento, of the most incredible rage, wishing us the worst from his hidey-hole. Bill really took it to heart, though he wouldn't show it. Never talked to the boy again, talked to me less. Personally I felt betrayed. I'd given Joel quite a good deal of money by that point. Well, blame ourselves is what we did, and it divided us. It was like a ghost lying there in the bed, our failure. But the first afternoon I saw young Ford, it occurred to me right away, the idea of being with him, a clean slate. Someone new. We had our little jokes, you see. I'm sure he thought we were just picnicking.

"But you must see, you must *see*, Cornelia, I never cheated on Bill. I did not betray my husband. I loved Bill, I loved him more that summer than ever I had, I adored him. But you'll have worked tremendously hard to build your life after a certain fashion, and then suddenly, one morning, you want something different. You want anything but what you have, you want it new and you want it just right then. It's terrifying, the desire's so powerful, you're just sick with it. Or perhaps I'd had too much to drink."

Cornelia tried to interrupt but Betsy wouldn't have it: "Either I'd had too much to drink or not enough. We were out behind the house. I asked Fordie to bring outside the record player so we could dance. I said I was worried he could return to school not knowing how to court a girl properly, and then what sort of hostess had I been? Oh, I'd planned it for days, it was such a hot summer. Though of course the boy could dance. He was dashing, he knew it, he was very well taught and groomed and turned out, boys were in those days and Ford especially. And there was a moon out. And even at dusk it was still so hot.

You smelled like honeysuckle. He put the record on and I instructed him on how to grasp my waist. Then we danced several times. And I kissed him."

Betsy was staring off into the woods. I asked, "So what happened?"

She laughed. "Well, nothing, dear. He wanted to see what came next, I could tell, and so did I, but that was it, just about as far as I was capable. Bill returned home the next day and Fordie departed a week later."

Betsy coughed and was seized by a fit. Her voice cracked and gurgled. Half an hour later, she threatened to drive herself home. I got her into my car after Cornelia gave her a hug and she and Betsy spent a few minutes discussing what dreadlocks required to maintain.

"A nice girl," Betsy said as we drove through the dark to Northeast Harbor.

"I'd never heard that story before. About the boy."

"A nice girl," she repeated, leaning on the door. "Be careful, dear. Now, let's have the radio, I want to sing."

We sang along to Dolly Parton's "Nine to Five." Halfway home, I was about to ask more concerning the almost-affair, but Betsy had begun snoring.

Our third day together was a Mount Desert belle. In the morning, I showed Cornelia my pick in the guidebook, Pemetic Mountain, one of the island's tougher hikes. I was packing the backpack when I noticed that my iPod was out of juice. I'd seen Cornelia unplug hers from her laptop before breakfast, leaving the white cord dangling like a tail, so I sat down and plugged in mine, and then stared dumbly at the password screen.

"I just wanted to charge my iPod," I said when Cornelia appeared.

"No worries. It's 'early bird special,' no spaces."

I typed it in. The password screen vanished.

"First thing I see," said Cornelia. "At home, when I open my lap-top, across the street is this sign for a parking garage. 'Early Bird Special, Monday to Sunday, seventeen seventy-four, plus tax.'" She laughed. "I've probably looked at that sign twice a day since I was a kid."

By eleven, we were halfway up the mountain, past the tree line onto granite slabs scaling the open ridge. Across the valley, a thin stream of cars was circling Cadillac, the island's tallest mountain, in order to buy their I CLIMBED CADILLAC bumper stickers at the gift shop.

Plainly, I could have used a ride. I was stopping frequently for breaks, nearly dizzy. Pemetic may have been my favorite hike, but I hadn't done it in several years, and crunching four Advil wasn't rescuing my knees. It didn't help that Cornelia had suffered a nightmare the previous night about dead animals, a mountain of babies piling on top of her, an apoc-alyptic shower of lab rats and minks and baby seals.

I was wheezing too hard to explain I'd never clubbed a baby anything.

"What's weird is that everybody agrees torture is awful. Russell the libertarian agrees it's the end point, full stop. So why is torture on humans so terrible, but not on animals? You think we're the center of the universe. Nature prefers us, we've been selected for superiority. So you extract information, it's justified cruelty and you supplant it, Uncle Victor, you're responsible for it, and I'd be acting unfairly to myself, to my principles, if I didn't hold you to it. And don't say it's for the good of research, as though research is more than means, is in itself noble, is not what brought about the fucking A-bomb."

She turned on me and shook a branch to make her last point.

Where had she read this? Where did she get the lungs?

We dropped our backpacks at the summit signpost. I sat down, closed my eyes, and listened to the blood thudding in my temples. I'd been thinking about Regina, trying to reconstruct her face at that recital, but it was a blur, a Polaroid that wouldn't come through. I put my head between my knees. Cornelia sighed, clopped over to me, fawnlike, and sat on my lap for a moment drinking water. I put my arm around her shoulder, though I could have shoved her off a cliff. Anything joyful and light needed crushing.

After a minute she whispered congratulations on surviving the hike, and I looked around. The view was stunning, panoramic from the ocean to the mountains. I caught my breath, feeling more fifty-eight than forty-six, but at least not sixty-four. Not seventy-nine.

I saluted Cornelia on proving me a war criminal. She started singing something old by Janis Joplin, then jogged me around by the hands, spinning us both until we were wheezing.

There was a whistle close by. We crept to the lip. About three minutes below, a dozen Boy Scouts in neckerchiefs and baseball caps and uniforms were climbing in a line, led by a man in a brimmed ranger's hat.

Cornelia grabbed me and started down the other side.

"Hurry, after them comes the Hardy Boys, and then Nancy Drew, let's go!"

They taught us in Boy Scouts that the most important component in a fire was kindling. Without lots of small dry branches, your fire would self-extinguish, or never catch in the first place. I collected sticks for ten minutes in the woods, stooping, cursing my sore knees. Afterward, though, I had a good fire burning in the outdoor fireplace, adding a glow to what remained of the sunset.

Cornelia made pasta and we split a bottle of white wine. I started on a second while Cornelia drank herb tea. The phone rang after dinner and she took it upstairs. It was the fourth time the phone rang since we had gotten home. The previous three had been from Betsy, but I'd checked the caller ID each time and elected not to answer.

Going in for more wine, I heard snippets of conversation floating down the stairs. The voice mail light on the machine was flashing. Cornelia came back and sat opposite me, deeply buried in her sweatshirt, her tea mug hidden up her sleeve. The night fell in around us. I thought about Russell sitting there, exactly where Cornelia was, only weeks earlier.

"Who was that?"

"Who do you think?"

"Did he want to speak to me?"

"No."

"Well what did he want?"

"It doesn't matter." Cornelia jeered, "He wants me to come home."

"Have some wine," I said, offering her the bottle. She drank straight from the neck.

"That's ridiculous, you're doing so well up here. Don't worry, I'll call him."

"Victor, don't."

"Anyway I want to. For other stuff. I won't mention you at all."

"Please, Victor."

I found Russell's number in my address book.

"I knew you'd see the light," he said.

"Russell, it's Victor. How are you?"

"Christ, I thought you were Connie. Did you just talk to her? What'd she say?"

"Nothing. I didn't talk to her."

"So what's happening?"

"Nothing. I'm just calling."

"You're just calling. Okay, listen, I've been rethinking. I think Connie would do better down here for the rest of the summer. I need her, okay? I tell you I broke up with that Ukrainian chick? Nightmare, I can't tell you. Slavic women are all kinds of fucked-up. But about Connie, I need her back home, preferably this week."

"Because you got dumped again? What about her job?"

"Hey, I know how it looks. On Connie's end, I talked to a chef who's a friend of mine—"

I interrupted, "You remember that fall, when Sara was out in California?"

"What?"

"Did you go out to see her? In California?"

"Buddy, are you drunk? Put Connie on the phone."

"I want to know is, did you go out there?"

"Did I go where?"

"Were you two having an affair?" I said.

"Jesus. I don't know who I'm talking to right now."

I heard the door slide open and slam shut. Cornelia went by in a blur, a hooded ghost running up the stairs. "Sara called you," I said steadily into the phone. "From Los Angeles, when she left me."

"She called me to talk. To talk about a fucking movie. Why you would think—we talked about her script. I read dialogue."

"Where did you get it?"

"Get what?"

"Tell me where you got the pages."

"The pages? Victor, I did not go out there. Are you listening, are you recording this right now? Because I don't want to hear a question like that again from my oldest friend. We are talking about two phone conversations, maybe three. I told her about a girl I was dating, I needed advice."

"Tell me about the movie."

"Okay, you're drunk."

"Tell me—"

"Put Connie on the phone."

"Send me the pages."

"This is over right now. Victor, put Connie on the phone. Will you put Connie on the phone?"

"Don't call here again," I said.

"All right, I'm calling Connie's cell phone, you go sleep it off. Good night."

In a childless marriage, there can be no secrets, Sara once said.

Technically, it was a line from *The Hook-Up*.

Three in the morning, I couldn't sleep, I was still drunk and the shelves in my music room were spinning. I wondered if Cornelia was awake. I cracked open her bedroom door. She was sleeping on her side, her hands clasped together near her face. One of the windows was open. I slid it closed and pulled a quilt down from the closet and draped it over her bed.

Downstairs, I went into Sara's office and turned on the light. I took her laptop out of the drawer and opened it on her desk, right where she'd always placed it.

A picture of popcorn. Right behind her laptop, slightly to the left, tacked to the bulletin board was a postcard of popcorn overflowing from a red bag.

I laughed when "popcorn" worked. I was making a mental note to tell Sara about it, when I realized what I was thinking.

On her computer's desktop were the usual icons, plus one that had been dragged to the center, a file named "In Progress." I double-clicked on it and Sara's screenwriting program started. "THE PERFECT HUSBAND," the screen said in big letters. "BY SARA GARDNER."

I booted up the printer, ran off a copy, and turned off the light. I stopped again by Cornelia's door. She was snoring. I must have stood there two minutes before I noticed that she'd kicked off the quilt. I put the screenplay down on the floor and slowly crawled around the sides of the bed, tucking the quilt into the crack between the mattress and the box spring. When I reached Cornelia's side, our faces were inches apart.

Her eyes popped open.

"What are you doing?"

"Tucking you in," I whispered.

"What?" She bolted up and pulled the sheet up to her chin. "Jesus, get out of here!"

The parking lot for the Somesville bookstore was jammed. Some people I recognized from Soborg, or maybe they just looked the type, happy people my age in river sandals giving friends the smallest of waves.

I'd spent the last days of my vacation alone. Cornelia hadn't mentioned the night I tucked her in, except to say nothing whenever we were in the same room. Two nights in a row, she'd slept elsewhere. The first night, she left me a note on the kitchen counter saying I shouldn't worry. Second time, no word at all.

Chapbook readings were bigger events than I'd imagined. I stood leaning against a shelf of cookbooks, trying to remember the name of someone in the audience I recognized when I spotted Regina sitting in the front row, facing forward. I tried willing her to turn around. Then a girl's hair caught my eye: third row, green streaks, Lindsay the roommate who was turning in her seat. Our eyes met. She didn't see as much as absorb me, then turn away with some inscrutable expression quivering around her mouth.

I wondered, Would antlers require four hands to carry?

The store manager shushed the crowd. Someone shouted back, "*You* shush, Barbara!" The manager thanked us for coming and begged us to forgive the lack of air conditioning. She introduced the readers, winners of the University of Maine's Aroostook Prize. When her name was called, Regina turned in her seat and waved to the audience. My face burned, but we didn't make eye contact. I looked around in case I knew anyone else in the crowd.

Too much, too much. I felt unsteady on my feet. I turned to leave, but three young people had just walked in behind me, stopping in front of the door.

The first two poets went quickly, reading abstract poems that meant nothing to me. A woman in a crimson velvet vest went next. She wore so many silver bracelets, the clacking noise nearly drowned out her voice. Her last poem was titled "Bush, Cock," which turned out to be pretty much the only words employed. When she finished, the crowd applauded loudly, some of them stamping their feet.

When Regina stepped behind the lectern, I slid partially behind a book display. She pulled back her hair and stared at her pages—my Regina of the pronounced shining cheeks where the glow from the skylights was caught trembling.

"Why, hello," Regina said slowly into the microphone, drawling her words and then smiling. People laughed. "Now, I don't know if I can top that, but I will try, I will try." She was gazing around. "As many of you know, I work at Soborg, but my calling, my true vocation, is to catalog my insecurities. So here we are."

She had them in the cup of her hand.

"This morning I was asked by my roommate where I got the title for this book. It's called *Fair Merman*, there are copies for sale in the back, please remember to tip your waitress. And I told her, I found it in a poem my uncle Mitch once sent me. He said he'd found it in a collection of old Scandinavian love poems. I figured: similarly cold environment, a good place to start. The piece I stole from is called *The Fishermen*, it's by Johannes Ewald. The stanza I borrowed from goes like this:

> *And if my arm so pleases you*
> *With solace and with peace,*
> *Fair Merman, then hurry! Come and take*
> *Both my arms, take two!*

"I just love that, I don't know why," Regina said after a pause, smiling to herself. Then she shifted her line of vision. She stared straight through me. Her mouth turned into a tight, thin line, turned up at one corner, but her eyes didn't change, as though she didn't see me at all.

"The first poem I'm going to read is actually something new. It's called 'Dive':

> *Someone drops a hat at a funeral*
> *And someone laughs. Two lovers, laughing,*
> *Invite four more to bed, a raft for diving,*

But I'm not there and neither are you.
No, we're at my place
Where I'm the play, you see, or so I hoped

The footlights showed
How love became ordinary
When it was not love, was rather
Applause we gave each other

For playing our parts at dusk,
And knowing the right films to see.
Whether you saw me, who knows,
You left behind your ticket stub.

See, I misplace my keys all the time.
I wonder how we forgot about love,
Yet I'm still brokenhearted

About the Friday matinées.

Take back your platform, diver.
Your swimming raft from which
To plummet solo, snorkel-less.

I'll find the lovers returned from the funeral,
Ready to mourn, and I'll be there
Without you, too busy diving."

Out I slipped, past the scrum, less than a minute to the road and ten minutes to the ocean, in floral shorts from my trunk, plucked from an antler. The water was surprisingly warm. I enjoyed a meditative pace out to Rockefeller Island, then swam farther, pushing myself, locked in a rhythm despite the waves.

I swam for twenty minutes, chopping my way toward Cranberry, before realizing how far I'd gone. I was somewhere halfway between Sutton and East Bunker Ledge, but I knew that from the map in my head, not the green blobs on the horizon, each alike.

The water was freezing. I realized I was mostly numb. I floated on the chop, a white dot in a vast black pool.

And I'll be there
Without you, too busy diving.

Something brushed past my leg. I gasped and started to crawl back toward the beach.

Then I panicked. Part of me as witness, part the swimmer. As if I were able to watch a home movie of myself panicking: breakers crashing over the swimmer's head, swamping his mouth. I watched while he tried a side crawl, but after a few minutes his triceps ached. The water was so cold, his limbs were heavy. His teeth ached from clacking. The scissor-kick motion made no effective difference.

This was how his mother used to swim, the swimmer remembered, her head kept above water to avoid mussing her hair.

The swimmer couldn't tell if he was any closer to shore. He crawled and forced himself to go slowly. The internal propulsion that had brought him out was no longer in his body. He counted to three hundred Mississippi. He promised he would do three hundred more.

I'm closer, the swimmer thought, but by how much?

He started up again, stopped, lowered his head, and treaded water, now numb inside his lungs, his lungs like metal-mesh bags. Center of a rimless sea, center of everything. This is an emergency now, the swimmer told himself, thinking it would give him confidence, but it made things worse. He could die. He could die. He crawled another three hundred seconds, backstroked three hundred seconds, and stopped again, the panic sweeping through him in cold arresting surges.

Odd thoughts suggested shock settling in: that, true, Lucy's antioxidants could thrash some serious axonal curling, but it was a dreadful wasting of precious reserves, wasn't it? Wasn't there also a tragic demise to consider, of the world's most cultured, Chopin-listening, bow-tie-wearing neurons in those deli-thin hippocampal slices?

See how the perfect human rests.

How the perfect human lies down.

See how he falls.

The swimmer floated on his back. Floated like a dead man. He thought about Betsy Gardner, his dead wife's aunt, discovering his body rolled up onto her cottage lawn, a corpse in the herbaceous border shrubs—oh, it made him laugh, a high-pitched hysterical laugh! How he found himself hilarious! And Regina, what ridiculous things she'd said. *We forgot about love, yet I'm still brokenhearted about the Friday matinees.* He never claimed to understand poetry, but was that what people nowadays called a poem?

> *The ocean is black*
> *On the surface. Weird.*
> *Normally it's see-through.*
>
> *But so cold. Arctic. Glacial.*
> *Victor suspects his vision*
> *Is creeping in.*

I began kicking, heading for land, feeling the cold encasing my legs. I added strokes, counting to one hundred this time, and then rolled onto my stomach and paddled before rolling onto my back again, back and forth so as not to wear myself out, for what felt like an hour until I was close to shore and I could half crawl, half surf up a break of slimy rocks. I tried standing, fell, and slammed my forearms, and I was too weak to resist when the black water swept me out and I was funneled a dozen feet back into the surf.

> *The waves like they're*
> *Winter preparing to laugh,*
> *Breathing me in.*

I flung myself forward, staggering, then another wave knocked me over and raked my shin against a boulder. I tried twice more to make land. It seemed ridiculous that there it was in front of me, just twenty-five feet away, but I couldn't reach it, the break was too large and there were wooden towers to avoid. I vomited into the water. Another wave pushed me over. I tried to take a step but couldn't get traction. I crouched low underwater and clawed for rocks and began to pull myself to shore, hunched over, scratching my stomach on barnacles.

It wasn't my position to walk, the ocean instructed, mine was to crawl.

The swimmer vomited again when he was ashore. The shoreline was mainly rocks mottled with pink and black. Like Hunter's Beach, was his last thought before he passed out.

The sun was setting behind bluffs dotted with beach grass. A green lawn led up to a cedar-sided mansion with two wings. There was a flagpole, a children's play set, and a dock big enough for a yacht.

I swore I'd never swim again.

The wind rapped metal grommets against the flagpole. The mansion was dark and empty, with the patio furniture under canvas wraps. I unlatched a gate and limped up the road. Two driveways farther on was an Episcopal church whose hanging sign I recognized. It seemed a miracle that I'd come ashore only a half-mile from the beach where my car was parked.

Legs and hands and stomach and forearms were bleeding. I zombie-staggered down the road to the parking lot. Halfway home, I thought I was going to black out. When I arrived, a rusting green Saab was just leaving, driven by a shaggy-haired boy. It took me a moment to place him: the bartender from Blue Sea, the one with the necklace. He passed, deliberately not meeting my eyes.

Cornelia was watching television. The living room smelled of marijuana. I collapsed by the picture window and Cornelia shrieked.

"I'm fine."

"Oh my God, you're bleeding."

"Cornelia—"

"I'll call nine-one-one. You're covered in blood!"

"Cornelia, stop," I shouted, and stood up, grabbing the window frame for support. "Go to the bathroom. There's a first-aid kit under the sink. Bring that and a towel and the quilt from the bed. And get a cloth and some hot water."

Half an hour later, all was on the mend. My injuries were cleaned and dressed, I wore five layers of fleece, and Cornelia had turned on the gas fireplace and made me coffee. She left for the grocery store. Two hours later, I was awakened from a nap for dinner straight from Blue Sea's menu: fried oysters, a blue-cheese-and-pear salad, and risotto with bacon, asparagus, and mushrooms. Cornelia watched me eat and brought me coffee when I finished. We didn't talk. I felt her eyeing me. I guarded myself against giving any sign that she could open a line of questioning.

"So who was the young man I saw pulling out?"

Cornelia sighed. "That's Dan. He's the guy I was telling Betsy about." She added a second later, "I meant to tell you, Betsy called."

"What did she want?"

"She said she wanted you to call her back ASAP."

I laughed and noticed my voice was weirdly high-pitched.

"I'm sure she did."

"There's another thing." Cornelia sat down next to me with a plate of sliced apples and more coffee. "A woman stopped by for you."

"A woman?"

"Like my age or so. A gray Civic. She had dark hair. Pretty. Said to let you know that Ramona stopped by—"

"Regina?"

"Whatever. She asked where you were and then who I was—"

"What did you say?"

"What? I said I was your goddaughter. Why?"

"Sorry," I said, "I mean, where did you say I was?"

Cornelia started cleaning the kitchen. "I said I didn't know. I said I'd give you the message. I mean, so there's the message. Look, do you need anything else? If not, I need to go to work soon."

The bedroom was incredibly hot. I opened the windows and stripped off my sweaters. I had to change my bandages but couldn't get the new ones to stick properly, so I left them on the floor. I thought about calling for Cornelia, then remembered she was gone. I took two Ambien, lay naked on top of the comforter, and fell asleep.

When I awoke, the morning sun was hot, blazing through the bedroom windows. I must have slept fourteen hours. Somehow I'd gotten under the sheets. I felt jet-lagged. Cornelia was tanning in the backyard, wearing a white bikini and sunglasses, listening to her iPod. She was reading something.

"The phone's been ringing," Cornelia shouted, compensating for the music in her ears. I was standing in the doorway, shielding my eyes.

"What are you reading?"

"I found this inside. It's like the lost screenplay or something?" She was only a few pages in. She held up the cover page.

"Where did you find that?"

"What?" she shouted. She removed her headphones.

"Where did you find it?"

"Upstairs?"

"In my bedroom," I said.

She took off her sunglasses. "Dan checked on you last night. He said it was all over the floor, flung around the room. With your bandages. You were lying on the floor naked?"

"Okay," I said. I remained standing there in my underwear. Cornelia put her sunglasses back on.

"Look, I'll be honest, you're weirding me out, Victor. I think you should get dressed. You got a little tweaked yesterday. Like, see a doctor, maybe?"

"Cornelia," I said. I stood there another few seconds.

I went inside and watched her through the living room window. I made sandwiches and set them out on the kitchen island. An hour later, I was skimming through a magazine when Cornelia ran upstairs to her room. I called after her. She returned in her sweatshirt, jeans, and clogs, saying she'd forgotten she needed to be at work early.

I found Sara's screenplay in the grass. I ate my lunch beside it, still in my underwear, then went inside and brought out a bottle of wine.

This would probably be the fourth time I'd read it in three days. But I didn't remember reading it or flinging it about the night before.

It takes an hour to read a screenplay.

Now someone else knows, I thought.

Cornelia returned home at midnight. From the floor in my music room I could hear her and the bartender laughing in the breezeway. They sounded stoned. It was funny, Dan had a high-pitched voice, especially as opposed to Cornelia's tenor. They were speaking Dutch for all I understood. The music was lovely *Eroica*, eternity's music.

Cornelia appeared and turned down the volume.

"Why are you on the floor? Are you drunk?"

I held out the scotch bottle to make peace.

"How was work?"

"Uncle Victor, this is Dan."

"What's up," I said.

"What's up," he said.

"Tomorrow will work," I said. "Look, I found pants."

I got to a squatting position and went upstairs. Someone turned off Beethoven. I swallowed some Ambien and squatted over the toilet. My scalp needed buzzing, it was starting to prickle around the crown, so I got out the clippers. Then my eyelids clamped shut.

I undressed for bed and barely made it under the covers.

Later—a few hours, maybe—I woke up to noises from downstairs that sounded like someone smashing cymbals.

My eyelids felt like metal shutters as a result of the sleeping pills. I went out to the landing overlooking the living room. The house was dark, the walls were concave. I figured out the cymbals: the children were playing techno music loud enough to destroy my stereo. The bass was rattling the pottery. It made my organs vibrate.

"Will someone please turn it down," I screeched, with an old man's voice, and grasped my head. I cried again just as uselessly. I was too tired to stand. I tried kneeling by the railing, but on the way down I banged my knee and crumpled over, pain bursting through my head. I shouted this time without words, a guttural sound invoking the invisibles, an ululation.

The music stopped. Cornelia appeared in the living room, squinting up at the landing. I couldn't get my legs to work, but managed to haul myself to a sitting position. I grabbed the railing to keep from falling over backward.

"Jesus, what's wrong with you?"

They both wore hooded sweatshirts, Cornelia and her giant, like two druids peering up with metal-shutter faces.

Kneel to the victor, I thought, then I blacked out.

There was hardly any sunrise, just instant sun. Someone had tucked me in. The clock read seven-fifteen. After I yawned, I smelled rot off the back of my hand.

The children were naked, asleep on the pullout couch. Dan's mouth hung open and dripped saliva on a cushion. Cornelia lay on her back, her dreadlocks coiled under her head like a boat's docking line. Her breasts were petite, her nipples very dark, almost purple. A tattooed butterfly fluttered next to the left aureole.

I saw Sara's screenplay through the music room door.

Saw Sara arriving at LAX, saw her standing at the Hertz counter, saw her driving to West Hollywood, to the bungalow she'd found at the last minute. I saw the car dealerships on every corner and their huddles of repossessed Porsches. Saw the walled-off fortresses and the street-level billboards hawking stars. Saw Sara writing at someone else's desk, in someone else's house, harking back to Maine.

Twice I lost her, three times she left me: to California, to death, and now to this.

Dan's starfish necklace lay on the coffee table. I hung it around my neck. It was a real starfish, with a piece of hemp cord cinched around the middle. On the table was a wadded-up piece of Kleenex. I held it to my nose, smelling the used condom inside. Dan rustled in his sleep and adjusted his arm, like an oar reaching out over water. Cornelia responded, turning to spoon against him. One of them farted.

I dressed for work, grabbed my briefcase off the dining table, and tossed it in the trunk.

It clattered against the antlers.

Cornelia was snoring when I tiptoed back inside and delicately placed the rack above their heads. I collected the screenplay, drove down to the beach, and read the first thirty pages in my car.

The movie was a thriller that began with a dinner date: a single, childless writer in her forties living in Bar Harbor is set up by her best friend with a widowed doctor newly arrived to the island. He's perfect husband material, says the friend. Must be some reason he's still on the shelf, the writer says. Still, she shows up for dinner, and waiting at the bar is an older Bruce Willis type: handsome, tall, and quietly projecting confidence. He tells her about his work as an infectious disease specialist. He's funny, he's smart, he's self-deprecating. She can sense he's good in bed, and her research that evening proves her out. They fall in love and marry three months later at Otter Cliffs. In her toast, the writer thanks her friend for tracking down the perfect husband, and in coastal Maine, no less.

Unfortunately, the honeymoon's cut short a few weeks later when an oddball cousin the writer met at the wedding, the one her husband referred to as his family's black sheep, urges her to investigate the previous wife's death. Wasn't it odd, the cousin says, that she died from the same disease the doctor made his specialty?

I left the car unlocked.

The sky was pale. Down on the beach, the air was warm and tinged with wood smoke. The surface of the bay was perfectly flat out to the ocean. I swam at an even chop past Rockefeller Island, went another five minutes, stopped, and doggie-paddled. The clarity was exceptional. I took a deep breath, took another, and dived, striking the water, and released the air slowly as I pulled myself down, kicking for probably twenty feet until my lungs were empty and I stopped. I touched seaweed on the bottom, and the wildfire started. I focused my attention on listing the alphabet backward, though by the time I reached K, I couldn't continue. I thrust my hands into the seaweed to find rocks. I tried holding on to whatever my hands could grasp, pulling up plant stalks and fistfuls of muck, but I needed air—the inferno was burning my body inside out.

See the perfect human enter a park. He finds a peak to climb. He climbs for two years through winter blizzards, across rushing creeks in spring, an alpinist on an island full of humpbacked mountains, the summits mostly bare. A deserted island, but he prefers it that way, to be alone and unobserved. Mourning as the best way to meet nature, dust to dust. Perpetual mourning. Occasionally he hears sounds from town, the hum of cars like animals prowling around the base of a canyon, but he sees no one, not a single person on the trails.

The perfect human climbs. He never tires. He is ceaseless in his state, where it never occurs to him that it should be any different.

Why should it?

The bay was full of sailboats. The closest to me was a sixty-foot cruiser with a kelly-green hull. A ladder hung off the stern near a small American flag with thirteen stars. I pulled myself aboard. Near the bow was an anchor and some loose chain. On a cabin door was a padlock someone had forgotten to latch. I laughed and quickly made myself a belt.

My hands were shaking.

I cinched the chain around my waist and clicked the lock closed.

Then I grabbed the anchor and almost dropped it from shock. It was a decoration. I'd thought it might weigh two hundred pounds, but it was as heavy as a crowbar. As a flute.

I had to piss.

I pulled off my trunks and kicked them overboard, opened the cabin door, and pissed down the chute, waving my penis around, urinating everywhere.

Then it came back to me finally, the name of the movie Sara and I had seen that first night we met in New York: the fucking *Umbrellas of Cherbourg.*

Darling, it's The Umbrellas of Cherbourg, *a pleasant little French musical. There's not much fucking involved.*

Go away.

You just peed on someone's boat. You're naked with a starfish around your neck. Victor, you haven't had your coffee yet. Allow me to play Poirot: You thought a toy anchor would pin you down?

Spur-of-the-moment decision.

Please, you've been working on this for weeks. How many sleeping pills did you obtain? And yet you left them in the glove compartment. So you could soberly attempt to drown yourself in a cove that's twenty feet deep.

I was going to—

It's barely sunrise. You're standing on private property. You're trespassing, you're degenerating, but one thing you're not is suicidal. Nice belt.

I wasn't the one who refused to wear a seat belt.

Oh, don't say this is about me. This is melodrama. Except in developing countries, melodrama is never by accident.

Nice. Tell me about the screenplay.

What about it? You found it. Congratulations.

It's the fifth card, the fifth change in direction.

What? Says who?

Not only am I a workaholic, I'm capable of homicide?

Darling, slow the horses. First, it was a rough draft.

You and Bruce weren't able to get it into development in time.

You really think it's about you? About us?

You wrote it, you tell me.

Well, it's not autobiographical, I'll start with that.

Sara, why couldn't you pick up the phone?

Why didn't you come after me? You bought a ticket.

I apologized a hundred times.

You're constantly apologizing, Victor. After a while, it sounds more wistful than sorry.

What should I have done?

Darling, what do I say? You could have flown out, bought me a steak, and made some big macho scene. What do you want me to tell you? Do you remember our marriage at the time?

I called Mark. I found his number after I got into your computer. He has no idea.

Trust me, where I'm standing, this is public knowledge. So what?

I don't have to give it to anyone. I could delete it tonight.

Assuming you get off this boat. But fine, who cares? Victor, you're not listening. Even if I were alive, it wouldn't mean that much to me.

Don't give me that. A scientist in Bar Harbor, married to a writer—

Did it occur to you I might have had other motivations?

Try me.

Frankly, I was just happy to be working again. I went out there with this fantasy of me as David Lynch. You know, writing my art-house opus. Oh, I wrote allegories out the wazoo, but nothing worked. Even I got confused. Each scene was like an extracted dead tooth. Then one morning, when I merely contemplated writing a thriller, something straight Hollywood, suddenly I couldn't type fast enough. The pages wrote themselves.

Sara, I need to know.

What?

Was there someone else?

Victor, what do you think?

Did Russell go out to California?

Oh, darling, if he had, wouldn't that fit your reduction so neatly.

You were never vindictive.

Among a hundred things you've chosen to forget.

I remember you every day.

But your memories aren't true. The more you recall something, the more false it becomes, remember? You taught me that. What are the signs of Alzheimer's? Memory loss, disorientation, poor judgment, problems with abstract thinking—

Sara, how could you do it?

You sided against me. You wiped out an enormous reserve of trust that night. Imagine Cornelia when she wakes up, penned in by antlers. Though I'll admit that was charming, in a Russell-y sort of way.

Oh, and that's a good thing.

You know, after you introduced us way back when, I always did have a slight crush on Russell.

I don't believe it.

He's vulnerable. He's a mess. Girls go for that sort of thing, you know. We like to get our hands dirty.

I never cheated on you.

You think I did?

I don't know what to think.

Listen to me: Neither of us cheated. We were loyal to a fault. What a perfect union.

I always hated your sarcasm.

Hey, at least I was there. At least I fought for us. What did you do? The fact that you sat on your hands was why we almost did separate.

You don't know what it's like to be left behind.

Really? Years ago you loved me, I was everything to you, and then what happened?

You edited me out of my role.

Or you couldn't evolve within it.

I loved you.

And I you, darling. Now come on, cheer up, wave your penis around the boat again, show it off to the beachcombers. Maybe you can work up an erection for old times' sake. Though I heard that's not really your thing these days.

Go away.

Let's talk about Regina.

Sara, I can't do this.

Doctor-client privilege? What, she was your bereavement therapy?

You don't know her.

I know her poetry, at least it's better than Uncle Bill's. And you think you've got a clue? A dancer and her impotent audience, e-mails and midnight phone calls, that's a relationship?

So we should have been more status quo, then you'd approve.

You called it an affair because you liked sneaking around. Being kinky with no commitment. Deep down, you believed you were cheating on me.

That's a lie. The deception was hers, it was her wish from the start.

But you fell for it. I'm dead, Victor. You think it's easy being your belly dancer?
Poor girl, trying to figure out what you wanted, putting on a tough face—

She loves dancing.

She loves you, Victor. Or she did. I think she's over it by now, post windshield
therapy. But imagine, trying to please a man who wants you so badly he won't
sleep with you?

That's not fair.

What have you learned, Victor? What have you learned? For your clever
little questions, what answers have you found?

I've done my trials.

Please, you've been dating a Ziegfeld dancer. And when that got too heavy,
you imported a little girl as your nurse.

You left me. You left me here.

Of course. Me, Ben Lemery. Me, the best of your days, your fugitive, your
amorous new body.

How can you—

What, darling?

No one's perfect.

Says the man who never grieved.

That's insane. I have grieved more than anyone could possibly—

No, you haven't. It is the one thing you have not done. You're like that case
study. Me dying was your trauma, I was the hippocampus surgically removed
from your life and you've refused to deal with the present ever since.

You have no right.

Well, tell that to the police.

What?

There's a patrol car in the parking lot. Seriously. He's saying something over
the bullhorn.

He says I'm trespassing. He says I have to leave.

Maybe you should put on some shorts.

What should I do?

Get dressed? Victor, do what you want!

What if I don't know what I want?

Do you remember why we were going to Italy?

A fresh start.

A new ending.

Show me.

Why did I return home from California?

I don't know. I never knew.

Because I loved you.

You loved me.

Because what we'd done to each other wasn't due to a lack of love. The point, darling, of that screenplay is that you never know what lurks beneath people, even when they're perfect on paper. Well, we were different. We knew the depths of each other. It wasn't about us, because I didn't need it to be. I sat there at my desk thinking, our last act can still be written together.

How many times have you seen The Perfect Human *since I died?*

I don't know.

Liar, it's a fifteen-minute film, you count everything. How many times have you identified with the man in the box?

Twenty-three.

And did you kill Ben Lemery?

I don't know.

Again.

How am I supposed to know? How can I possibly?

Go back. You were a child, you were watching TV. Why should you have gotten up and gone over to his house?

But I knew what he was planning. I didn't tell anyone. I'm responsible.

Fine, but you've never taken responsibility, have you? You've held on to this virtue of being unsure, unable to trust your memories when instead of grieving and getting over it, you've squatted in the middle, clutching your precious relativity, and now you've cracked. Real life isn't relative, Victor, a chair is a fucking chair, we do things or we don't, and either way there's a cause. Did you kill him? Did you kill Ben?

No.

But when Cornelia brought her boyfriend home, weren't you jealous? When Russell called, weren't you afraid he'd reclaim your private chef, the daughter we never had?

You left me.

Like a dog, darling, you smelled her boyfriend off that tissue, the other male in your domain. And Russell, whom you despise—

What?

You hate everything about him, and still you're full of envy, for Russell's sins, for Cornelia's whimsy, for Regina's daring, for Lucy's awareness, for Betsy's tongue and Joel's addictions. For life, you hate them, yet you wish more than anything to be right there alongside.

Fine, it's true.

What you wanted from Regina and Cornelia, Victor, you wanted from spite. Against me for dying, just when you were being drawn back into life. So to drown, this would be your revenge against me, whom you hated, whom you hate.

Yes.

Then grieve, Victor. Grieve now.

Sara, everything I regret—

Grieve, Victor, for yourself.

But I don't know how.

five

Betsy's funeral was scheduled for a Wednesday morning, followed by a lunch buffet reception at Jordan Pond. The sunlight was white on the rocks, yellow on the water. Joel and I took the early ferry in together from Little Cranberry to Northeast Harbor, though we drove in separate cars from the parking lot: me in the Audi, Joel in Betsy's Cutlass Ciera because he'd recently bent the front axle of his Explorer on public property.

In the week before she died, when she overheard death making plans, Betsy told Joel and me exactly what she wanted for her memorial. More precisely, she let us know what she did not want: no obituary in the newspaper, no program announcement at a church.

"If any of the snobs want to miss me, they can put a plaque up at the polo club: Betsy Gardner was not a member."

To be cremated and have her ashes buried next to Bill's in the plot in Bar Harbor was Betsy's wish, and at graveside to have a short testimonial read by Joel, followed by a reception at Jordan Pond, with floral arrangements of mountain laurel and red sweet peas. Only family would be invited, and only the members she liked: Joel, me, Sara's sister, Miriam, and a few relatives from Bill's side I'd never met.

Miriam, who lived in Kansas City, sent us a foam cooler of frozen brisket. She said that she and her husband would come right away. She said she was glad to hear from me and hoped I was well, and that I might find a way to talk to God about my grief.

For the funeral I wore a green tie Betsy had once given me for Christmas, with a pattern of whales having sex. Already a small crowd of people was milling around the entrance. The cemetery was small, overlooking Bar Harbor, surrounded by a pine forest and wild ferns. Joel was nowhere to be seen, though we'd left the ferry parking lot at the same time.

The air was absolutely still. I was a little breathless when I arrived, my throat constricting. I couldn't get out of the car. My blood seemed to get slower by the second. I avoided looking through the windshield and turned up the radio, some man yelling at me about immigration.

I felt a hundred things flowing through me, with no sieve to catch them.

Miriam stepped away from a stout pair of old women in hats and came over, opened the car door, and hugged me around the waist once I was standing. She looked like Sara only in the nose and eyes, the rest of her was petite and round, but still it was Sara who was standing in front of me.

"I always run into you at funerals," Miriam said, and patted my chest with both hands.

I saw not Sara but Betsy in her face, I realized, which cheered me up, oddly. Miriam introduced me to her husband, a recent acquisition, Gary, the potbellied music instructor, a jazz saxophonist my age with a mustache, who nodded more than he spoke. Miriam was recounting a favorite story about Betsy when Joel arrived, parking Betsy's car at the bottom of the cemetery.

The fluorescent orange stripe on the driver's-side door was brightly visible in the sun.

Joel and I had spent a lot of time together in the preceding weeks. He was red faced and sweating, grizzled on the chin and jowls, wearing a wool blue blazer that didn't fit him, carrying a bouquet of lilacs. I met him halfway to the gate and he squeezed my biceps but wouldn't meet my eyes. He hitched up his khakis, passed me the flowers, and strode off to speak with the grave diggers, an old Mainer and a young Hispanic guy both wearing neckties tucked into their overalls.

We slowly gathered around the burial site. Joel greeted everyone. He started by reading from a piece of notepaper, "My mother was not a religious person. She did not believe in God. She did not believe in a lot of things. She'd be laughing at us right now. My mother was an idea woman. A political person. My mother loved conversation, though she was not much of a 'people person,' either."

Joel stopped and his head jerked, as if he'd just woken up. The woods were full of buzzing cicadas. Miriam reached out to take Joel's hand and began reciting the Lord's Prayer. A number of us joined in. When we finished, Miriam looked around warmly, her small eyes twinkling as though she did this every weekend, and made a brief speech about Betsy meeting Saint Peter, seeing the "No Smoking" sign, and attempting to turn her walker around, but God needed a bridge partner and hauled her back.

A woman to be remembered, said Miriam. A modern woman who knew the satisfaction of mental combat. A woman who loved Mount Desert Island. Loved people untrammeled by the fashions of the day, who were unafraid to appear foolish, and she let us know in her own particular way, never to be repeated, that she loved us.

Back at the cars, Miriam told her husband that she'd be driving me and Joel to the reception. We slid into the backseat. "You boys look terrible," Miriam said, staring in the rearview mirror. "You'd think somebody croaked."

It was the day after my boat incident that I'd moved out to Little Cranberry for what remained of the summer. I was lucky the Rockefellers decided not to press charges, had been Betsy's opinion, and the Bar Harbor police captain agreed. "You're luckier than most of them," he told me when I was released, and I assumed he was referring to the island's other flashers. "Family doesn't like the newspapers. Now, if it was up to me—"

He was the same officer who'd been called out to the scene, the one who responded after a grandfather Rockefeller reported a nudist on his sailboat. He and his grandchildren had been looking for hawks through a telescope, and spotted me instead.

The captain followed me out to my taxi. "Must be pretty high standards up there on campus." He was squinting at me, though it was dark outside.

Back at the beach, I got the pills out of the car and chucked them in a dumpster, along with the starfish. It was nine p.m. by the time I returned home. I found my front door locked and Sara's BMW gone. Inside, the living room was tidy, as if the maid had come through. I went up to Cornelia's room, expecting it to be empty, but her purple backpack was still in the corner.

I sat on her bed and massaged my legs. I was sweating through my clothes. I had no idea what the right thing was to do, just probably the opposite of whatever my gut said, considering how well it had guided me recently.

A rock roach crawled in from under the door.

I packed a bag and drove straight to the Cranberry ferry. The lot was deserted. I parked and cut the engine and prepared to wait for the next boat, a seven-hour wait. A motel up the road was open, the occasional minivan buzzing around; otherwise the area was dark and empty.

I rolled down the windows. The air was cold and salty. My scalp tingled.

And what Sara said came back to me slowly. There in jail, there sitting on Cornelia's bed, it had been with me all day, but I couldn't see her. I tried to see her and closed my eyes, but my memories were whitewashed. I tried to sleep with the driver's seat cranked flat, but mostly I cried. I called her under my breath and remembered her shoe size. Her long fingers. I remembered when I held the box with Sara's ashes over a stream near the house, how long the moment lasted until I tipped it over and then how quickly it was done. I remembered how happiness on her face was a look of sharing. How much I loved her. I remembered with painful clarity, with the words piped into the car, the moment when I'd asked Sara what she knew about writing screenplays.

I sensed people watching me from inside their rooms. Peering through binoculars. Through the windshield, it was as if the motel's orange lights kept exploding. Memories rose from their soil beds and passed me, trailing wisps, axons that wouldn't connect to any greater whole, and dissipated in the air around the car.

The air was so salty I could feel it on my teeth.

After the boat docked at Islesford, I called Betsy's house twice from the ferry manager's office, but no one answered. The Islesford harbor resembled Northeast's, though it was smaller, more industrial, less layman-friendly. Fishermen at that hour were few, either hanging around on the long piers or cleaning gear. A wall of rigid, bristling trees in front of me was gauzy with fog.

I bought a grilled cheese sandwich at the harbor grill. After I said I was Betsy Gardner's nephew, the bartender said of course he knew her, she insulted his food regularly. He gave me vague directions, and after a long walk, I was standing outside the cottage. It was perched on the coastline, gray-shingled, rotted by the sea air and winter sleet, gradually collapsing. There weren't any neighbors. The front door was unlocked. The house inside smelled like Cape Near, of old birch shelves and ocean air and cigarettes, and newspapers in sheaves growing mold. The quiet was deeper than I'd ever before experienced. I spent the day reading an Agatha Christie novel in Betsy's living room, and then exploring when I couldn't sit still. The refrigerator was empty. For dinner, I found two cans of tuna fish and ate them while I studied Betsy's map of White House conspiracies. I couldn't make any sense of it. Clusters of cabinet members drawn by arrows to subcommittees and names of corporations, as if someone had fired Post-it notes from a shotgun.

A paper trail she couldn't stop adding to, I thought.

I slept on a cot I found stored away in the basement, woke at dawn to the summer light, and lay there for three hours, studying the sky through the small window, hearing the wind drag tree boughs across the roof.

Betsy pulled in at lunch and parked her golf cart on the lawn. She didn't seem surprised to see me, but was pale and shaky, smaller than usual in khaki shorts, a Shetland sweater, and a yellow slicker that reached down past her knees. Her legs underneath were thin as broomsticks. At arm's length, peering up through her glasses under the beach hat, she wanted to know if I'd come to fix her roof. I said, How else would you get me out here? She harrumphed and squared me in the eye, then told me where to find the ladder.

"I heard about the boat," she said, leaving it at that.

The temperature dropped quickly after dark. We drank a bottle of wine before getting to dinner, except Betsy only kept tuna in the house and I'd finished the tuna, so we opened a second bottle of wine and put on additional sweaters. She told me between cigarettes where she'd been, up at the hospital in Bangor. They'd made her stay over the previous four nights. The cancer they'd removed years ago during the mastectomy had returned, metastasized into a dozen lymph nodes on her right breast. The voice mails I'd ignored at the house had asked me to drive her up to the hospital, but since I never called back, she'd phoned Joel.

"I'm very disappointed in you, Victor." She let it hover in the air. "Why don't you get a goddamn cell phone? Even I have one."

"Maybe I will."

"Truth is, it's to my benefit you're so selfish. Joel and I had some conversation. It's a long drive. I like him."

"People change."

"Well, some can't," she snapped. "I'm dying, Victor. This time it will work. I'm very depressed, I don't know that you'd care."

A moment later, I said, "I can't lose you."

We remained seated. Betsy carefully stubbed out her cigarette.

In the morning, I wandered out through the fog to the shed. The roof truly was in rotten condition. A third of the shingles had come undone and the rest looked ready to fall off in the next storm. I worked steadily at removing the bad ones and patching a number of small holes. I'd done some roofing one summer during school, and it looked as if Betsy's roof dated to about the same period. Betsy weeded below me while I worked, and then went in for a nap. In town by the docks, I inquired at the market where I could buy proper supplies, and the proprietress put me on the phone with a hardware store in Northeast Harbor. They said they'd have them for me on the ferry the next morning.

The roof took an additional four days. At lunch, Betsy brought out tuna sandwiches and yelled at me not to fall. She wasn't sure, she said, if her accident insurance covered people who were naturally unfit for labor.

At night, I read Agatha Christie novels aloud to Betsy until she nodded off, then I'd stay up listening to country music or talk radio, whatever I could dial in for company. I didn't sleep much myself. I'd packed a fresh copy of Sara's screenplay, and I forced myself to read it again. I asked Betsy on the fifth night if it would be okay if I stayed another week. In the backyard there was a hammock strung between two locust trees. "You look just like Uncle Bill," Betsy said one afternoon when I was lying out there, reading the screenplay, and she went in and got her cane just to come visit and hold my hand for a minute.

One morning I unpacked a number of science journals I'd thrown in my duffel bag, and out fell the Gardner genealogy. I'd forgotten I'd packed it. I picked it up and went and found Betsy, watching television in her room.

"This book isn't very current," I said.

"Dear, you're saying I'm out of date?"

"Your generation is barely mentioned."

"Well, Father *was* an admiral. You don't reach that level in the Navy thinking about your children."

I saw a deer the next day in Betsy's front yard and named him

Bananas. Twice I telephoned Cornelia, but couldn't reach her. I left messages at the house, letting her know where I was and how to put out the recycling. I apologized about my strange behavior. As for work, after lunch one day, I requested a sabbatical over the phone while sitting in Betsy's living room, shuffling a deck of Uno cards. Given rumors about what had happened in Seal Harbor, Soborg had no problem if I wanted a little personal time away from campus.

Lucy was less accommodating when I called her afterward to cede control.

"I don't understand. What's happening?"

"I need some time to myself," I said. "Time to think."

"Think about what? About the *Nature* paper?"

I explained that I'd phoned the editors and requested they remove me as principal investigator and give her the primary authorship. She said that made it even worse.

"I've never been a producer for the Victor Aaron show."

"Lucy, I know."

"Honestly, until recently I didn't think you saw me that way."

"I didn't," I said. "I don't."

"Who gave you the right anyway to go off the reservation and make a decision like that? Since when do I need top billing? That's what you think I care about?"

"I'm sorry, Lucy."

"If you want to retire, if you're giving up, then let me know that. We'll work out a schedule and I'll figure out how to get the hell back to New York. But at least show me the courtesy, after all these years, to include me in the decision."

"I understand."

"You do? Don't you see how once again you've shut me out?"

The next morning, I called Lucy back and she was willing to talk, but only because she had in her hand that day's *Bar Harbor Times*. Apparently I'd made the news. Lucy read aloud from the police blotter describing one local resident, Dr. Victor Aaron of Somesville, as "a public nuisance," having trespassed on "the deck of a prominent Seal Harbor family's Sou'wester, nude."

Some Soborg PR representative had managed to keep my title at the lab from making the news, but otherwise the details were correct: the bike chain, the "public urination." Hearing Lucy laugh, I was filled with pride. I'd officially been made a local, and all it took was pissing off the right people, or on them. And then the humiliation sank in.

Everyone I knew would see this. It would appear on the Internet, be e-mailed through chains of colleagues, be republished on listservs. What would the National Institutes of Health think of my state of mind the next time I applied for a grant? Was my tenure really so secure? What about my reputation?

Before we hung up, I asked, "What about Deke?"

A long pause. "I don't want to talk about that."

"Lucy," I said, "I really am sorry."

"So am I," she said.

I couldn't sleep. Betsy's spirits checked in and out. For a full day she wouldn't talk to me after I'd made fun of Andy Rooney's twitching hands. Several times she went with Joel to see her doctors and came back angrier, more resolved not to seek treatment. But she had her sprightly moments. So impressed was Betsy by my escapade that she cut out the police blotter and had a print shop in Northeast Harbor enlarge and frame it so that she could hang my prize above the toilet.

"I always knew you had it in you," she said.

After considering it for days, I called Mark, Sara's agent. I told him about *The Perfect Husband*. I promised to put my copy on the mail boat first thing. He was over the moon.

"Best thing she ever wrote," I said.

"I can't wait," he said.

"How's Mother?" Joel asked.

"Today, pretty cheerful, actually."

"Not her mood, her health, Victor, how does she seem?"

"She's like she's been. It's a good week. She talks about you all the time."

"Well, we've got a private party practically every night, I don't need anything more shoveled onto my plate right now."

"Joel, I didn't mean—"

"Forget it. Sorry. This is tearing me up. Tell her I'll come out soon. Tell her that."

"I will."

Two more weeks of foggy mornings passed on Cranberry, evenings lost drinking and playing cards with Betsy, betting on who'd pay for the wine the next morning. I didn't know where I was or what I was doing. The evening in the ferry parking lot seemed like months before. I missed work, though. I missed knowing what I'd accomplished between one point and the next.

One Wednesday evening, we attended a potluck supper at St. Mark's of Islesford. We made cocktails and spent an hour getting ready. I found an old tie of Uncle Bill's and Betsy decorated the brim of her gardening hat with daffodils. We were drunk by the time we arrived in the golf cart. The white chapel with the pea-green steeple was bursting, maybe forty people milling around folding tables in the yard. Betsy hobbled off to catch up with friends, and I wound up in conversation with a short woman in a flapping rain poncho and the kind of glasses they gave out free at the optometrist's. She looked like a welder on a camping trip.

"You're new around here."

"I was married to Betsy's niece."

"The girl who died in the car accident."

"That's right."

"Sara, she was a duck on the field hockey team, back when. Well, all are welcome."

"Thank you. The food's delicious."

"Am I religious?"

"I'm sorry?"

"Well, are you? You go to church?"

"Oh, no."

"No. Who does these days?"

I snuck inside to look around. Behind the hall was a small, pine-paneled sacristy with an altar and a coatrack supporting vestments. No one was around. With creaking joints I knelt on the prayer bench and felt the symptoms of an episode start and dissipate. No tears, but I was woozy. Got up for some fresh air and stumbled into a conversation between the welder and the elderly parish priest outside. I apologized for interrupting them. The priest gripped my hand, a powerfully strong grip. He said I could call him Ken. He looked like a retired Elvis: white pompadour, muttonchop sideburns, and a thick sunburned neck. He invited me to stop by some time for a tour. I said I'd be sure to do that.

Lucy called late that night. It was two in the morning and she was still in the lab. She'd been entertaining visitors, Brian and Trinny Fowler, a wealthy Boston couple looking to sponsor some research. Occasionally rich people would call us up, seeing a donation to science as a component of their philanthropy. Mr. Fowler, Lucy informed me, had made his fortune building a microchip company, and Mrs. Fowler had spent most of it on face-lifts.

"Like someone Saran Wrapped her face. Why these women do these things, Victor. But his mother had dementia, and he's worried about his grandchildren. Anyway, I gave them the tour. They'd never seen a mouse room before. The wife asked if I was normally there at night, 'among the rats.' I said yes, that I usually worked late, and I tried explaining how we do not actually go into the mouse rooms at night so as not to disturb them, but then she interrupted me, she said, 'Well, it doesn't seem like much of a life for a lady.'"

A pause. "They said they'd send a check next month. Otherwise I could have killed her." A longer pause. "You know Deke called last night."

"Really?"

"He calls during downtime. He'll probably call in five minutes."

"What does he say?"

"He talks about patients. It's all slapstick." She laughed wearily. "They fist-bump instead of shaking hands, to avoid germs. Logical, right?"

"We should try that."

"Then he says—this is last night—that every time something crazy happens, he makes a note on his Palm Pilot to tell me about it later. He has a file going back to last winter."

"To when he proposed."

Lucy stopped. I could hear that she wanted to tell me more. Maybe I wouldn't have heard that before.

"He says he misses me. That he still loves me. I just don't under-stand people sometimes." Her voice was shaky. "It's like, I'm on this side of the river and everyone else is over there."

"Lucy, if you love him, you know it," I said. I wished I had more to give. "Do you love him?"

"Yes."

"I'm on your side, Lucy," I said.

Without my work, without the lab, systems slowed down. I felt paler. I knew I was losing weight. I stopped at the church one after-noon on my way to meeting Betsy for lunch, and Ken the priest was cutting grass in hiking shorts, no shirt. He was fit, tan, and freckled. His pompadour magically stood aloft. He invited me in for iced tea. He explained how he and his wife, Dorothy, lived on Little Cranberry in the summers, but during the year they looked after a small parish in New Hampshire, where his wife's family came from, in Warren. I asked them what they did at night on the island.

"Mostly watch television. My wife has a thing for the police shows."

"Which ones?"

"Doesn't much matter. You know there's one, someone's always abducted at the beginning, then the FBI track them down in fifty-nine minutes, minus commercials."

We both laughed. "They always get their man?"

"Sometimes it's a woman. Now they messed up one episode. A little girl, they didn't find her, that's what Dot said. Personally, I couldn't watch it, I had to leave the room. Put a child in a situation like that on TV, I don't have the stomach for it."

"Do you have children?"

He looked at me for a moment, then nodded. "Three. Three daugh-ters, four grandchildren. Scattered like seeds. They're out west, Wyoming mostly, we don't see them as much as we'd like."

"You ever worry one would be kidnapped when they were kids?" Ken paused. "Tell me, where's this going?"

"I don't know," I said truthfully.

"Well, every parent does, imagines a scenario like that. You don't have children? We had a panic one year. Beautiful girl, cheerleader, abducted outside the mall. Kind of story you don't forget. She's kidnapped, missing for weeks, then they find her strangled up near Winnipesaukee. Hard to talk about now. See, we were advised to make home movies of our kids so they could be shown on the news, that was when the shock really hit, the realization that it could happen to us. We took Julia, our youngest, she's now got two girls of her own, we took her down to the park in town. I remember I bought a camera specially for it."

"Have you ever watched it again?"

"You know what's funny, I've scavenged for that tape a hundred times. I wanted to show it to my granddaughters, so they'd have proof their mother was a little girl once, too. But I can't find it for the life of me."

In the July/August issue of *Neuroscience Report*, scientists at the University of Arizona reported employing light-sensitive genes (which were in themselves a marvel: genes that actually could be controlled as easily as light switches) to aid spinal-cord injuries. Using rat models, they'd partly severed the rats' spinal cords at the second vertebra so that messages couldn't pass very easily from the brain to the lungs.

Cornelia no doubt was outside those scientists' offices that very moment, with a megaphone and a rocket-propelled grenade.

The rats then had trouble breathing because the lungs weren't receiving proper instructions, so the scientists injected a protein, channelrhodopsin-2, or ChR2, just below the injury spot. They knew ChR2 would make the correct neurons fire to cause the rats' lungs to resume pumping, but ChR2 also happened to be light-sensitive. Shine a very, very small flashlight on it, and it got to work. A few days later, and after figuring out exactly when and how frequently to switch on the lights, tests found that the rats' diaphragms were working properly again. The blood was plenty oxygenated. And after the flashlight was turned off, the rats' breathing continued normally for thirty-six hours.

The implications, sitting there on Betsy's couch, were wild enough to strike me naive. An on/off switch for respiratory function? For anyone with a comparable spinal-cord injury, the idea that someday they could use a miniature flashbulb instead of a respirator would have to be pretty thrilling. Extensions became fresh and green in my imagination. Why not control pain by a switch, why not impotence, why not memory loss?

I phoned Cornelia at the restaurant the next afternoon.

"So what's today's special?"

"Oh my God," she said, "this grilled halibut for the past three days. It's easy, but people are going nuts. I'm subbing on the grill station, so it's like 'Ordering two "buts,"' 'Ordering four "buts,"' all night long. I've been in the weeds all week."

"You still like it?"

"You know, kind of. There are complicating factors, as they say."

"As who says?"

"Forget it. What's up?"

I took a deep breath. "I wanted to apologize, Cornelia."

"Over the phone. Okay."

"For what I did. For how I behaved."

"So it's, like, you're the kid, I'm the parent."

I laughed. "Sort of."

"Well, all right, but—"

She stopped. I tried to hear what I should say next. Mostly there were restaurant sounds, men yelling in Spanish.

"But what?"

"Well, seriously, what were you thinking?"

"I'm sorry, Cornelia."

"I know, but why do all that?"

"I don't know. The important thing is that it had nothing to do with you. It was my own fault, my own issues."

"Well, I mean that's reassuring, or completely *not*. Honestly, Victor? It was fucked-up. Dan and me were totally freaked out. He said you took his necklace?"

"Yes."

"Well, he doesn't want it back. We're actually not talking right now so much, but whatever, that's like a whole other subject."

"I'm sorry, Cornelia. I was pretty messed up. I've *been* messed up, I think. I'd like to say I don't remember what happened, but I do."

"Yeah, well, I saw the newspaper. Everyone's seen it. Joel has it framed above the bar. It's like the only thing anyone's talking about around here. You're totally famous now, you know."

She told me Joel had offered her a full-time position at Blue Sea through the fall, and she would probably accept. I congratulated her. I said I thought I'd be living on Cranberry for the foreseeable future, at least through my sabbatical, so she could stay in the house as long as she wanted. I told her Dan could live there, too, if she liked, assuming it was okay with her parents.

She asked me if I'd heard her when she said they weren't talking anymore.

She said she was worried about me. She said she'd asked Joel to look out for me, and that Joel had told her I was fine, that Betsy would kick my ass if I stepped out of line.

On CNN one evening, a woman in small-town New Mexico was interviewed about seeing a "ghost car" rip through town. Numerous residents had seen it, an old maroon Charger running on horses loud enough to wake the dead, drag-racing the main strip and through subdivisions, knocking over mailboxes, killing a dog. And never with a driver behind the wheel. There was video from a bank's outdoor camera, but when the news segment zoomed in on the footage, the pixels showed no driver. Police twice had set up roadblocks, but hadn't caught the beast. "The Headless Hoodlum," the local media called it, and eyewitnesses had every possible theory: Navajo witchcraft; a remote-controlled vehicle from Area 51; teenagers crouching down with jury-rigged mirrors; an immigration scheme piloted by Mexican dwarves. People wanted the mystery solved. They wanted the truth. Mainly, they worried their dogs could be run over.

I turned off the television and thought about Regina, as though the TV's glow were a catalyst, and my on-switch responded: Regina projected into my thoughts and around the room, and me breathing quickly.

I couldn't contact her. I couldn't *picture* contacting her. Knowing she must have seen the police report, my humiliation was too specific. Regina believing that whoever this lunatic had become, this monster, he'd been in her bed for months, preparing for his big day.

So she'd wonder, Was I involved in that degeneration? Was I responsible somehow?

They were selfish thoughts.

Much worse, she'd think, what does it say about me that here's the man I brought home, being arrested for such behavior?

I brushed my teeth and remembered Regina's brother, her fifteen other lovers, her professional accomplishments, and her age. My ego was still exaggerating. The true chagrin was more depressing: that she'd picked a bad apple. She'd pick a better one next time, and when Regina remembered me years later it would be for pissing in public.

As would many around the island, I thought. People who knew my name or face would feel that they'd uncovered the truth, that the ghost car's driver was merely defective.

Lucy informed me over the phone that the news hadn't spread very far. Turned out the *Bar Harbor Times* didn't publish its police reports online. My indiscretion would be fodder for puppy cages for a few more weeks, and then would be gone.

But still alive in memories, I thought. Ones people wouldn't be quick to let go.

I needed more to do than read science journals and watch television. Being away from work was making my skin crawl. If I was going to rot, at least I could be productive.

In youth, you're judged for talent. In middle age, for how much you've produced. Later years, for endurance, for stick-to-itiveness when the sky's darkening. That, at least, was a quality I'd never lacked.

I sat Betsy in the living room for an hour after lunch, switched on an old tape recorder, and got her running. She didn't ask what it was for. Perhaps she'd been hoping someone would do this, finally her date with Charlie Rose. Over two days, I arranged twice more for interviews, going slowly so as not to tire her out. We talked about the Bar

Harbor debutante season, her coed years, her travel to Japan and Chile after the war for Bill's engineering projects. When Betsy finally asked what it was all for ("You're not blackmailing me, are you, Victor?"), I declined to say much, excused myself, and snuck away to the study upstairs, and opened the admiral's book.

The final chapter, I decided, would be recorded if not artfully, at least accurately, and slid in on loose-leaf.

But it was Joel, not Betsy, whom I spoke with most, and not about genealogy. We were constantly in touch about Betsy's health, her insurance coverage, her preferred doctors, her radiology appointments. We'd talk late at night once Betsy was asleep and the last dinner service at Blue Sea was finished, and after a few conversations we started to talk less about Betsy and more about ourselves. Joel must have started it. Perhaps he had no one else to confide in, or he figured that with my recent scandal, I wasn't one to judge. There were problems at the restaurant, new menus to nail down, staffing issues to fix, tax headaches that never eased. The burden of his addictions and trying to get to AA meetings on a steady basis. A proposal from well-heeled regulars to open a second Blue Sea in Bar Harbor kept him awake at night out of fear that his headaches would double. His girlfriend had recently dumped him.

"I told her, 'I've been straight with you from the beginning, I'm not the marrying kind.' Jill said, if that restaurant's not a wife, I've never seen one."

Our conversations weren't unlike talks I'd had with Russell, but I found myself saying more, thinking or holding back less. I told Joel the whole story of what had happened on the boat. Eventually I told him about the antlers and Cornelia and Dan. "You are one perverted old man," he said, but he laughed as he said it.

I told him about Sara's visitation and my efforts to resummon her, and he didn't laugh. He didn't say anything at all.

One night Joel called with bad news: his sponsor in AA, the man who had gotten him sober in the first place, a surrogate father figure named Michael who was a retired pilot for Colgan Air, had gone into the hospital with a malignant glioma, a brain tumor.

"Lucky me, he had the sense to go up to Bangor for evaluation. So I see Mom in the morning, Mike afternoons. Small miracles, right?"

But Betsy remained our primary topic, our central concern. She'd started to slur her speech. In the span of two weeks, between me and Joel, we drove her to Eastern Maine Medical five times because she refused to stay overnight for observation. Several opinions we sought out concurred: the prognosis was grim. Betsy took it, though, as if someone were giving her a repair estimate on her car, one she could whittle down with negotiations. The small summer library on Cranberry had an Internet terminal, and once I'd shown Betsy how to use it, she began printing off reams of white papers for her appointments, equipping herself so that she could grandstand the doctors and expose their ignorance when it showed.

"Honestly, she's grinding me down," Joel said over the phone. "You know what? I'm losing the will to compete with her. I wouldn't bet on ten Marines against Mom right now."

Betsy made a show of trying to smoke in the hospital waiting room.

None of us was strong enough, Betsy least of all. After the fifth trip to Bangor, she informed Joel she would never leave Little Cranberry again. Chemo would be too painful to redo. It was indescribable, she said, an inhuman procedure. Joel replied, in that case he'd move out to

Cranberry, too, at least come out during the day and take the ferry back for the dinner service. I told him I thought this was a terrific idea.

"Yeah, well," he said, "I wasn't looking for your okay."

"Joel, I realize that," I said.

The first day he came out, he showed up on Jake's golf cart, Jake the owner of the harbor grill, affable but haughty. We'd never become friendly despite how many grilled cheese sandwiches I'd ordered, but Jake and Joel were laughing like brothers. When Betsy went out, the three of them may as well have been a family posing by the mailbox for a Christmas card.

"Victor, what's up," Joel said, going by me through the doorway.

He spent his days at the house helping Betsy plant a vegetable garden, the two of them hoeing and smoking side by side.

"You're raking all wrong. Who taught you how to garden?"

"Mom, I do this for a living."

"You do what for a living? You cook dirt?"

"You remember when I was out in California?"

"You were out of it in California. Drugging, whoring, what have you."

"Actually, I was in charge of the restaurant garden. That was four times this size, easy. Dozens of tomatoes, fruit trees, good soil, too, none of this rocky shit—"

"Joel, watch your mouth."

The more time we spent together, though, the better we got along, both me and Joel and us as a threesome: preparing lunch, arguing about Iraq. Joel was a studied neoconservative, an Internet addict in his free time. Betsy would attack his positions while he tried to explain to us what a blog was. After the first week, though, Joel withdrew: ignoring the garden, arguing with either of us over nothing as important as politics, shouting in Spanish over the phone at his cooks, disappearing for a day or two with no word to me or Betsy as to where he'd gone.

One Wednesday afternoon, driving Joel down to the dock in the golf cart, I told him it was silly that he ride the ferry back each time.

"Sure, look at the two of you, like you need company."

"What are you talking about?"

"What?" He wiped his hand down his face. "You're the son here, we both know it. Excuse me, the favored son."

"That's not true."

Joel laughed bitterly. "Hey, listen, not that I don't appreciate it. Trust me."

I asked Betsy that night if she thought Joel was drinking again. She said she assumed so, there'd been liquor in the air one morning but she hadn't mentioned it, fearing she was just smelling her own breath.

Our suspicions were confirmed by a phone call a few days later from the police, after Joel had parked his Explorer on top of a bench in Northeast Harbor. The police captain there was an old friend of Betsy's and he'd let Joel off with a warning, presuming he spent the night at Betsy's house and also replaced the bench.

I took the ferry over in the morning. Joel got in the car, fetid and blotchy. He slammed the door and fixed his sunglasses on his nose, a pair of gold Gucci wraparounds some customer had left behind at Blue Sea. "So Mike died, if you're curious," he said, flipping down the visor for the mirror.

"Your sponsor?"

He stared straight ahead down the street.

"Can we just go?"

"Joel, I'm sorry," I said.

When we reached the house, Betsy was standing in the doorway.

"Ooh, pretty glasses. Some girlfriend buy you those?"

Joel didn't reply, just went inside and around the corner.

"Well, you look like a girl," Betsy yelled. "Maybe you can pick up one of these lesbians around here."

That night I moved out of the guest bedroom and went down to the basement cot.

Incorporating Betsy's history into the family genealogy didn't begin well. Grant proposals I knew, not family stories. But I wouldn't give up. One morning while I was at my laptop, Joel and Betsy were outside arguing over repairs to the storm doors, and I picked up the phone. I didn't hesitate. I called Regina's lab, her director picked up, and I asked to be patched through. The conversation lasted thirty seconds. We made a date to meet a few days later.

"So it's true what I saw in the paper?"

"Yes. Regrettably."

"Well, that's insane," Regina said. Her voice sounded shaky. "I know what crazy looks like, either this is a good facsimile—"

"I will explain everything. As much as I can."

She was quiet. "Fine. But you don't get to call me again afterward."

The next day, I had an accident in church. I'd started going, partly to see Ken for conversation, mainly because it was a quiet place to think. One moment I was kneeling fine, but when I tried to stand up, I fell over.

Afterward, when I was forced to call out for help, I had a fight with Ken about going to see a doctor.

"I'm a regular forty-seven-year-old."

"You're a pain in the ass."

"I thought you were a man of God."

"Take up swimming, how about," he said. "Works wonders for the elderly. Get yourself some water wings."

Regina met me, as scheduled, at the ferry landing Thursday afternoon. The dock in Northeast Harbor was full of people squinting from the sunlight, waiting to go out to the smaller islands with cardboard grocery boxes between their feet.

Regina was sitting in her car with the engine running. Her hair was pulled back in a ponytail, hidden under a baseball cap. She wore blue jeans and a ribbed yellow tank top and flip-flops, the backs of which were caught in the cuffs of her pants.

She smiled without pleasure as I got in the car.

"So, status report. Catch me up. Do we go to the beach?"

"How about just a drive," I said.

"Look, let's get this out of the way. I am here to satisfy my curiosity. I will not be dragged back."

The light turned green. She focused on driving.

"Regina," I said, "I am ashamed about my behavior. About a lot of things. This isn't easy."

"Like it is for me?"

It was a sunny summer morning. We were just another couple out for a weekend drive, going to check out a yard sale with our coffee tumblers in the cup holders.

"I'm not sorry about the antlers," Regina said.

I added hastily, "I would not expect you to be."

She laughed. I noticed that her hair was wet, as if she'd just gotten out of the shower.

"I mean that you don't have cause to be sorry. I'm sorry that I hurt you."

"You're sorry you hurt me how? By fleeing my reading? The time you ripped a poster off my wall?"

"None of it was your fault."

The wind died down as she turned off the main road onto Sargent Drive. We drove through the woods, coming out into sunshine.

"Well, that wasn't something I was considering. I'm just shocked to see you. Driving with a public nuisance. I mean, I just want to be filled in, then I'll drop you off."

"You saw the newspaper."

"I told you on the phone."

"Well," I said, "the story's pretty much all there."

"And now you're out on Cranberry, lying low."

I was sweating through my undershirt. Her car was too small for me, forcing me to bend my legs so that my knees rested on the door, but I didn't want to reach down and adjust the seat. We quickly went around a turn and I put a hand on Regina's shoulder for balance and she jolted away.

"What are you doing?"

"Sorry—"

"Look, I'm pulling over."

Regina got out, but left the engine running. The inlet the road over-looked, Somes Sound, was supposedly the East Coast's only fjord. Sara had told me that, adding it could be just a rumor, some island lore. A local legend. The road there was meandering and narrow, hugging the sea cliff like an Italian route for testing Ferraris.

The day we got our new cars, Sara and I had raced from one end of the road to the other, at one point driving side by side, death defying. Sara won, not wearing her seat belt.

"I heard about your swim, you know. The one after my reading."

"How?"

"Your goddaughter. The girl who works at Blue Sea. The other night I was eating there, she remembered me from the time I stopped by your house. She told me all about it. The day a poem almost drowned you." Regina laughed. "She said she thought I'd want to know since we were colleagues, that you were staying out on Cranberry until the coast was clear. Since we were colleagues."

There was a long silence. Regina took off her the cap and threw it into the car through the window. My embarrassment forced me to stare at Regina's face. She was dignified, I was a mess. I leaned against a wooden barrier, and she sat looking up at me from a large, flat rock, blinking while she redid her ponytail with two hands, her elbows fanned out.

I said, "I haven't been myself in a long time."

"Since before we met."

"Probably."

She nodded, staring out. "Part of me knew all along."

"Regina, I didn't realize."

"I happen to really hate dishonesty, you know? What a waste, when the other person is lying. What a waste for them."

"When I said I cared about you, I wasn't lying."

She looked up at me. "Why say that?"

"What?"

"Will you listen to yourself? It's, like, Alzheimer's of the emotions. You know what, forget this."

Regina got in the car. I followed.

"I think studies find that people, in general, are naturally suggestible," she said. "You know, at work, in court. All it takes is a leading question from the opposition, suddenly they're astray. We're so busy searching, we don't stop and see."

I said a moment later, "I think you're right."

She laughed under her breath. "See, with you I was so busy trying to analyze what we were, I never actually looked. It's like, bodies are complicated, not people. We get brain scans, we go to therapists, we try to pin things down. But finally, when we come up for air? We forget the water was only two inches deep."

"You're saying we're superficial."

Regina stared at me. One of her hands was on the emergency brake. "Your wife died. With me, you got easy sex cheap. When I started wanting more, you panicked. The end. My bad."

"You know, Lindsay had you pegged exactly right," Regina said, shifting into reverse, "you're just this little boy."

We drove back to Northeast Harbor. Traffic accumulated by the mile, first one car in front of us and another, then two behind us, until we were a wagon train of sedans going west at twenty miles an hour.

"Regina," I blurted out, "I did care about you. I still do."

"Oh my God, just stop."

The light before the harbor was notoriously slow to change. Regina stared up through the windshield. I clasped my hands and pushed my toes against the floor, thrusting myself back hard against the seat.

Regina reached around, grabbed a book, and dropped it in my lap. "You don't call me," she said. "I won't call you."

When the light turned green, she drove down to the ferry and out the loop for exiting cars.

After a fashion, I was back to my old ways: I worked morning, noon, and night documenting Betsy's life. Cognitive-functionally, I clocked maybe a seven out of ten. One afternoon, Joel came down the basement stairs. He was sweating, pink from too much sun, growing a beard and gaining weight. He smelled like booze. He asked what I was doing. I played him some of what I'd recorded that morning with Betsy, her describing how the admiral had moved the family to Hawaii for two years. Joel walked away, saying I was wasting my time.

"Worse than that, you'll give her a bigger head."

Joel and Betsy now began most days with a dignified European lunch featuring wine. By dusk, fights broke out, screamers mainly consisting of amnesiacs' roulette, blame games fought to exhaustion.

"Liberal attitudes never start at home."

"What is that supposed to mean?"

"If you're such a humanitarian about towel-heads, why ship off your own kid?"

"Oh, so you think we had an easy decision?"

"Hilarious. Yes, I do."

"Well, your father believed in tradition. His father went to St. Luke's, Bill had a lovely time there, why wouldn't you, unless you deliberately fought against it? The grounds were beautiful, terrific sports teams, a good choir."

"Honestly, Mother, you know I saw kids get their heads slammed against a wall."

"Now you're exaggerating."

"My Latin teacher? He broke my index finger with a fucking Bible."

"Well, had we *known*, Joel, your father never would have stood for such *malfeasance*."

"Of course he knew."

"You told him?"

"He wanted me down there getting my ass whipped, that's obvious. It was the same headmaster in place as when he was there. How many times did I ask to come home?"

"You'll remember, if you didn't remain through graduation, then how would you have gotten into Yale?"

"Well, that worked."

"Not our fault, dear. *We* didn't light the school on fire."

"Dad didn't want me around. The serving utensils were more useful. Not like you ever stood up to him anyway."

"Oh, allow me to confide in you, Joel, I am terribly sorry, but you'll find, perhaps I didn't *want* to confront him on this topic. This will not be comfortable to hear, but I did not adore being a mother. It wasn't my strong suit. Would you believe, could you imagine I had aspirations of my own? Do you fancy it was easy then for a woman to want something more for herself than darning onesies?"

"You know what? Both of you were lousy parents."

"And you, you were an *ungrateful* child."

"What was I supposed to be grateful for?"

"Don't interrupt me. Your generation, you were good for what? Escape, excess, and misanthropy. You were an advertising campaign. What would you know about duty? About adversity? Responsibility?"

"Well, I'm not the one who abandoned my kid to pederasts."

The house was quiet. I worked undisturbed for ten minutes. Then I heard ice cubes being broken out of a tray and thrown in a glass. Joel came downstairs with a big gin and tonic.

"Okay, what have you got on me?"

"Some stories from your mother, that's all," I said. I opened a folding chair next to the desk. "You're welcome to correct them."

"How about I give you the original version. We'll go old-school, straight from the source."

For three hours he recounted his life story, filling up his cup twice, watching me take down the outline as though I were some antique automaton he'd found in the basement.

His patient chronicler, neither judge nor jury.

"Victor, you need to know something."

"What is it?"

"I don't know how to say this. I've begun looking around to move."

"To move? To move work?"

"I'm just putting out feelers," Lucy said. "You know, maybe bio-tech. I don't know where it sits with me. The timing feels right."

I was crushed. "No, of course, it's a good idea."

"You mean that?"

"Well, it's sudden."

Lucy laughed darkly. "Try having your research partner go AWOL."

"I understand."

"It's not because of you, Victor. Not completely." She sighed. "Deke is moving. To California. He's taking a position at UCSF."

"But that's wonderful. I mean, if you're going with him."

"Are you asking me?"

"I just assumed."

"Like I said, I don't know."

"Lucy," I said, "I'm happy for you. I already miss you as it is."

"Yeah," she said after a second. "You, too."

With Betsy's and Joel's entries finished, I left the Gardner book alone for a week. Only Sara's and Miriam's entries remained to be included. People had suggested occasionally that I write a book about Alzheimer's disease for the lay reader, a look at current research from

the inside perspective. Now was the first time I'd seriously considered it. I began swimming again. Some days I lay in the hammock
and read an old mystery. I got a haircut, I gardened, I drove the golf
cart to pick up groceries. There were moments when I thought I'd
never leave, that here was paradise. Twice I had dinner with Ken
and his wife, Dot, who looked just like Pat Nixon.

One Thursday, a foggy morning with an overcast sky, Joel found
Betsy dead when he went in to help her into the shower. Joel stumbled
downstairs. He was wearing a T-shirt and boxers. He ran outside.

Betsy was crumpled on the floor in a nightgown by the curtains,
her eyes wide open, her glasses knocked off a few feet away.

The fog had settled in the grass. Joel went past me into the kitchen
and poured out two full glasses of gin. He laid his arms on either side
of my neck. His face was flushed underneath his beard. He would
see to the coroner, he said, I was to call the lawyer, the family, and arrange the funeral, whatever his mother said she'd wanted. We embraced, then we toasted with our juice glasses. Joel poured himself
more, became sullen, and fell into an easy chair.

I walked around through the fog to shake off the alcohol. My knees
creaked, my back ached, my mind wouldn't go one stop past the
obvious: *dead, gone, cold*. I refused to accept any of it. I walked to the
ferry dock and sat down on one of the benches. People would appear
from the fog, then fade away. There were watchers in the trees, all eyes
on me.

One gull, guarding a pyramid of lobster traps, wouldn't stop
screeching.

Who's to say the whole island couldn't sink in the fog? And if it
did, who would mourn us? Fifty years down the road, who remaining
would remember us and what we'd done?

The week after the funeral, I stuck it out on Cranberry alone, rarely leaving the house. Joel moved back in with his girlfriend, Jill, in Manset, then was kicked out again, and then I didn't know where he was. He disappeared. His cell phone went straight to voice mail.

I called Lucy, but the lab told me she and a friend had taken a last-minute vacation to Tortola. I left a message. I sought occupation at all costs. I swept the floors, vacuumed bedrooms, mowed the lawn, cleaned out the shed. Ken and Dorothy brought over a big pan of lasagna, and I stored it in the basement freezer, which I'd just emptied out and defrosted.

Joel showed up unannounced one chilly, cloudless night with tidings of September. He had a twelve-pack of beer and a bag of cheeseburgers. We sat in lawn chairs in the backyard and looked out over the water, listening to the frogs and bugs. I had to go in for jackets, bringing out some of Bill's, two old flannel work shirts. The lights of Bar Harbor were clumped together in the distance, as though the town were a far-away cruise ship.

Joel threw one of his cheeseburgers into the ocean. "Honestly, I can't feel any worse. My tongue is like fucking a layer of fertilizer."

"That's the McDonald's."

"I don't mean the food."

"Joel, it takes time."

"Well, great." He tipped a beer my way. "Thanks for the expertise."

"Hey, screw you."

I got up and walked down to the water.

"You think I don't have regrets?" he shouted. "I fucking wake up, I've got a dozen things I wish I'd said, then the next morning, they're still there, plus I've come up with two more my old scoutmaster confessed to me in a dream while he's driving around in a clown car. How do you get rid of fucking *that*?"

"Quit drinking. You should get back to work."

"Yeah, well screw you, too, Dr. Disappear-O. Work cures all, my ass."

"I'm serious."

"She collected bums to feel better about herself. Me, my dad the drunk, now you." Joel laughed. "Hey, no disrespect, but who's more fucked-up than He Who Pisses Naked While Trespassing?"

I went inside and searched, found it, then returned with a notebook I'd discovered in Betsy's desk while I was cleaning house: a collection of all the reviews Joel had ever received, clipped and glued in chronological order.

He paged through slowly. Half he hadn't seen before, he said. He cried like a baby.

We must have fallen asleep outside because I woke up at five in the morning, still in the same chair. Joel was gone. Someone had spread a blanket over my legs.

I read Regina's poetry book several times: in bed at night, outside at lunch, first thing in the morning before work. I understood her poems better each time, and that perhaps they didn't need to be understood through logic so much as felt, like music.

And I worked. I wrote about Sara's life, a skeletal outline. It went badly.

Betsy's lawyer flew up from Boston about a week after Joel's nighttime visit. We met one afternoon in the dining room at Blue Sea: the lawyer in his suit, me in my gardening clothes, Joel in his baseball cap and chef's uniform. At least his eyes looked clear. The room was busy with cooks draping long sheets of pasta over the dining tables. I noticed Cornelia was absent. She hadn't been at the funeral, either, though I'd invited her. Dan the boyfriend was polishing wineglasses. He avoided looking at me and stayed behind the bar. I considered shouting out that I'd thrown away his necklace.

The lawyer explained the terms. A third of the savings would be split between Miriam and the few relatives I'd met at the funeral, another third would go to an Acadia preservation group. The remainder and all of Betsy's assets and possessions—the bonds and life insurance, the house, the car, the cottage on Cranberry—were Joel's. I was left a painting I'd always liked.

"You're welcome to come back," I said to Joel when the lawyer was gone.

"Well, it's my house now, isn't it?" he said. He put a hand on my shoulder. "Sorry. I'm stressed, I quit smoking again. Tell you what, I'd appreciate it if you continued living out there for a bit."

Then he noticed something, spun around, and screamed at a young woman preparing ravioli. Apparently she wasn't cutting consistent shapes.

There was a message on the answering machine from Cornelia when I got back to the cottage, her voice hemming and hawing.

"So, hey, Uncle Victor, hey, so I actually decided not to take the job with Joel. But please don't be mad, I'm irresponsible, I know. And you did so much to help me, I totally realize that. So I'm calling from Logan, I bought a ticket last night online. I just don't know if I want to cook for a living, you know? Except I totally fell in love with wine at Blue Sea, there's so much you can learn, so I think I'm going to try working for my dad. See if I like it, you know, the business from the other side.

Anyway. But please don't worry, I'll mail you the keys tomorrow, I took a taxi to the airport and the car's in the driveway. And with everything that happened, I still totally loved this summer. I just don't think I'm an island person. Oh, and I broke up with Dan, in case you see him. He was a pothead anyway, plus he was like sleeping with this waitress, can you believe that? Anyway, rambling, I know. Okay. Bye."

A week later, Joel called. He told me his plan was to move into Cape Near sometime in September, and that he wouldn't be doing anything on Cranberry for at least a year. He said, would you consider closing up the camp, or just staying there through October?

"It would be a privilege," I said.

"Thank you."

"Are you back in AA yet?"

"What, for dates? Honestly, half the reason people go to meetings is to meet somebody as screwed up as they are."

He laughed and hung up.

I did an inventory of Betsy's possessions. I went to church when no one was around, and I found no company there, but I utilized the quiet. I caught up on my reading. I was dying to get back to work. Forestalling the obligation to write a short history of Sara's life, I asked Miriam about hers over the phone. Pleasant childhood, pleasant college experience, unpleasant early divorce, a second marriage that lasted two decades and bore two lovely children, then the husband died from cancer, later she met Gary. "I really think I've done all right," she said, laughing cheerfully. "You know, it matters that you say it when it's true, Victor. You've done all right."

I planned trips to visit Ken and Dorothy in New Hampshire come fall. I puttered around the island, trying to fix the exact date in mind when I'd stage my Soborg comeback. The Little Cranberry people had ceased taking notice of me, and they accepted me at their town socials. People paid me compliments about Betsy, even Sara: anecdotes about my wife, reminiscences, questions about *The Hook-Up*. One afternoon, I was cleaning out the attic and I noticed a yellow Post-it note stuck to my shoe.

"Rumsfeld knew Saddam???" it said in Betsy's handwriting.

One night, Mark called, Sara's former agent.

"How are you. Look, let's talk. *The Perfect Husband.*"

I sat down at Betsy's desk. "What did you think?"

"Victor, first, Sara meant the world to me, you know that. I miss her. I miss her all the time."

"I know," I said.

"And nobody wants the long-lost script to appear more than me. But okay, this is business. What are we looking at, really?"

"I think it's a rough draft."

"Well, it's a first draft. And truthfully, that's the problem. I mean, it's barely readable. The main character's a walking cliché."

"I don't know," I said, feeling hot, "I thought it was true to life."

"Yeah, okay, there are some decent lines. But true to life doesn't put people in theaters. I read a hundred scripts a week. Why do people go to the movies? Because they're not real. They're so not real, they're super-real, they're Frankensteins without the stitches. But the stitches here are obvious. I'm not saying there's no gold in the premise. Look, I like the local color, I buy the whole serial-killer-as-disease-specialist thing. And if anyone could mine her own material, it was Sara. End of the day, though, what we lack fundamentally is Sara's vision. If she were alive, she'd write forty more drafts before she was satisfied. You and me, this isn't what we do. I wouldn't even know where to start."

"Yeah," I said, "me neither."

Mark sighed. "Look, never say never. Maybe there's some way to get this touched up. I'll think on it, yeah? I'll let you go. Call me next time you're in L.A., okay? All right?"

One night after a bottle of wine, I almost phoned Regina. Instead, I called her the next morning, when I was sober and aware of my motivation. I wanted to call and wish her good luck in her graduate program, and to wish her well, that was it.

"She doesn't work here anymore," the receptionist said.

"She left?"

"I'm sorry, who's calling, please?"

I almost hung up. "This is Dr. Aaron," I said. "I'm off campus."

"Dr. Aaron, I'm sorry, I didn't recognize your voice. No, Regina finished last week, last Monday. I can give you her e-mail address if you want. Did she work for you at some point?"

And then that afternoon, as if responding to my signal:

From: belletter@umich.edu

To: vaaron1118@yahoo.com

Subject:

Victor,

I go into this e-mail without knowing why I write, or necessarily what I want to write, but hoping that by writing, by satisfying the compulsion, whatever I mean to express will come out clearly. The need will be sated. Need to explain, need to bear witness for those who can't speak for themselves. A humanitarian impulse.

Please excuse the purple prose. I'm trying to live up to the occasion and be a lady.

A lady, they say, knows when to leave.

I believe you, Victor Aaron, to be among the strangest men I've ever met. Not only as recent reports demonstrate, but earlier, a priori, when I first sought you out for a lover because you were tall and intelligent and from New York, and you possessed that older-guy thing. All that lured me to bring you under harness. The challenge of it. The hunt.

But where other men would buck a woman's sway or submit to it, it's like you didn't recognize what was happening. You operated by other laws, ones tied beyond this world. I figured this out last night. Your wife had died and everyone knew but you.

I hope you don't find that cruel. And I hope you're doing better. I hope the new windshield didn't cost too much and that you leave your island.

Please don't reply to this e-mail or contact me again. But wish me luck as I embark on yet more debt and more studies. I still don't know what I'll do when I grow up, but I want more than ever to do something. Something worth doing, and not just for show. La Loulou is retiring; maybe just Regina will be good enough for what comes next. My brother will be nearby and at the very least he's interesting company. So I've got that going for me, which is nice.*

Yours sincerely,

Regina

*You won't get this reference, but don't stress out. Some things you shouldn't change.

The tourist season ended after Labor Day. Numbers on the ferry dwindled and the temperature dropped. We saw fewer visitors to scout the pie stands, and there weren't as many drowsy summer people to nod to when I walked the lane into town.

I'd started collecting rocks off Betsy's beach. They were like the ones at Hunter's, coral with black spots, or gray and ringed with pink stripes. There would be some specific cause, I thought, for why those markings developed, and though I'd never been curious about geology before, it became a preoccupation. Most days, I found myself spending an hour or two with my pant cuffs rolled up, wading through the tide and storing my most interesting specimens in a bucket. I made a mental note to seek out someone in the geology department when I returned to the university. As sediment, were these rocks unique to Mount Desert Island? Why pink and gray, these tiger stones, and from what material causes? Had they turned up at Cape Hatteras, on Miami beaches, or was it only in Maine that they'd settled? What had brought them there?

By day I was finishing Sara's entry in the Gardner book, as much of her life as I could remember. The end was in sight, but what had begun as a paragraph was approaching twenty pages. At dusk I'd check in with the lab, and some nights I joined Ken and Dorothy for dinner to watch police procedurals on TV until I was tired. Some nights I was. Others I stayed up until three a.m. and still couldn't sleep without a couple of drinks.

I called the lab on Wednesday. I knew Lucy had recently returned from the Virgin Islands.

"Nice vacation?"

"You know, not bad. First day, I'm unpacking, I pull out a drawer to put away my tops, and this iguana jumps out, we're talking twelve inches nose to tail, and lands on my chest. Gripping my jog bra with its claws. Other than that, I think this may have been the first time I actually relaxed. On the second-to-last day, but still."

"So you went with some girlfriends."

A short pause. "I said yes, Victor."

I laughed and had to hold the phone away for a moment. "Of course you did," I said. "How wonderful. Congratulations. I'm very happy for you."

Now Lucy laughed, too. "Thank you. I don't think my mother's accepted it yet."

"Are you happy?"

"I am. I'm trusting."

"So what does the engagement ring look like?"

"Oh, it's a Specialized."

"A what?"

"A Rockhopper. Deke thought it was time I tried mountain biking, something we can do together. Isn't that cute?"

"Probably a lot of biking near San Francisco," I said. "Lot of labs out there, too."

She exhaled lightly. "I've heard that," she said.

It was nine o'clock, a Thursday evening, when Joel showed up, banging on the door. "I've been drinking," he shouted from the yard.

"Seriously, I'm fucking tearing my skull apart out there, thinking about this shit," Joel said, pacing in the kitchen. His bulk was full of energy, the opposite of drunk. "You know, the only time of day my mother was good for, my father was good for, was happy hour?"

"Joel, come on."

"Hey, it's in the blood, man, this is programming speaking. You're the gene guy, am I wrong?"

"Yes and no," I said. He stared at me, his eyes like knuckles. "A lot of it, introns, we're clueless about. Ninety-five percent, some say."

"What did you do, tell me that."

"What did I do when?"

"After Sara. Your 'coping mechanisms.' The scientist's guide to grief, or whatever."

"I did nothing."

"And that worked?"

"Not at all."

"So then you end up on a sailboat."

"Something I regret," I said, "on top of everything else."

He waited a second, but didn't stop staring. "So you figured I'd be drinking."

A statement, not a question. I said, "Can I get you some water?"

Joel was rattling his head. He couldn't seem to stop grinding his teeth. He laughed under his breath, then went outside, plopped down in one of the chairs in the yard, and lit a cigarette. I sat down next to him and for some reason this propelled him up a second later, dragging the chair. He lifted it and slammed it against a tree, over and over, warping the frame, until he flung the poor thing ten feet out into the ocean.

We watched it bob in the water. There wasn't any current to pull it away.

"You want to know what I've been doing, right?" He turned, flicking his cigarette butt in the water. "Fine, I took two tabs of Ecstasy. Happy now? This afternoon, off one of my cooks. How about that? Unbelievable rush. Nearly burned my head off. Then, an hour later, my sous-chef kicks me out. Of my own kitchen. At least I think he did. I mean, I was blissing out like I've never seen. But you know what? I drove over to Jill's. Like, why not? Genius. See I had this incredible epiphany. I wanted to share how I'd become, like, one with the universe and shit. But by the time I get there, it's gone. It's transformed. And I'm going schizo. Like I was chopped in two, me the watcher and then me, you know, independent of that. Like my thoughts were disappearing down a black hole and I couldn't catch them. I saw myself disappearing. Like, whatever I was, I wasn't anymore, or what I was was being sucked out somewhere else, and I was left watching it get sucked away. Or whatever. So that was what I wanted to tell Jill about. I ring the bell. Next thing you know, Jill's there and I'm telling her how I've gone crazy, I'm crying, and then she puts her hands up, so I'm quiet and she tells me, that's it. I could save it. She didn't care. This was the end, she'd call the police if need be, but I couldn't come back, ever. Then she slammed the door in my face. I mean, now *that* I can fucking understand. So I mean, that's exactly what I'm thinking now, you know? Just stop. Just stop. A nice, simple exit. Slam the door on this shit. I mean, *look at me*. What am I adding to the world right now? Fucking what, man?"

He was pacing around the yard in the dark. He saw my bucket of rocks, picked it up, started taking out the rocks and one by one throwing them far out into the water.

I took the bucket away and got Joel inside and gave him one of Betsy's sleeping pills. He lay down in the cot and passed out with his boots on. I called Ken and asked him if he knew any support services. Turned out Cranberry had a weekly AA meeting falling on the following afternoon, held in his church of all places.

We went down together the next morning. I introduced Joel to Ken in the church driveway. Ken said he'd always been a fan of Joel's way with scallops.

I looked at Joel. He nodded. "It's going to be okay," Ken said.

Ken called that afternoon, around the time the meeting would be getting out. "We were sorry we didn't see your buddy this afternoon."

"What are you talking about?"

"He said he was going to join you for lunch, then the two of you would be coming back together. Not true?"

I slammed down the phone. I called Joel's cell and left a message. I called Blue Sea. I called Jill. There was a knock on the door and through the screen I saw Ken.

"I'm sorry, Victor. I shouldn't have let him out of my sight."

"He's an adult. I'm sure it's fine."

Just stop. Just stop. A nice, simple exit.

"Can I help?"

We jumped in his golf cart.

"Just get me to the ferry."

From Northeast Harbor, I didn't know where to start. The island was full of bars and restaurants and gas stations selling beer. I drove home to change clothes and think. Weeks since I'd left, it was an odd sensation, driving down the road to my house. The woods looked oddly unrelated to any life I'd lived there before.

My answering machine had a single message.

"Victor, this is Joel. Look, I gotta run. You're not going to see me anymore. I need to start over someplace. San Diego, Austin, just someplace warm. I know you're the worrying type, so I thought I'd call, seriously you've done a lot for me. But anyway, it's cool, I've done it before. I just can't hang around here anymore, this island's full of ghosts. I don't know how you do it, but I can't."

Caller ID said the call originated from Cape Near.

Betsy's car was in the driveway when I pulled in. The front door to the house had the screen door propped open by an old gardening bench. I found Joel out back, sitting in the lawn chair Betsy always favored, facing the woods. An army duffel lay fully stuffed in the grass.

"I'm bullshit," he said after a second.

"Yeah, I know."

He laughed. "I'll tell you, you know the one story I like? About school? It was my thirteenth birthday. My parents neglected to visit, they didn't call. No surprise, they'd shipped me away since I was seven. For presents I think I got some new shirts and a ten-dollar bill. But I remember the card my mother sent. I still have it, it's in the safe-deposit box. On the front there's this photograph of a little boy laughing, with his hands tucked down his pants. And on the inside she wrote, I can quote it, 'By this point you've probably learned how to entertain yourself. Pleasure's rare enough, you should grab it when you can. Love, Mom.' Fucking, I was flabbergasted. It took me a second to figure it out. Not like the other guys were getting advice from their mothers, you know, pro—whacking off.

"I figured out later on, though," he said, "when I wasn't such a prick, that that card was a lot more who my mother was than some Oxford shirts."

"Joel, you don't have to go through this alone."

"People say that."

"Why don't you come back to Cranberry? Regroup, get a fresh start."

He turned and gazed at me. He looked exhausted, but also calmer than anytime recently. "Tell you what," he said a minute later, staring down the lawn, "that grill out there, in season? You could wipe them out with a taco truck."

We went out together that evening. I telephoned Lucy again and discussed recent progress. I was due back at the lab in two more weeks. Perhaps I'd commute by ferry, as Betsy had always envisioned. The ending, as of yet, was unwritten. Joel grilled salmon steaks for dinner and we split a bottle of mineral water. Joel watched the news, shouting at Tom Brokaw, then went to bed early while I sat in the living room and reread my genealogy entry, now a total of a hundred pages, making final adjustments and rewriting through the night, drinking coffee, until six in the morning, when I printed out a copy and left it on the table for Joel to review.

I went outside and tried the water. It was freezing. I went for a short swim anyway, toward Bar Harbor, where the lights were being absorbed by the sunrise. Then I went inside and added a postscript to Sara's section. It wasn't quite right for a book, but it would fit on an index card.

> *Sara,*
> *These lines I'm writing for myself. Not for us. Not for you.*
> *How was I to know grieving took faith? The same for living.*
> *I know it. I name it.*
> *I'm beginning to know the distance between me and*
>   *everything else.*
> *And I have the faith to collapse it.*
> *I leap.*
> *Our love exists apart. Underneath me, above me and all around.*
> *I hold your face in my hands.*
> *And I let go.*

author's note

My deep gratitude to: Ann Baldwin, Crans Baldwin, Leslie Baldwin; Julie Bleha, Jessica Francis Kane, Woodwyn Koons, Chris Lee, Andrew Womack; Josh and Juliet Knowles; PJ Mark; Sean McDonald, Emily Bell, and everyone else at Riverhead; the scientists who allowed me to pick their brains and mangle their research; Mary Baldwin; and my wife, Rachel, for everything.